CPAC

D1715645

OCT - - 2005

NOOSE OF FATE

NOOSE OF FATE

A Western Quartet

T. T. FLYNN

Five Star • Waterville, Maine

First Edition
First Printing: September 2005

Published in 2005 in conjunction with Golden West Literary Agency.

Set in 11 pt. Plantin by Ramona Watson.

Printed in the United States on permanent paper.

Library of Congress Cataloging-in-Publication Data

Flynn, T. T.
    Noose of fate : a western quartet / by
T.T. Flynn.—1st ed.
      p. cm.
    ISBN 1-59414-158-4 (hc : alk. paper)
    1. Western stories.   I. Title.
PS3556.L93N66 2005
  813'.54—dc22
                                    2005014202

NOOSE OF FATE

TABLE OF CONTENTS

The Fighting Breed

T. T. Flynn completed "The Fighting Breed" on November 28, 1936. It was the twentieth story he had written that year. It was accepted immediately upon submission by Popular Publications' *Star Western*. The title was changed to "Ranch It—And Die!" upon publication in *Star Western* (4/37). The author was paid $360. Flynn added an aspect of grim reality to the violence in his stories, and not even his protagonists were immune.

I

That evening, in the little office of the Clear River lawyer, old man Hardwick gave his final price—and a bitter warning: "You're buyin' trouble, grief, an' death. The price is sixteen thousand. Six thousand cash, the rest notes. It's open for ten minutes. Will you deal?"

Steve Raglan finished rolling a cigarette. He flicked a match into flame and silently inhaled. His eyes were expressionless as he searched Hardwick's tired, bitter face and estimated the shrewd features of Smith, the lawyer. In his middle twenties, Steve Raglan was wiry, hard under his sheep-lined coat. The bite of the cold evening wind was red at the roots of the day's stubble on his jaws. Steve had ridden out of Clear River early in the day and had just returned after dark.

Steve said with a pokerface: "Most buyers'd run from that offer."

"It'd be on my conscience if I didn't tell you," Hardwick replied. "Your partner an' you are strangers hereabouts. I'm takin' away enough bad memories without not warnin' you. I'm sellin' because the rustlers got me licked. I can't stand off the Barr brothers an' the gun slicks who run at their heels. I can't prove the Barrs rustled me down to a saddle string . . . but I know it. I can't prove they kilt my boy an' caused his mother to die in a month of a broken heart . . . but it happened. I ain't much with a gun. I'm licked down inside. I'm quittin' . . . goin' back East with my youngest girl to live."

Steve Raglan looked away from that lined, bitter face. In a moment of uneasiness he wondered if life could ever mark him as old Hardwick was marked. Then, because he was young and had never known grief, Steve smiled confidently.

"It's a deal. We'll take a chance on these Barr brothers. Grubbing out placer pockets all summer an' fall has paid us well, but we're cowmen. I've heard a little about these Barr brothers since we hit this range. Four of them, each one snakier than the other, I hear."

The lawyer glanced hastily at the door, as if afraid someone might have overheard. But old Hardwick, who was getting out, spoke his mind harshly: "Four wolves, mister! They've always run in a pack like wolves! They got too vicious for Dodge City an' had to move on before the oldest was twenty. They all moved together. Since they've been in these parts, they've had their way. Ain't any big cattle outfits to run 'em out. They do a heap of their skullduggery out away from here, but I know wolf sign. The four Barrs cleaned me . . . an' they'll be at your hams when you get fat enough to drag down."

"How about the fifth brother?" Steve questioned.

Hardwick smiled grimly. "A hard-shootin' *hombre* named Bassett kilt Pete Barr when Pete tried to bully him. The other four brothers rode out after Bassett that night. Three months later they caught him in Utah. They dropped a rope over Bassett's ankles an' dragged him slow all night over salt flats an' cactus until Bassett was cut to pieces. An' they passed out word they'd do worse to the next man who cut a Barr's hide. I'm playin' fair with you, Raglan. I've got another offer if you don't want to deal."

Steve Raglan stood up, smiling grimly. "I'll go get my partner, Tex. I'll give you half now . . . three thousand cash. Tex is packin' his half."

"That will do," was the lawyer's prompt reply. "I will give you a receipt against the sale, the money to be kept by my client if you do not sign the final papers."

"Make it out," Steve directed.

The clerk at the hotel shook his head. "Mister Travis hasn't been in yet."

Steve frowned. "No idea where he went?"

"He didn't leave word. Le's see . . . I saw him come out of the bar this afternoon."

"Was he drinkin'?" Steve demanded quickly.

"He'd had a few. I didn't notice who was with him. Two men, I think."

Steve turned on his heel with a curt word of thanks. He was swearing under his breath as he hurried out of the hotel.

Tex drinking! Big Tex, good-natured and square, had been on the wagon all year and sworn he wouldn't touch a drop until they had a piece of land and some cows. But Tex had to do it that way. When Tex got past two drinks, he was off with a bang. The bigger Tex's roll, the bigger the bang.

"I should 'a' known that big buckaroo had an awful itch under that fat money belt," Steve groaned to himself as he headed down the street to the first saloon.

This was Saturday night. Clear River stores, sidewalks, saloons were filled. There were seven saloons and the hotel bar. Steve reached the sixth bar empty-handed.

One of the bartenders listened to his question. "Tall *hombre* with a gray Stetson, an ivory-handled gun, and a wild look in his eye?"

Steve nodded. "He oughta have one hell-awful wild look by now. Where is he?"

The barkeep hesitated. "Not aimin' to start any trouble, are you?"

"I'll comb his hair for drinkin' today," Steve promised. "He's my partner. There's business waitin' for him. If you know where he is, let's have it."

The barkeep shrugged. "Through that back door," he directed. "Second door on the right. He's been sittin' in a poker game for a couple of hours."

"Hell an' hell's fire," Steve groaned. "And he'd bet his spurs against aces full when he's drinkin'!"

"I reckon he's lost 'em by now." The barkeep grinned. "They've called for plenty drinks."

Steve cursed again as he made for the back room.

Through the second wooden door in the passage Tex's loud voice was audible: "An' I raise you twenty an' keep raisin'! Sweeten it, boys! You've won enough! My cards is man-killers lookin' for a ride, an' there ain't no pick-up man! Ride 'em if you think I'm bluffin'!"

Steve stepped inside. So quickly did he appear, without warning, that he was half in the door before the nearest man saw him and gave a quick start—a guilty start. A hold-out card under the table edge was brushed to the floor.

Steve swept his gun out. "Everybody sit!" he commanded. "Tex, what in hell are you doing in a poker game? Come over here and take a look!"

Four players sat about the table—Tex, and three others—and a heap of money and bills was in the center.

One of the three was a cold-eyed professional, vest open, sleeves rolled up, his long supple fingers toying with his poker hand. At Tex's left, sitting with his back to the door, was a lean man whose high-crowned hat perched far back on his head. His worn leather coat hung open in front, his scuffed riding boots were hooked around the chair rungs. He turned an angular sneering face over his shoulder, but made no other move. He snarled to the man across the table: "Jack . . . who brought *this* in?"

The fourth man's face was covered by a short black beard. He was, Steve guessed, younger than the beard made him look, but his manner demanded watchfulness. His glare across the table was surly and threatening as he dropped his cards face down.

"Who'n hell are *you?*"

Tex missed all that. Tex was riding high and open. A bottle at Tex's elbow was half empty, and another bottle across the table was hardly touched. They had been loading Tex with whiskey. Tex whooped with delight and came out of his chair, waving his cards.

"Steve, you got here just in time . . . I'm on the prowl an' fixin' to jump! Lookit this hand! Lookit the pot! Comb out your pockets, Stevie boy!"

"Shut up, you ory-eyed fool!" Steve rasped angrily. "You won't win on this draw! Pick up your money an' get outta here!"

"Who don't win?" Tex yelled. "Take a look at what I'm holdin'!"

Steve stepped quickly to the left as Tex blundered before him, waving the poker hand. Steve barely saw it—but he had known it was coming. The bearded man behind the table went for his gun. And Tex was in the way. . . .

II

There was no time either to yell a warning, to stop that draw, or to get over in the clear. Steve kicked out past Tex's shin at the table leg just beyond Tex. His boot drove the table back hard against the bearded man as a gun muzzle whipped over the table edge and crashed flame and lead.

Tex staggered, and the two other gamblers were diving for the floor. Steve threw himself to the left so he could shoot past Tex. His shot topped the bearded man's second gun blast. The heavy slug tore into his broad chest and knocked the man halfway around in the chair. The bearded man's gun hand dropped into the pile of money, sending gold and silver cascading to the floor, and the bearded man's glare died like the flame of an exhausted lamp. His body moved convulsively. A strangled gasp issued from his lips, then his head sagged over, he crumpled down on the table edge, and slumped off the chair to the floor.

Sobering fast, Tex said stupidly: "He drilled me through the arm."

Blood was already drenching Tex's coat sleeve, and powder smoke was rank in Steve's nose as he backed to the closed door, covering the two men.

"Get up, you two!" he ordered. "Tex, grab what you've got comin'! It was a crooked game!"

"The hell it was," Tex muttered.

The sallow gambler stood up with his hands high. His face was pale, furtive with fear. The lanky man looked stunned, malevolent.

"You killed him," he said. "He's dead. Jack Barr's dead."

Steve rapped at him: "Jack Barr? Was *he* one of 'em?"

"The youngest Barr brother, mister," said the lanky man. "God help you when the rest find it out. They'll peel your skin an' roast you over a slow fire."

Tex snorted as he swept money off the table. Blood was dripping from Tex's wrist. He ignored it. "We've kept our skins so far," said Tex. "You can tell these Barr brothers we aim to wear 'em a while longer. Steve, I ain't got time to count this. If the game was crooked, I hope I'm getting too much."

Under Steve's orders, the two came to him with their hands up. The lanky man had a single-action Colt. The gambler had a Derringer in an inside vest pocket. Steps were audible in the passage; louder voices came from the barroom.

"Stand back!" Steve called. "We're comin' out shootin' if there's a gun trained on us!"

The gambler lifted his voice. "Jake! Watch out! I'm comin' first! Don't let anybody sling a gun at me!"

The gambler opened the door, stepped into the dim passage.

Men who had crowded into the hallway were already backing off into the safety of the barroom. Not a half dozen stood their ground as Steve, with Tex at his back, pushed out with a gun in each hand.

Crouching, Steve backed along the passage toward the back door, his guns covering the men in front.

"A Barr brother's dead in there," he clipped out. "His game was crooked. He went for his gun when he thought he had a chance . . . drilled my partner's arm before I dropped him. We're leavin'. Don't try to stop us!"

A man who looked like he might be the owner invited: "Keep going, stranger. The other Barr brothers'll take care of you."

A moment later they were both outside, running through the night behind the Clear River stores toward the hotel. Tex's arm, Steve noted, was bleeding badly.

"Got to get to the hotel room first, Tex."

They entered the hotel through the back door, and ran through to the lobby stairway. A group of men was lounging there, and, as they rushed up the stairs, Steve looked back. He saw a man pointing them out to two other men.

Steve locked the room door. "Peel your coat," he panted.

While Tex did that, Steve got out their rifles, threw their blanket rolls on the floor.

Muscles had been ripped and torn below Tex's elbow. Blood was pouring out, dripping down on the carpet.

Steve slopped water from the pitcher into the wash bowl, wet a towel, swabbed the arm, looked at it. Talking fast, he yanked a sheet off the bed, tore strips from it.

"You played hell, Tex. I've bought a ranch . . . the Hardwick land an' all the beef we can find on it . . . an' now I've killed one of the Barrs."

"What of it?" Tex grunted. "He asked for it."

"There's three more brothers. It means a feud. We've got to kill 'em sooner or later, or they'll get us."

"Hell," said Tex, "only three of 'em?"

A few turns of bandage on the upper arm eased the blood flow.

"Unload your money an' get down to the livery stable with these blankets an' rifle," Steve ordered. "Got any money in your belt?"

"Some." Tex grinned sheepishly. "Hell, Steve, I played the crazy fool, didn't I?"

Steve grinned back as he stuffed money into his pockets.

"It ain't the first time . . . for either of us. Get the pack horse ready to go, just in case. This town has grown too small."

Tex was a head taller. His sombrero shaded a broad, good-humored face. But now Tex's eyes narrowed.

"Maybe I better go with you," Tex said.

"I'll handle this," Steve insisted tersely. "Hole up at the livery stable, where you'll be some good if hell curries our backs."

Old Hardwick was still in the lawyer's office when Steve hurried in. The two men stared wordlessly as Steve dropped handfuls of money on the table.

"Count it," Steve ordered. "If there's three thousand, gimme a receipt. If there ain't, an' you'll deal on what I've got . . . write it out."

Smith, the lawyer, dropped a coin he had picked up from the table and uttered an exclamation. He was staring at his fingers.

"Blood," he gulped.

"Keep countin'," Steve snapped. "My partner was shot in the arm when I busted up a crooked poker game he was in. I had to kill one of the Barrs."

Old Hardwick stared at him wordlessly. Visibly upset, the lawyer stammered: "You k-killed one of the Barrs?"

"Keep countin'. Here, I'll help you."

The lawyer's hands were shaking nervously as he stacked gold and silver and smoothed out bills. His eyes jumped to the door every few seconds.

Hardwick shrugged, began to move aimlessly about the lamp-lit room. "You're as good as dead," he muttered. "I oughtn't to take your money. It's like robbin' a corpse."

Steve grinned as he counted through a stack of gold pieces. "You never robbed a livelier corpse. Here's seven hundred. How much you got there?"

"Twenty-four hundred and eighty-two dollars and thirteen cents."

"Gimme the hundred and eighty-two. Keep the thirteen cents for luck. Make out a receipt. Same as the other. Steve Raglan. Tex's name can get on the other papers later."

The lawyer was blotting the receipt when feet tramped into the front room. He jumped. Steve drew his gun, stepped over beside the back door. The glass was painted. He could not see outside. A key was in the lock. He turned it.

The connecting door to the front room opened. A tall, slack-chinned man with a sandy mustache stepped in. A sheriff's star glistened on the front of his coat. Two men, deputies evidently, carrying rifles, backed him in the doorway.

Steve said: "Far enough, gents. My business isn't over."

The sheriff was uneasy. He bit his lip. "You're the man who shot Jack Barr?"

"What does it make me?" Steve asked shortly. He spoke to the seated lawyer, who was staring in fascination at the scene. "Gimme the receipt."

Steve leaned his rifle against the wall, took the receipt, stuffed it in his pocket. His pistol kept sheriff and deputies covered.

"You didn't come to arrest me?"

"I want the straight of it. I'll tackle that when I hear your story in my office."

The sheriff was irritable, uncertain. A weak man, Steve saw, who wanted no part of this, who probably had been pushed into it by others.

"I'll tell you now," Steve said. He told the circumstances of the shooting, ending with: ". . . and Barr went for his gun. I drilled him. How does that strike you?"

"I'll look into it. Pass over them guns an' come along. You'll be safer with me. The other Barrs are in town. They'll be after you."

Old Hardwick grinned derisively. "Bailey," he said to the sheriff, "if one of the Barrs howls acrost the street, you'd duck for cover. They've got you tamed. Everybody knows it."

"Keep outta this, Hardwick!"

"Damn your yellar-striped belly!" Hardwick burst out bitterly. "I'll have my say. I wouldn't be in the fix I am today if Clear River had a sheriff worth a lead *peso*. You know the Barrs, an' you know this man done a good turn for the county when he kilt Jack Barr. Go out an' disarm the Barrs an' warn 'em to keep the peace, if you aim to do right."

"I'm runnin' this, Hardwick," warned the sheriff angrily.

"An' you're runnin' outta here," said Steve. "Back up, Sheriff. Close that door."

Through the small front room Steve glimpsed a crowd around the front door. Word must be spreading fast that the sheriff was in here. The Barr brothers would hear. They might come in the front and back at any moment.

"You gonna let him get away with this, Bailey?" one of the deputies growled.

19

Stung, the sheriff warned: "Put up that gun an' come along or I'll outlaw you. Half an eye can see you're in the wrong if you follow it out thisaway."

"Git!" Steve cocked the gun. And, muttering, the sheriff crowded back on his two men and closed the door.

"Blow out that light," Steve directed Hardwick.

The sheriff's voice called at the front door: "I want a dozen deputies quick!"

Hardwick blew out the light.

"I'll get the rest of the papers later," Steve said through the darkness.

Hardwick answered him back through the darkness: "There won't be no later for you, Raglan. You're a dead man now. I'll wait at the ranch till I get word the Barrs have finished you an' your partner."

"You're fixin' to settle there, then." Steve chuckled. He threw open the back door, dived out, low and fast, into the darkness with his gun cocked. Then, not an arm's length away, a livid muzzle-flash stabbed out.

The report was deafening; powder grains burned his face, but Steve had come out fast, crouching low so that the bullet tore through the back of his coat and missed him. Steve fired twice at the flash and kept going.

He must have gotten the man, for no shots followed him. One of the Barr bunch, he guessed, who had slipped around to the back door on a chance he would come out that way.

Steve wiped at the powder burns on his face as he ran, and smiled grimly. Hardwick's words were fast coming true. Kill a Barr brother and you scratch trouble.

The one-eyed livery stable man gave him a puzzled look. "Didn't you meet your partner?"

"Meet him where?" Steve snapped.

Two lanterns gave dim light in the pungent interior of

the stable. Horses were stamping in the stalls. Here were quiet and peace, although down the street a crowd was milling in front of the lawyer's office.

The liveryman scratched his chin. "Kid came in here an' told your partner that you wanted him to ride to the big cottonwoods this side of the river ford. Here's your horse."

"Who was the kid?"

"Hell, mister, I don't know all the kids. Seems to me I've seen this button with Ace Loftus, the gambler. Might be one of his'n."

"Has Loftus anything to do with the Barr brothers?"

"You'll have to ask Loftus that, mister."

Steve had his answer from the liveryman's sudden unwillingness to talk. He asked one more question as he shoved his rifle into the saddle boot and swung on his horse.

Steve stormed out of the livery stable at a gallop. Back along the dimly lighted street the crowd was still surging before the lawyer's office. The river ford was half a mile away, on the west edge of town. Steve rode fast, apprehension tightening under his belt. Another time Tex might have questioned the kid closely. But tonight, filled with remorse, not knowing what had happened at the lawyer's office, Tex was primed to obey orders.

The galloping horse drummed loudly against the night quiet as Steve rode recklessly toward the ford. There might yet be time to warn Tex, or to join him.

A half moon hung, cold and white, against the black sky. The cottonwoods at the river ford towered darkly as Steve raced past the last houses. Reaching shadowed trees, he reined in, looked about. The night quiet closed in. The hard-breathing horse sent twin jets of vapor pulsing into the chill air. Water glinted under the moon as it rippled over the river stones. The early winter wind raked through the dry cottonwoods. But there was no Tex. Tex's horse and pack horse were not in sight.

"Tex!" Steve shouted.

Fifty yards back, at the corner of a small adobe house, two dogs ran out barking. Steve called again. He heard a house door close and drew his gun.

One of the dogs yelped from a blow as angry words in Spanish silenced both. Through the wan moonlight a dark figure came hesitantly.

"*¿Señor?*"

III

Steve rode to meet the man. "I don't savvy much Spanish. Talk *Americano*. I'm lookin' for a man who rode here to the ford. Didja see him?"

"Weeth one pack horse, *señor?*"

"That's right. Where'd he go?"

"Thees other mens she tak heem with one riata. Hees yell an' swear, but they drag heem an' tak heem."

Stunned, Steve looked down at the uneasy Mexican.

"You mean," he asked, "somebody roped this man outta the saddle before he used his gun? Wasn't there any shootin'?"

"No shoot."

"What'n hell were *you* doing?" Steve flared. "Why didn't you start in to report it? What'd they do to him? Where'd they take him?"

"*Aí, Dios* . . . *quién sabe?* We hear the *caballos* come there, *señor*, by *mi casa.*" The Mexican pointed to the

shadowy area beside his house. *"Cincos hombres, señor . . .
five men. They tell me tak dogs in. Thees man come fast
weeth pack horse. When hees pass by, they drop la reata an'
drag heem to el río."*

"You mean," said Steve, sick with fury, "they dragged
him through the river?"

"No, *señor* . . . they are laugh when they tak heem from
the water an' then they all ride away. I say to *mi esposa* . . .
'Thees bad . . . w'at we do?' She say . . . 'Ees notheeng.
One *Americano* treek.' *Dios*, w'at I do? W'en you call, I
come to see, *señor*."

With cold intensity Steve leaned over.

"Which way'd they go? Across the river? West?"

"¡Si, señor!"

Steve fumbled in his pocket. "Here's five dollars. *Cinco
pesos*, savvy? Go in to the sheriff. Tell him the Barrs have
kidnapped the man Jack Barr was playing poker with. Tell
him Steve Raglan says, if the sheriff's half a man, he'll take
his posse an' get that man back. Tell it to everyone you
meet. Savvy?"

"¡Ai . . . g-gracias, gracias!" stammered the Mexican.
"¿Los hermanos B-Barr, señor?"

"Scared stiff of the name, huh? Well, do the best you
can. They won't cut off your ears . . . if you keep out of
sight."

As Steve's lunging, plunging horse stormed recklessly
across the shallow river through showering water, Steve was
cursing aloud with a terrible intensity. Tex trapped,
dragged on the ground, hoisted on his horse, rushed away.
The Barr brothers—Ory, Clyde, Tom—were behind that.
No guesses were needed as to why Tex had been roped and
carried away unharmed. There were slower ways to die than
by a bullet. And Tex would meet them—big, grinning,

good-natured Tex, who hadn't even shot Jack Barr.

Now, under the serene moon, with the Clear River lights fading behind, Steve Raglan came face to face with the thing that had lined old Hardwick's face and broken his spirit. One man against many, with no help to back him up. Steve smiled now—a savage grimace, his lips drawing back. He'd made the buy for Tex and himself. He'd bought death for Tex, as Hardwick had said—such a death probably as not even the Barrs had dealt out on the lonely Utah salt desert to the man they had relentlessly trailed.

This side of the river ford, west, was the Hardwick Ranch in the small wooded hills and breaks that ended some twenty miles away in the first range of the mountains. There was good grass, sweet water, tight fences, and sheltered winter range there on the Hardwick land. It was his land now—his land and Tex's. But Tex, who had bedded by hundreds of campfires with the thought of his own land and brand in his mind, would never see that vision come true. Tex had vanished into 10,000 square miles of tangled range; there was not moon enough for tracking. And six-guns and one rifle were not much to throw against a killer bunch, ready for the one man who might come after them.

Miles beyond the river Steve dismounted in the sandy bed of a dry arroyo and searched the sand with a cupped match. There were plenty of tracks—wheel tracks, horse tracks, cow tracks, crossed and tangled in the sand. But none looked as if it had been made in the last hour.

Steve groaned as he dropped his last match and stood up. It was useless. Not until daylight would it be possible to go back and try to pick up the trail. And back there by the river ford he would be fair game for the Clear River sheriff. A weak man, stung by his weaknesses, he would try to vindicate himself by attacking the lesser of his evils. That would be Steve Raglan, and not the Barr bunch.

Daylight was a long time away. The horse had been ridden most of the day. Steve decided to ride on some miles to the ranch he had bought. There should be a man or two around, a fresh horse, a bite of food before he started out after Tex again.

Steve's lips drew back off his teeth again as he swung into the saddle. After he found and buried Tex's body— then the Barr brothers would get a taste of what it meant to be hunted to the bitter end. A one-man hunt, with blazing guns for any Barr man met.

You're buyin' trouble, grief, an' death! Again the echo of old Hardwick's warning came to his ears, and Steve Raglan spoke aloud to the emptiness about him: "I bought it . . . I bought death. An' now I'll peddle death, damn them, an' see how they like it."

Miles beyond the arroyo, Steve cut onto the Hardwick Ranch road, up a wide draw. He closed the wire gate and rode over his own land—his and Tex's.

Two steers stood in the moonlight and watched him pass. Only two. The Barr bunch had gutted the beef. There was, Hardwick had said, some left. But a man would have to search it out to make the slim tally. There were haystacks that would not be needed; there was a ranch house built in hope and filled with hopeless memories; there was a bunkhouse, windmill, corrals, and a shed or so. And there was the land, the grass that were worth just what the Barr bunch made them worth, and no more.

Steve rode around the crest of a small hill and reined short of a bloody red glare staining the night a mile or two ahead. Sparks spewed up as he looked, and the glare brightened against smoke whirling toward the high, white moon.

It burned, Steve thought as he surged into a gallop, like

25

one of the big haystacks back of the ranch house. The wind already was driving the sparks in brilliant whirls across the night. Steve's heart leaped at the hope that Tex might be there ahead, alive or dead. At full gallop he drew his rifle from the saddle boot, made sure the magazine was full.

As he got closer, he saw two haystacks were burning. A smaller glare to the left, where the house was, began to grow. A bunch of horses burst across the road some hundreds of yards ahead and thundered across the range, hazed on by two yelling riders who did not see the lone rider on the road.

Steve lifted his rifle, then lowered it. The light was too uncertain; they were traveling away too fast to hope for a hit.

Then ahead, at the fire, sounded thin sharp rifle reports. Steve rode fast toward the sound.

IV

He swept over a rise, and stared, the red, raw scene of destruction lay down the slope before him. Haystacks were tinder piles. Flames seethed inside the house and licked from windows and doors. The shots, as Steve stopped and scanned the scene, were coming from the bunkhouse and the edge of a piñon pine grove, off to the right.

Steve marked two spots over in the pines where rifles were barking viciously. He rode back into the trees, tied the horse, and cut off to the right in a crouching run toward the rifles firing at the ranch building.

The bunkhouse was keeping up a spirited reply. Steve could see corral poles down where the horses had been run out. Ahead of him, among the trees, a hoarse voice called a questioning challenge. Caught off guard, Steve kept on, cocking his six-gun. An eerie red glow seeped back into the first trees. Steve made out a silhouette of a man not forty yards ahead. A rifle was trained on him. He swung his horse behind the nearest tree.

The rifle crashed and bits of bark flew out as the bullet grooved the tree side. Steve plunged out toward the man, pistol crashing. In his mind was only one thought, one hope—that this might be one of the Barr brothers. This might be a man who had helped to kill Tex.

He saw the figure stagger, saw the spurting muzzle streaks of a six-gun, then he saw that gun muzzle waver. Steve stopped and placed his last two shots with cold care. The dark figure lurched over against a tree trunk, slid down. The man was twisting on the ground, groaning heavily as Steve reached him with rifle cocked and ready.

The man still gripped his gun. His rifle lay on the ground by his feet. Steve twisted the short gun out of weakening fingers. He dropped to a knee, reloading hastily.

"How many more of you?" he asked.

A strangled oath was the answer. The man was clutching his chest. He had a mustache, was tall and spare of frame. With a fierce surge of exultation, Steve recognized the lanky man who had been gambling with Tex.

Through the trees, some distance away, a voice shouted: "Loftus! Are you all right?"

"Ace Loftus," Steve said. "So *you're* the one who sent your kid to the livery stable. Where's my partner, damn you?"

Steve had the man by the throat before he realized what he was doing. He released the throat. Loftus choked, then rolled flat on his back, and quieted. A laugh rattled in his throat.

"So you're the one who got me? Couldn't have wished it better. The Barrs'll even it up when they ketch you."

The voice called again, no nearer, but uncertain this time. Only the one voice—and there had been only two rifles here in the trees.

Loftus tried to answer. A strangling gurgle was the best he could do as his throat filled.

"Where's Tex?" Steve demanded harshly of the dying man.

Loftus gasped for breath and laughed again. "*I* figgered how to get him," Loftus gasped in obvious pain. "Wisht we'd knowed you was comin' this way. Ory Barr said shore they'd ketch you in Clear River. But he'll get you. Ory, Tom, an' Clyde'll follow you through hell."

"Is that fellow who's calling you one of the Barrs?"

"Wisht it was. Tom went with the horses. Ory an' Clyde stayed in Clear River to look for you. We turned over here when that yaller-bellied sidekick of your'n told that you two had bought this Hardwick place."

"Did Tom kill Tex?" Steve rasped.

The other man had stopped calling. He might be slipping through the trees toward them. Loftus was fast growing weaker. Steve had to bend over to get the reply.

"Your sidekick ain't dead . . . yet. Don't know when the boys'll get to work on him. But it'll be good, damn you, it'll be good. You can find him at Squaw Falls. Why don't you go get him?"

Loftus choked again, tried to clear his throat, and could not as dark blood gushed from his mouth. Then he was suddenly very still.

There had been, Steve was sure as he stood up, derision in Loftus's voice when he mentioned Squaw Falls. The idea had meant a last flash of macabre humor to the dying man.

28

Steve had never heard the name, but a load went off his mind—while fear remained. Tex was alive. But agony and horror were evidently ahead for him.

The rifle fire from the bunkhouse had stopped. No more shots were coming from the edge of the trees. The voice had ceased and only the sullen undertone of crackling flames filled the night.

Steve slipped away, lying prone on the ground. His gun ready, he tensed for sign of an approaching figure. After dragging minutes, a stick snapped suddenly farther back in the trees. Steve inched around, faced the spot.

The haystacks were burning down. The house roof caved in with a monster shower of sparks and flame. The brighter glare, striking back in the trees, picked out a furtive movement near where the stick had cracked. Then the light faded.

Eyes glued on the spot, Steve lifted his rifle, cocking it. He had to wait another five minutes before he made out another vague movement, much closer. He sighted fully on it, waited until he was sure, and squeezed the trigger.

He knew while the shot rang in his ears that he had killed the man. But he crawled carefully toward the spot, taking no chances. A man's body sprawled motionlessly there on the ground with a hole through chest and back. Steve left the dead man there. He had been a Barr man. That was enough. Steve walked out of the trees toward the bunkhouse, waving his hat.

A rifle barked at him. The bullet kicked dirt close to his feet. The distance was too far to call above the hiss and crackle of flames. He put his hands up and kept on. He was allowed to approach the bunkhouse, with the heat of the fire scorching his side.

"It's a friend!" he called.

A woman's angry voice answered through the shattered bunkhouse window: "Drop your guns! Open the door and back in! If it's a trick, you'll get shot first!"

Steve backed through the doorway, with the gun muzzle prodding his back. The same voice, cooler now, commanded: "Close the door, Gus. See if he has a gun hidden anywhere."

The fire glare shone through the window. By its light, Steve recognized Gus, a cowpuncher he'd seen from a distance when he had first inspected the ranch. Gus was an old cowhand, stooped and white-haired, who limped with a stiff leg and munched an enormous quid of tobacco behind his white, drooping mustache.

"Clean as a whistle," announced Gus after his hands went over Steve. Gus squinted. "Say, ain't you one of the fellers who rode over the place the other day with the boss?"

"Uhn-huh. I'm Steve Raglan. I bought the ranch tonight. Came out here to sorta take over and found the Barr bunch had jumped it."

The gun muzzle had left Steve's back, but, as he started to turn, it touched his side again. The woman demanded suspiciously:

"How do you know the Barrs did this?"

Steve chuckled. "I just killed a couple of 'em back there in the trees. Talked to one before he died. A couple more lit off with the horses. They'll keep going, I reckon."

Then, for the first time, Steve saw the girl. Red light through the window stained her young face. Her blonde hair was caught carelessly back over her shoulders. The man's sweater she wore sheathed her slimness as smooth bark might sheath a proud young sapling. Her small chin was pointed; there was a dimple in her chin for softness and for hardness her eyes were direct, challenging.

She said: "I'm Connie Hardwick. And so you bought the ranch?"

Steve felt foolish. He had expected a welcome—and enmity was unmistakable in her voice and manner. Hardwick had mentioned a daughter, but Steve had not seen her when he and Tex rode over the ranch with the old man. For some reason he had expected the daughter to be older, to be harsh and bitter like her father, and to be beaten and spiritless, whipped by circumstances. As a matter of fact he had not expected her to be out here at the ranch. He had taken for granted she was probably in town.

He was not at ease with this slender, pretty, challenging girl, with fire in her look and determined assurance behind the rifle she held. The best he could say was: "Yes, we bought the ranch . . . my partner and I."

"Where's your partner?"

Steve's face hardened. "The Barrs got him. I tangled with Jack Barr in Clear River tonight. Had to kill him. The Barrs got Tex by a trick. I lost the trail and rode out this way to get a fresh horse. It'll be daylight before I can pick up the trail again."

Connie Hardwick said: "You're trying to catch up with them . . . *alone?*"

Steve nodded. A man chuckled from the shadows at the back of the room. Steve hadn't seen him lying in a lower bunk. Middle-aged, unshaven, the man's stiff-splinted leg lay on top of the blankets.

"You've made a good start to run this ranch." The man chuckled again. "Started on a Barr an' dropped two more of their men before midnight. Yes, siree, you're all set now. Damn this leg . . . excuse me, Miss Connie . . . but I'd hafta be laid up with the fun just startin'!"

31

2

"What are they going to do to your partner?" asked Connie Hardwick.

"It doesn't help to think about it."

There was enough to see dawning pity in her eyes, to see that she understood how the thought was burning in his mind. Her dislike apparently had vanished. She opened the door and stepped outside. Steve followed her. He was conscious of grizzled old Gus, planting himself watchfully in the doorway with a rifle. Gus wasn't trusting anything yet. But Gus didn't matter as Steve walked slowly with Connie Hardwick toward the burning house. She seemed to have forgotten him. She was biting her lower lip. Steve guessed she was on the verge of tears. He looked away.

Only when the glare was bright and the heat was scorching their faces did Connie Hardwick stop. She stared at the destruction before her. Her voice was sad, and fierce, too, with youthful protest.

"Why did this have to happen to us?"

Steve tried to comfort her. "It's our loss . . . the deal is made."

Scorn flared into her face as she looked at him. "Your loss?" she cried vehemently. "What are you losing? A few dollars! We've lost everything! I was born here and I love this place. So did my mother and my brother. They're gone. It . . . it had to happen, I guess, but the ranch was left, and their memories are here. They loved it, too. And now all that's gone. I tried to save it . . . I tried to keep Father here, but he wouldn't listen to me."

"You wanted to stay here and buck the Barrs?"

Connie Hardwick's lip curled. "I'd stay here and fight them until they killed me!" she cried angrily. "This was *ours!* A lifetime of work went into it. Before I'd throw that away and run from a pack of cowardly wolves, I'd die fighting them!"

Steve thought: *You're beautiful!* Fascinated, he watched the angry glare of flames play over her proud, defiant face. There was a spark there that caught tinder in his heart, and he knew that men like the Barrs would never break the spirit of such a girl.

She must have read his thoughts. She looked startled. Their eyes locked; her eyes were wide, wondering. Color sprang into her cheeks. Then she looked away.

"That's how I feel," she said unsteadily.

"And that's how *I* feel," said Steve softly. "I'm sorry I bought something you didn't want sold. It's your'n as long as you want it. There's plenty of room here." Steve grinned as he spoke the grim truth. "It'll probably all be here for you after the Barrs get through with my partner and myself."

Her stricken eyes sought his face again. "You're sure the Barrs are going to kill you both, aren't you?"

"I reckon so," Steve agreed.

"And you still mean to fight them . . . alone?"

"Somebody's got to do it."

They were close together. Quick tears were in Connie's eyes as she looked at him. "You're a brave man, aren't you, Steve Raglan?"

"Maybe I'm a fool, Connie Hardwick." Steve grinned, and he wanted to say more. He wanted to shout it above the sullen crackling at his back. A man was a fool to feel this way about a girl he had just met, a fool to feel exultant about it, and a man who felt that way was a fool not to be brave enough to say it. Steve wasn't brave enough.

From the bunkhouse doorway old Gus's shout reached them.

"Here comes your father, Miss Connie!"

V

Hardwick spurred a lathered horse up to the bunkhouse ahead of two other riders. He leaped from the saddle and caught Connie in his arms. His voice was hoarse with anxiety.

"Honey, when we first saw the fire, I thought I'd lost you, too."

With new clarity, Steve saw how fear had haunted Hardwick, and how those who a man had lost could make him weak at the thought of losing more.

Connie hugged her father. "If anything happens to me, the Barrs won't do it. When the first haystack went up, I ran for the bunkhouse to be with Gus and Tom. They hazed off the horses and fired the house. I think that's all they wanted to do."

Hardwick's two companions dismounted. The first man down was middle-aged, broad-shouldered, and solid with a weather-beaten face that was now hard with silent emotion. The other man was younger, about Steve's age. He wore a high-crowned sombrero and a handkerchief around his neck for a muffler. His short overcoat was caught in by a gun belt he had strapped on the outside. He stood there, spreading his cold hands to the heat of the burning house as Hardwick turned to Steve.

"So you dodged 'em an' got out here, Raglan? You had luck, but it won't last. The Barrs did this, I reckon," he said bitterly. "Burned you out already. An' you ain't got a chance to do anything about it. That yellah son-of-a-bitch sheriff has outlawed you."

34

"For killing Jack Barr?" Steve asked.

"For killin' Kink Luvane, one of the town rats that tries to curry favor with the Barrs. Kink was outside the back door when you went out. I heard him shoot first. I tried to tell Bailey, but he wouldn't have it thataway. He swore you was a killin' fool on the loose, had run into Luvane out back, an' dropped him in passin'. He's set to get you for that, which'll help him dodge the question of the Barrs."

"Is he gonna dodge the fact that some of the Barrs got my partner while all that was happening and carried him off? They're fixing to do a worse job on him than that fellow they trailed over into Utah."

Hardwick shrugged helplessly. "A Mex run in an' tried to tell Bailey somethin' about it. Bailey told him he was lyin' and drunk. Then he had him locked up fer the night."

"Might as well put the Barr brand on the sheriff," said Steve bleakly.

Hardwick nodded. "He's a yaller skunk. Scared stiff he'll be put in a corner someday where he'll have to stand up to one of the Barrs an' bull it through against all of them. Which ain't helpin' you any, Raglan. You've paid your money over, your buildings is burned down before you get out here, an' Bailey is ridin' around in the dark with a half-hearted posse lookin' for you. It took me twenty-six years to get run out of here . . . an' I reckon you've made the same point in three, four hours."

Connie spoke sharply. "Don't talk like that, Father. Steve . . . Mister Raglan . . . isn't whipped. He's going to stand up to the Barrs and fight."

Hardwick's two companions eyed Steve with new interest.

Old Gus joined them. He spat toward the blazing house.

"Couple of the Barr men is up there in the trees to stay,

from what this feller says," Gus observed. "He's tallyin' 'em fast. Jack Barr an' Luvane in town . . . an' two more out here. Adds up mighty near one an hour. Come daylight, at that rate"—Gus cackled—"he'll have 'em whittled down to rabbitweed size."

The younger man in the short overcoat asked tersely: "Either of those two up in the trees a Barr?"

"Nope. A fellow named Ace Loftus is one," Steve told him. "I don't know who the other one is."

"I'm Bill Stratton," the speaker introduced himself, "and I've got a small spread north of here. Been feelin' the Barrs some myself. This here's Henry Conners . . . Hen for short . . . an' a rooster when it comes to gettin' his back feathers up. Speakin' as a neighbor, I'm mighty glad to meet somebody that's started cuttin' at the Barrs."

"Wonder you haven't rounded up the whole range years ago and cleaned out the Barrs," Steve said bluntly as he shook hands.

Henry Conners grinned sheepishly under a brown mustache and put in: "Nobody's wanted to take the lead. Each men figgered he'd be stickin' out his own chin without much help."

Steve grinned thinly. "I've got my chin out. How about a little help?"

"Now you're talkin'," Bill Stratton said promptly. "It's been buzzin' in my mind since we got here."

Hardwick shook his head. "You can't get 'em to pull together. The Barrs can call on every man who hangs out at Squaw Falls. You can't get at 'em, an' later they'd come out an' get you one by one . . . like they got me."

"Squaw Falls?" Steve broke in. "Where's that?"

"West of here," said Hardwick, "up Squaw Creek Cañon. Used to be a couple of mines there on the flat. They called it Gold Flat then. The mines shut down an' everyone moved out. The Barr brothers settled there. The old Squaw Cañon road cuts back through Squaw Valley an' tops a bunch of trails back in the mountains that ain't used much any more. From Squaw Falls you can dodge back into the mountains an' lose yourself from forty posses. The Lord only knows how many wanted men drift in there off the mountain trails, stay a while, an' move on. Cattle run in that way just vanish. Strangers off the range ain't wanted there, an' every rancher here knows he ain't safe from day to day so long as Squaw Falls stays like it is. It's like havin' a boil on your neck that's ready to bust any minute." Hardwick shook his head hopelessly. "They've done enough to me. I'm getting out."

Connie flared: "I'm not. I'm not going back East. I won't let them run me off."

Her father looked at her in amazement. "What kinda talk is this, Connie?"

"Fighting talk," Connie Hardwick snapped, her eyes blazing. "I didn't want to go to begin with . . . and after tonight I *won't* go. Every time I fired a shot at them, I was more sure of it."

Connie looked at Steve. Her eyes told him that it was after talking to him she had made her decision.

Hardwick pointed to the fire-gutted house, blazing fiercely beyond them. "All your shootin' didn't stop this, Connie. An' . . . an'. . . ." Hardwick swallowed.

Connie knew what he wanted to say. "And it didn't help Bud," Connie said. "But Bud didn't run from them. It broke Mother's heart, but I won't let it break mine. Everything you've worked for is here. Why . . . why, don't you *see*, Father, you can't run and leave it? You can't end everything by running away. You never ran before. You can't do it now."

Steve spoke slowly. "The Barrs have taken my partner to Squaw Falls. Hell will be a picnic to what they'll do to him there. Maybe it'll happen to him before I get there. Maybe not. But I'm goin'. Tex'd come after me. If he's alive, he'll be expectin' me."

Bill Stratton spat. He looked as if he were swearing silently. "Squaw Falls," he muttered softly.

Old Gus grinned crookedly and shifted his huge chew to the other cheek. But Hardwick shook his head. "You haven't got a chance, Raglan."

Steve grinned coldly. "Who wants a chance? I want Tex . . . and the Barrs. While I've got a gun, I've got as much chance as the Barrs. You're looking at it crooked, Hardwick. I'm not running from the Barrs . . . me, I'm *hunting* them. Looks like the trouble around here's been too much running and no hunting. The Barrs have talked mean and scared you all to death. If you'd get your backs up, you'd put 'em on the run."

Bill Stratton cursed softly, so Connie, beyond her father, could not hear. "Right you are," he said louder. "An' I'm for endin' it. How about it, Hen? You feelin' like a man tonight? You feelin' like totin' a backbone out to the other outfits around here?"

"Feelin'!" Conners exploded. "I've been listenin' an' boilin' to the poppin' point. Your house or my house may be blazin' like this next. Hell, yes. Raglan, stick around, an' we'll git a crowd together that'll make any Barr choke on his cud. To hell with Bailey. We'll tie him on a hoss an' shove him up to Squaw Falls ahead of us."

Steve shook his head. "Knowing you're backing me up as soon as you can'll be something to take along. I'll be going ahead of you. I've got to get to Tex quick, while there's a chance he's still there."

Old Gus squinted at him. "Walk into that nest of rattlers an' you'll get stung from hocks to head before you know what's happenin', young feller."

"Jack Barr and Ace Loftus are the only ones, as far as I know, who have seen me," Steve declared. "They're both dead. Draw me the lay of the land around Squaw Falls . . . and I'll try to drift in from the mountains off the outlaws' trail. It'll be the last thing any Barr man'll be looking for. Betcha they won't believe it after they see it." Then Steve chuckled. "Being an outlaw myself now, I oughta make a go of it without any trouble."

Old Gus stared at him. A broad grin spread over the wrinkled face. "Damn it . . . 'scuse me, Miss Connie . . . you mean it. Thought there wasn't any of that spirit left on this range. In the old days we'd've chased them Barrs out so fast their sign would 'a' smoked. I was on Gold Flat when the mines fust opened, an' I know them mountains for a hundred miles around like the back of my hand. Git me a hoss an' I'll put you smack where you want to be, young feller. The Barrs know me . . . but maybe I can keep outta sight an' do some good."

Bill Stratton was grinning. "That makes two of us, Raglan. The Barrs know me, too . . . but I'll tag along an' be around if I'm needed."

"Thanks . . . I'm not asking that," Steve refused.

"I'm tellin' you," Stratton retorted. "I ain't married. What I'm riskin' is my own. Hen . . . you don't need me to get things rollin'. You can outtalk five of me."

"You're a liar . . . but I can this time," Conners promised. "I'll stop home on the way to the Cross J. Shorty Carr's Cross J men an' mine'll make a good start. Hardwick, I reckon you'll be takin' Miss Connie to Clear River tonight. It'll be safer."

Connie was wiping her eyes. "Clear River?" she scoffed. "I know where to find some horses they didn't run off. The buckboard and harness aren't destroyed. I'll take Lon Purdy over to your place, Mister Conners, and stay with your wife." Connie looked at her father. "You'd better come too, Father. You can go to Clear River tomorrow."

Hardwick shook his head. His face was flushed. He was like a man shedding a bad dream. Hardwick's shoulders, Steve noticed, were straighter.

"Who said anything about Clear River?" Hardwick answered his daughter. "You're right, honey. Runnin' ain't the answer. Seemed like I was alone, with just you left . . . an' there wasn't nothin' to do but get away an' hang onto you. Listenin' to what Raglan aims to do makes me ashamed. I'll side you over to Conners's an' then make for the O Bar O. An' when they get through listenin' to me at the O Bar O," said Hardwick with a new rasp of firmness, "they'll be plenty ready for the warpath."

VI

Steve, Gus, and Stratton were ready to ride out from Hen Conners's Cross J two hours before daylight. Old Gus spoke up. "We'll hafta cut north anyway. You'll need blankets. A man don't hit them mountain trails this time of year 'thout somethin' to roll up in. Ef you're comin' to Squaw Falls offa the owlhoot trail, you better look like it. 'Sides, Miss Connie might have a might of trouble with the buckboard."

Connie Hardwick saw them off from the Cross J front door. She was slim and straight in the black before dawn chill.

"Good luck," Connie said.

"Thanks," replied Steve gruffly.

Steve looked back as they rode away, and looked back again and again, until the spot of light that was the door closed on Connie Hardwick.

Then Steve looked over his horse's ears, west, toward the mountains. He would, he knew, probably never see that door again, or ever again see Connie Hardwick. It was like coming out of darkness into golden light—and riding on into a colder, endless dark.

Old Gus rattled on cheerfully: "Now, boys, I'm takin' you over the old Highgraders' Trail, 'cross the flank of Shotgun Mountain. Guess it's brushed up a heap, but I can get you through. It'll put us on the North Fork of Sheephead Creek. We'll cut the Ringo Trail. A dozen forks offa the Ringo way'd take you anywhere back in the mountains . . . an' a feller still can stay on the trail an' cut southwest to the big valley an' git himself on the Sweetwater way to the border."

"Ought to help a man to drift into Squaw Falls from that way," Steve mused.

"Shorely, shorely," Gus agreed readily. "Now, lissen careful. I'll give you the lay of the Ringo way north toward Gold Rock. You can talk then like you've rode in that way . . . or bluff it out, if you can get by with bluffin'."

Old Gus talked the sun up, riding tirelessly with one leg stiff in a lengthened stirrup.

They crossed the flank of Shotgun Mountain through brush that had almost obliterated what trail had existed years before. North Cañon held chill mist; the north fork of Sheephead Creek brawled and leaped between fringes of ice that formed a silvery fretwork along the banks. And they came into the Upper Park in the mid-morning, on horses that plodded wearily after the long cold miles of climbing.

By noon they had ridden out of the south end of the park. Toward the middle of the afternoon Gus reined on the shoulder of a cliff that suddenly broke away to their left in a dizzy drop.

"There you are," said Gus, spitting into space. "There's Squaw Creek down there, headin' into Squaw Cañon. Three miles down you'll find Gold Flat, where the mines usta be, with Squaw Falls just below. Right by the falls the road's so narrer a mule wagon just usta be able to squeeze through. The Barr brothers have barricaded the road there an' put a gate in. An' they've barricaded the second bridge down from this end with another gate. You gotta cross that bridge or you can't go on. A thousand men can't get in at them Gold Flat renegades once they've holed up. An', son," said old Gus, squinting from red-veined eyes, "once you're inside them barricades . . . you're *in!*"

"I've been thinking," said Steve, squinting down into the rock-rimmed mountain valley far below, "that once the Barrs get in there, they could be held in."

"That's one way of lookin' at it . . . if you got somebody to hold 'em in at both ends." Gus spat over in space again. "Ain't ary use'n Stratton an' me tryin' to go to the falls with you. We're knowed. But come dark there's a little pocket down there off the cañon head we can tie the hosses in an' ease down the cañon to a ledge near that second bridge. Give us any light a-tall an' we can pick 'em off as fast as they come hellin' up the road. That is," said Gus dubiously, "if anything happened to make 'em come outta the flat. Might be tomorrow night or after afore Conners brings anyone up the cañon or gits anyone around this way. Soon as you take that trail down the cliff there, an' get down to the flat, you're in a rattler's den."

42

Steve grinned. "It'll be my call to rattle. I'm obliged to you two for comin' this far. If you don't hear any shootin', you'll know I got in with the rattlers anyway."

Stratton said nothing as Steve waved and headed down the trail, knowing they both considered him already a dead man. He wondered, as he rode down toward the pine tops far below, if Tex also had brought this cold dead feeling of fatality to the outlaw camp.

Squaw Creek wound through the grassy mountain valley, where rustled horses lifted their heads in the distance and stolen white-faced cattle grazed. Some of them were probably Hardwick stock.

The sun still washed the eastern side of the valley, and the sheer rock walls of Squaw Cañon were purpling with chill shadows. The rocky road was a ledge skirting the deeper bed of Squaw Creek, whose cold blue current leaped and frothed over water-smoothed rocks.

A mile and a quarter down, the first bridge of old rotting logs carried the trail across the creek chasm to the opposite wall. You crossed by that bridge, Steve noted, or you didn't get across. One gunman under cover could hold it against ten.

Another mile, and there was the second bridge, hanging forty feet above the rocky streambed, and fifty yards from the other end of the bridge the trail burrowed through a shoulder of rock that jutted out over the stream. A massive gate of old mine timbers had been swung across that tunnel mouth.

The sagging log bridge trembled as Steve's horse walked across. A rifle barrel eased out through a slit in the gate like the warning tongue of a snake.

A gruff voice called: "Where you headin', stranger?"

"Where the Barr brothers an' the whole damn' lot of

you'll be headin' if you ever get smoked out of this cañon," Steve replied, riding on. "Open up that gate. Are you afraid I'm packin' handcuffs an' a roll of head-money dodgers on you curly wolves?"

A loud guffaw burst out beyond the gate. "Sounds like hell-fire on a blizzard ridin' down the creek! You're just the gent I been wishin' for, stranger. Ride in. Jackknife, quit your grumblin' an' grab holt of that end."

You could like a man who talked like that, Steve thought, as the heavy gate creaked slowly out. He rode into the dark shadows inside the tunnel mouth. Two men were in there, and two horses were standing some yards farther on.

One of the men held a cocked six-gun. He wore old overalls tucked inside older riding boots, two coats, a muffler, and a weather-beaten sombrero that looked new beside his seamed and dissipated face.

"Jest take it easy," he warned in a whiskey rasp.

He looked like a broken-down grub-line rider who had kept going for years on whiskey. But his stare was level, his gun steady, his manner dangerous.

The other man was younger, taller, and powerful. His movements were quick as he hauled the creaking gate back in place and heaved a huge wooden bar up into its supports. He was grinning as he turned around.

"I'll bet you can sing a mean middle in a quartet," he said, squinting up. "You're needed, stranger. I'm Happy Jack Harris. This is Jackknife. He ain't got another handle. Claims he's all blade an' cuts mighty mean. Tally up, stranger. Where you headin', what's your name, how come you aim to pass thisaway?" Happy Jack was smiling.

Steve guessed the big fellow would grin just as cheerfully while he cut a man down with one or both of the two guns he carried. Happy Jack had the wild, reckless look and manner that marked him as unfit for a lawful life. Here was a man who would hit the outlaw trail with a whoop and gun his way through life with a smile and a joke. But his smile might mean what it said—or it might mask death.

"The name," said Steve readily, "is High-Low Henderson. I'm from plenty of places I've passed through, an', if I like your bump in the road, mebbe I'll stay. I aim to bed down, eat a bean, an' get a wink of sleep without watchin' the back trail."

Happy Jack chuckled. "High-Low, you're home. The bean is cookin'. We all sleep sound. If you look right, drag an easy loop, an' handle your gun, the Barrs'll let you hang around. You know the Barrs?"

"Heard of them. Kinda run things, don't they?"

"They give orders an' back 'em up," said Happy Jack. "Which keeps the cañon peaceable. Grudges shoot it out. Troublemakers get run out or drilled quick. Women ain't allowed. If a man ain't for the Barrs, he hightails quick. Jackknife, the relief'll be comin' along. You watch the gate while I side this man down to the flat."

Jackknife hunched his long neck inside the dirty muffler. "Suit yourself," he grumbled with a scowl at the newcomer. "Mebbe the Barrs'll like his singin' . . . an' mebbe they won't." He spat. It was plain he had taken a dislike to the stranger.

But Happy Jack was in good spirits as he took the down trail with Steve. "The Barrs went to Clear River a couple days ago. One of 'em got hisself kilt. Hell'll be poppin' over it. They brought in a feller about daylight, an' hazed in a bunch of hosses a little later. My guess is Squaw Falls is on the warpath an' a good gun hand'll be welcome."

Steve grinned thinly. "Doesn't sound like the Barrs take to havin' a Barr killed."

Happy Jack sobered. "Mister," he said grimly, "I've never seen a man that'd make me back down, but I'd wade into a she grizzly an' her cubs bare-handed before I'd shoot a Barr. Think that over if you got a quick temper."

"Did they bring in the man who did the killing?" Steve questioned.

"Nope. His partner, I hear. Tom Barr come in with the hosses. I heered him tellin' this feller what he was gonna get. Tom worked on him a little . . . not much. Tom had to leave. When he gets back, the fun'll start."

"What'd Tom Barr do to this fellow?"

Happy Jack shrugged distastefully. "Ain't my business. Better keep out of it." Happy Jack gave him a narrow look. "You sound curious. It ain't healthy."

The brooding dusk was somber. Sounds were magnified. The widening cañon seemed to be swallowing them. The world beyond the high rock walls was far away, completely cut off.

Steve could feel the tension tightening. Would any man at Squaw Falls, he wondered, know him? Had one of the Barrs seen him at Clear River with Tex?

Galloping horses drummed up the cañon toward them. Two riders met them, paused briefly.

"Who is it you got there, Happy?"

"Fellow off the Ringo Trail."

"Tell him to speak soft. Tom Barr just come in. He's lookin' for blood."

Night was dropping fast when the cañon began to murmur with the roar of falling water. The sheer wall beside them drew back. They rode around a turn, and the ghost town of Gold Flat brooded before them in a rock-encircled pocket opening off to the right.

Log cabins were bunched together, and a two-story building towered above the others. Horse corrals were in the open; past the corrals, old mine dumps made shapeless piles near the frowning rock walls girding the flat.

Happy Jack said: "There's an extra bunk in my cabin if you want it. You buy your meals with Preacher Riley . . . two dollars a meal. The preacher's chink cook drawed fancy wages from a rich family in Denver until he filled the soup full of strychnine an' run for it. The boys call him Judas an' make him sample the grub first."

They rode into the outlaw camp. The log cabins were old, rotting. The two-story building was larger than Steve had thought.

They dismounted at a hitch rack. Other horses were tied there. The lower part of the big building was brightly lighted. It had once housed a huge barroom, a dance hall, and a store. The barroom and store were again in use.

Men were loitering at the bar. Long tables stood on the dance floor. Twenty or thirty men were eating at the tables. The noisy clamor one would have expected was absent. Men stopped eating and stared at them as they walked in.

They were, Steve saw, hard-looking, armed, cold, and watchful, as men become who lived constantly on guard. But Steve's attention was held by a coffin resting on a wooden trestle opposite the bar. The coffin was open. A body was inside.

Steve knew before he moved forward with Happy Jack that he was once more going to see the man he had killed.

And he did.

The sensation was eerie, creepy. It was as if Jack Barr's

cold, bearded face had malevolently followed him to Squaw Falls.

A wooden peg leg thumped on the floor as a man limped from the nearest table. His face was broad and pink. A benevolent fringe of white hair encircled his bald head.

"New boarder for you, Preacher," Happy Jack said.

Preacher Riley shrugged. "Better see Tom Barr first. He'll be here in a minute."

Steve saw every eye in the place studying him, and breathlessly he waited for recognition. But the clatter of horses and forks on tinware began again. No one challenged him.

Steve drew a soft breath of relief. "How about a drink?" he said to Happy Jack.

A hook-nosed barkeep served them. The liquor was burning inside when Steve saw a man enter from a doorway at the back of the old dance hall. Steve knew him at first sight. This was Tom Barr.

VII

Tom Barr lacked the black beard of his younger brother. His black mustache was cut short, but his black hair had the same curl. His guns were ivory-handled, his boots expensive and well-kept. He might have been a prosperous rancher. Yet his face was sullen and lowering.

Preacher Riley jerked his head, said something in a low voice as Tom Barr passed him.

Steve put his back to the bar and waited. Tom Barr stopped before him, shoulders hunched, head thrust forward challengingly. He was red-eyed, haggard.

48

"Who in the hell are *you?*"

"The name is High-Low Henderson."

"Never heard of you." Tom Barr turned his head. "Anybody know this man?"

No one did. Tom Barr turned back. "Where you from?"

"I came from the Blaze Bit country, over the Ringo Trail."

"What you want?"

Happy Jack interrupted: "He's on the owlhoot, Tom. Wants to hole up here."

"You look familiar to me," Tom Barr said to Steve.

Steve shrugged. "Maybe so."

All sounds had stopped. Their voices were audible to everyone. Steve knew he was on trial—before a merciless jury of hunted killers.

"You any good with a gun?"

"Pick your test."

"Cocky, ain't you?" Tom Barr seemed about to sneer, then he changed his mind. "Stick around. Maybe we can use you." He breasted the bar. "Gimme my bottle, Johnny." Brooding blackly, he ignored Steve and Happy Jack.

They went to the tables. Eating had been resumed. Preacher Riley directed them to two empty plates.

"Dive in," he directed.

Tom Barr hung over the liquor counter, brooding and drinking. Twice he walked to the coffin and stared down at the dead man. Finally he began to pace between the bar and the coffin, while the men watched him covertly. Black fury was plainly seething in Tom Barr.

Steve's plate was half empty when Tom Barr, muttering to himself, strode back past the tables. His red-veined eyes were staring ahead.

The gray-bearded man at Steve's right hand cursed softly, and an expectant silence fell as Tom Barr vanished through the rear door.

Across the table a sly-looking, fox-faced man with a reddish mustache chuckled. "Tom jest can't wait for his fun."

Steve moistened his lips. He could feel his heart thumping. He sensed what Tom Barr's fun would be. But even at that, the sudden scream of pain that rang out at the back of the building made Steve start.

One scream—that was all. Then a fateful silence. It was easy to visualize teeth clamping hard on a bloodless lip to stifle more cries. Several of the men were grinning. Others were sober. More than one looked angry. Steve felt sick with helpless rage. He was trembling, fighting down an impulse to jerk out his gun and make for that closed door. It would, he knew, be suicide. One man against two score guns didn't have a chance.

Then the door opened. Tom Barr returned, wiping the blade of a knife on his leg. A crooked smile was on his face as he returned to the bar. Glass in hand he faced the table.

"You'll really see something if Ory and Clyde bring back the man who killed Jack," he promised.

Steve pushed back his plate. "I'm tired," he said hoarsely to Happy Jack. "Where's your cabin?"

Outside, Happy Jack spoke as they rode away from the hitch rack. "I know what you're thinkin', High-Low. Tom Barr's a devil tonight. Better forget it."

One of the outer cabins was their destination. A light burned inside. A lean-to at the back already held one horse. Jackknife came out with a lantern as they unsaddled.

"So, Tom Barr figgered he could use a new man?" Jackknife said after watching a few moments.

50

"He like to fell on High-Low's neck." Happy Jack chuckled.

"You don't say," Jackknife grunted. "I wonder what Tom Barr'll say when he hears his horse wears a Clear River range brand. Stick 'em up, Henderson . . . you've got explainin' to do!"

Steve was picking up his saddle. Happy Jack was a step to the right, heaving his saddle up to a wall peg. Steve jerked his saddle up and straight-armed it at the gun covering him. Jackknife's shot blasted into the leather. The flying saddle knocked Jackknife staggering as Steve's roaring gun dropped him. Steve jumped back to cover Happy Jack, who had gone for his gun.

"Drop it!" Steve yelled.

Happy Jack's arm streaked above his head. The horses were stamping and crowding away from the spot. Jackknife's lantern was on the ground, smoking dimly, and Jackknife was writhing beside it. Steve secured Happy Jack's gun belt.

Jackknife gave a convulsive twist and lay still.

"I hated to risk it with that brand," Steve said. "Can I get in the back door to that fellow Tom Barr is torturing?"

"So you put one over on us," said Happy Jack over his shoulder. "An' the Barrs'll swear I helped you. Well, you're a dead man now. They'll hunt you down here in the cañon in two shakes."

"I'm huntin' my own self . . . huntin' me some Barrs," Steve said. "Hold still, Happy. You ain't a bad cuss, but you're in my way."

Happy Jack tried to duck. Steve's gun barrel thudded dully, and Happy Jack pitched forward.

Steve took his rifle, Happy Jack's rifle, and Jackknife's gun and belt. It made a heavy load, but he had to risk it. Guns now were all that stood between Tex and himself and death.

51

There was still a chance he could ride to the barricade and gun his way out, but that would do Tex no good. He left the horses there, skirted the cabin, and started running heavily through the dark. Steve was grateful for the black shadows down here in the cañon as he skirted the outer cabins toward the rear of the two-story building.

As yet there was no great alarm; no guards were out at the back of the building. The rear windows were dark. There were three doors. Steve tried the door at the right, behind the barroom. It opened.

He found himself in an unlighted passage, heavy with kitchen odors. Ahead of him, on the left, light came from an open doorway. Pots and pans were clattering in there.

A man stepped out carrying a tray under his arm. He turned toward the other end of the passage without seeing Steve flattened against the wall. He kicked open the door and vanished into the big room which held the tables. Steve sucked in a breath of relief.

Two doors opened off the right side of the passage. Steve tried the first door. A hinge creaked as the door opened inward. Then he tensed as from the darkness he heard Tex's voice snarl.

"Back for more of it, huh?"

Steve closed the door behind him. "Tex," he breathed.

"Steve," Tex groaned. "So they got you, too."

Tex was at the back of the room. Steve put the guns on the floor, struck a match. A low oath leaped past his lips.

Tex was standing upright, facing the back wall. His ankles were tied to spikes driven into the logs. His arms were spread-eagled and lashed to other spikes. Tex was stripped to the waist. Blood caked his back. Raw cuts had been gouged in the flesh.

"They won't live long enough to get what's comin' to

them," Steve said through his teeth. "Hold still, Tex.
They're after me, I reckon. We got fast work ahead."

"Steve, you jug-headed idjit. Why'd you walk into a tight
like this?" Tex staggered as Steve cut him loose. Steve had
to hold him up. "Been tied there since they brought me in,"
Tex mumbled.

In a few moments Tex was able to stand. His shirt, vest,
coat had been tossed in a corner. Tex put them on in the
darkness while Steve's husky whisper explained what had
happened.

"Who wants to get outta here?" Tex gritted. "I want that
snake, Tom Barr. We won't get any help from Hardwick's
neighbors. Make a run for it, Steve. I'll stay here an' clean
up."

"Here's a gun belt an' a rifle," Steve said. "Sounds good
to hear fightin' talk. Trouble with these Barrs is they ain't
had any fightin' to do. First off, while we got a chance, we'd
better fire this rat's nest. If we're ever gonna ranch it, we've
got to clean out this place."

Tex managed a chuckle. "If you was twins, Steve, we
could clean 'em barehanded. There's a lamp full of oil on
that table in the corner."

Steve piled tables and chairs against the wooden parti-
tion at the front of the room. He dashed lamp oil over the
bottom of the pile.

"All set?"

Tex was at the door looking out. "Wait," he breathed
sharply, and softly opened the door.

Heavy steps were coming back from the barroom. An
angry voice was saying: "Must be twenty of them comin'.
Maybe more. The fools'll never get past the barricade. I
wish I knowed whether the son who kilt Jack is with 'em!"

Tom Barr's voice answered: "We'll get him if he is. If he

ain't, we'll track him down like a dog. We got this one to start with, anyway."

Tex stepped out, bawling: "Come get him, damn you!" His roaring gun caught up his last word. It was then that Steve tossed a match into the oil.

A billowing fountain of flame puffed after him as he dived for the doorway, rifle in one hand, six-gun in the other.

Tex's gun clicked empty. Tex had the hall to himself. One man was down on the floor. The swinging door at the end was closing behind men who had scrambled back into the barroom.

Tex's yell was exultant. "I got the dirty snake!"

Tex had killed Tom Barr. The barroom beyond the door was in a state of pandemonium. Steve grabbed Tex's arm. "Get outta here before they bottle us in!"

Tex dashed out the back door, re-loading as if there were no pain in his wounded arm. "Scared 'em to cover," Tex chortled. "The other two Barr boys, or I'm a liar. They may be catamounts from the canebrakes, but they can dive to cover pretty fast."

Steve and Tex were running, doubling back into the night the way Steve had come, trying to reach the shelter of the nearest cabins before they were trapped there behind the big building. Pursuit was boiling out the front; men were racing around back on horses and on foot.

Another of the back doors flew open. A gun spit fire after Tex's lumbering retreat. Tex shot back.

A voice bawled: "Back toward the corrals! Two of 'em!"

Steve cursed the wan moonlight now seeping down into the cañon. Every open space was a trap. They reached the shadows behind the nearest cabin, and Steve panted: "How far down is the barricade by the falls?"

"Quarter of a mile it is . . . maybe less."

"We've got to get there. Hardwick's neighbors are comin'."

"Hell of a chance we got," Tex gasped.

They were running between the cabins now, making for the river and the trail in a wide half circle that would bring them out on the other side of the clustered cabins.

Steve burst past the corner of a cabin. A rider yanked a horse around in the open space in front. Steve shot from the hip, and behind him Tex opened up. The horse bolted away with the rider hanging low over his neck. Behind them yells announced discovery of their new position.

"They'll ketch us in the open in a minute!" Tex bit out. "Maybe we better hole up an' stand 'em off!"

"An' get burned out or blowed up when they get around to it. Tex, I got an idea. Follow me!" And Steve broke straight for the creekbed.

Here at the flat the banks shallowed out. The high cañon wall threw a black shadow over the rocky streambed and part of the cañon trail. Thirty yards from the trail they left the last cabin and were running through the open. Guns began to blast, bullets were singing about them as they dashed down the black-shadowed bank and waded into icy, knee-deep water.

"Are you crazy? We're cornered acrost here!" Tex cried violently, looking up at the sheer dizzy height of rock beyond the water.

But along here there was a rocky rubble slope at the base of the cañon wall. Bushes grew undisturbed. Not for some time would the belt of black shadow give way to the moonlight.

They clawed up the steep bank and hurled themselves behind low bushes, dropped behind protecting rocks as lead began to spat and ricochet about the spot.

Back across Squaw Creek, in the moonlight, they could see men running and riding, hunting them. Steve thrust out his rifle, lined a horseman in the sights, and squeezed the trigger. The man dropped.

Tex got one of the leaders on foot; a moment later Steve got another one. Then, across Squaw Creek, there was a break for cover.

Stooping, crawling, dodging from rock to rock and bush to bush, they advanced downstream along the heavily shadowed foot of the cliff.

Tex chortled: "You did have an idea, Steve. Lookit that fire comin' up! They'll be lit up for us to pick off a in a little while."

Flames were gushing out of the back corner of the building, licking up the dry log walls.

"Listen," Steve said. "They're shooting downstream!"

Through the low roar of the falls coming endlessly out of the narrowing cañon below, the faint sharp crackle of rifle fire was audible. From cabin windows and doorways across Squaw Creek, guns sowed lead among the rocks and bushes about them.

A ricocheting bullet smashed a rock by Steve's head. Steve groaned, clapped a hand to his eye, dropped flat.

Tex was beside him a few seconds later. "What's the matter?"

Steve did not answer for a moment; he was gritting his teeth against pain when he did.

"My left eye's gone. Punctured clean. Save your cartridges, Tex. You'll need 'em. Come on. I can see outta the other eye."

VIII

Invisible, undetected, they left the zone of gunfire. Behind them, flames rapidly gushed higher from the doomed building and sparks were beginning to shower down on the other cabins. Looking back, they could see men carrying possessions out into the open.

Downstream, the roar of the falls grew louder, and the gunfire down there at the barricade rose and fell time and again as attacks were beaten back. Half a dozen riders galloped down the trail, plainly visible in the moonlight.

"Don't shoot!" Steve warned harshly.

They were advancing fast along the base of the cliff now. The slope was getting steeper, narrower; the rocky streambed was growing deeper below them.

Blood was on Steve's lips where his teeth had bit hard from the agony in his eye. The cañon turned, and suddenly ahead of them Squaw Creek poured over a rocky lip into a black chasm. The silver moonlight made it eerie and awesome. The glinting water rushed over the rocky bed to the drop, and a sullen roar poured up from below. Damp mist floated up in the chill air.

The narrow trail across the way went on past the falls, angling down along the side of the cliff, as it had been blasted by the mining men of long ago. The stout barricade was there above the lip of the falls, blocking the trail. Well back from it, riderless horses were being held in a bunch. The moonlight showed men and guns behind the barricade.

"Got 'em blocked. They'll never get through," Tex said hoarsely at Steve's shoulder.

"What'n hell d'you reckon we came down here for? To jump over the falls?" Steve said harshly. "Pick a good rock an' get to work on 'em. If we last long enough, we'll clean the barricade out."

Tex swore with delight and crawled over behind a boulder.

Their first shots dropped some renegades who were behind the barricade. Men who knew they were across the creek realized what was happening, and a storm of shots answered their muzzle flashes.

Tex swore loudly. "Creased my leg!"

"Pour it into 'em," Steve answered.

More outlaws dropped there, behind the barricade, as bullets spattered about Steve and Tex. But there was no rush up the trail by Hardwick's men. They did not know what was happening. The water's roar drowned out their shouts.

Steve stood up and started down the bank. "Hardwick's men are gonna hang back too long. There'll be another barricade up around the turn. Boost me up the bank over there, Tex. I'll open the barricade an' get 'em."

"You can't make it!" Tex called. "You'll go over the falls!"

Steve was already sliding down over water-worn rocks into the icy current. Half-blind, lashed by pain, he waded out above his knees—and the racing current caught him and sent him staggering, floundering toward the awesome drop a few yards away.

Tex's big hand caught his shoulder, steadied him and urged him straight across the driving rush of the current. Somehow, they got across. The water shoaled, their boots gushed water over dry rocks, and the trail was a rocky shelf ten feet straight up.

"Drop your rifle an' go over the edge with your six-shooter cocked, you fightin' fool!" Tex yelled.

Tex braced himself and hoisted; Steve's feet settled on Tex's shoulders, and a heave sent him scrambling over the trail edge. It was madness and suicide, but he never stopped to think of that. He only knew it was the one thing he could do. Through a hail of gunfire, he jumped for the gate, his six-shooter spitting. How he gained that timbered barrier he never knew. The heavy wooden bar seemed almost impossible for him to lift. He struggled with it, and then the gate was swinging open.

He glanced once over his shoulder, crouching there in the shadows, pressing fresh shells in the cylinder of his hot gun. The gunfire was keeping up its deathly crackle. Through stiffened lips he sobbed curses, wondering what had happened to Hardwick and the rest. Then, through the flashes of gunfire, he made out a shadowy figure crawling over the trail edge. Tex!

For a split second, Steve saw Tex paused there, bring up his gun. There, almost at once, he saw Tex's form sink down, saw an arm reach out wildly, the fingers clutching for support, as he slid farther and farther back toward the drop, toward the streambed.

Suddenly Steve was up and running, dodging like a jack rabbit back to where Tex's hand was clinging desperately to a clump of scrub growth on the brink of the bank. He slid to a stop, his left hand grasping Tex's wrist. Then he twisted, gave all the leverage of his back to hauling Tex up again.

Through the open gate rushed a bunch of men toward them. Six-guns blazed in their hands. Tex scrambled up. "Come on, you curly wolves!" yelled Steve. "We got 'em cut off. Make for the gate!"

Together, shoulder to shoulder, Tex and Steve charged

those half dozen renegades. For an instant, under the withering fire of their guns, the bunch who had run out the gate hesitated. Then, as Steve and Tex kept up their mad charge, their guns bucking in their fists and the light from the burning buildings flickering weirdly on their powder-grimed faces, the outlaws broke and ran in wild panic for the safety of the barricade.

But they were too late. A pound of hoofs, mad shouts, and the thunder of guns cut them off. Hardwick's men came pounding up, a part swerving to wipe out what was left of the men outside, the rest to charge inside the open gate and take after the fleeing outlaws.

Steve and Tex stood by the barricade and watched them go. They were men he did not know by name or face, but not strangers. They were neighbors now, and friends for the years ahead. They were men who were riding to fight for their ranches and families, grim-faced, determined men who had at last thrown off the shackles of fear and taken the law into their own hands.

They found the saddled horses of dead men at the barricade. Tex turned toward the stream, to wade over and race back along the rubble slope to a vantage point where he could use his rifle. Steve swung into the saddle with difficulty and rode back up the trail. It was only then that he realized he had been hit in the left arm; already it was growing useless. Blood was oozing over the shoulder. And the agony in his eye would not stop. But he rode, although he sensed he was not needed. Nor was he.

Old Gold Flat had become a hell pocket of flame and destruction. The great two-story log building was a fonting inferno of flame that spewed sparks to the cliff tops, far above.

Showering sparks had fired other log cabins. Every

60

building on the flat was doomed. Riderless horses were dashing wildly about. Already the tide of battle was receding up the cañon as the outlaws fled from a spot no longer worth fighting for.

Steve rode into the red glare and blistering heat near the big building. There in the open a closed coffin rested. Tom Barr was stretched on the ground beside the coffin. Another man, a bearded man, strangely like Jack Barr, was crumpled on the ground a few paces away. Steve held his terrified horse there for a moment, staring at them.

Three of the Barr brothers—dead by the wild violent code by which they had lived. At most, only one more Barr lived. Never again would the Barr bunch be a name to terrify. The Clear River range was scoured clean.

Tex came limping across the creekbed, swearing because the fight had outdistanced him.

"Ain't you had enough?" Steve asked. "Help me fix my shoulder an' get your leg fixed. We ain't needed."

Hardwick said the same thing when he galloped back with part of the men. Hardwick's shoulders were back and he looked strangely young as he dismounted in the red fire glare and spoke to Steve and Tex.

"You two dealt the winnin' cards. What's left of them has scattered back in the mountains. Gus an' Bill Stratton were layin' back up there near the trail an' cut half a dozen down when they tried to get past. Gus said they must 'a' thought the mountains was full of guns the way they broke an' ran. We're shut of this nest of snakes for good. . . . My God, what's the matter with your eye?"

"Lost it," said Steve.

"You better get back to Conners's ranch an' have it tended to. I had orders from Connie to see that you got back all in one piece."

"A one-eyed man ain't much to bring back."

"You don't know Connie," said Hardwick.

And Steve found out his first hour back at the Conners ranch, that an eye more or less made no difference to a girl in love.

Brothers of the Damned

This was the first story T. T. Flynn completed in
1937. It was sold to *Star Western* for $300. The title
was changed upon publication to "Blood Bondage of
the Lawless" in *Star Western* (7/37).

I

Six miles to go—and no gun trouble yet. Cass Maxton relaxed on the jolting stagecoach seat, high above the horses,
and watched the clear shallows of Lonesome Creek torn
into froth by the four-horse team. The coach lurched,
swayed through the rocky ford, creaked and groaned as it
met the steep bank.

Perry Boyle, gray-mustached and lanky, threw his long
whiplash in pistol-like reports over the ears of the lead
team.

"*Hi-yi,* you spavined, wind-busted sons!" Perry bawled.
"Walk into it! King, you lazy, crow-bait loafer, pick it up!"

The stage rattled and groaned up the long winding grade
to the rim rock far above. Perry Boyle directed a thin
stream of tobacco juice over the side and grumbled:
"Rather a damn' sight be a muleskinner in a freight outfit,
then you can make talk the critters understand. Haulin' a
stage fulla pink-eared ladies an' gents cramps your talkin'
like hell."

Cass Maxton chuckled. "That preacher's wife inside got you boogery, Perry?"

"Hell of a time to be haulin' a preacher's wife," growled Perry Boyle, snaking his long lash out again. "A box o' gold to be rushed to the railroad . . . an' no chance to talk to them damned hosses to make 'em run."

"You got the trip behind you now, Perry."

Perry Boyle shot a glance under shaggy gray eyebrows to the shotgun Cass Maxton held across his lap. "I'll be worryin' till I see that gold in the express," he said flatly. "Havin' the sheriff packin' a shotgun an' a rifle on the seat by me may be safe business for the Queen Mine that's shippin' the gold . . . but it don't make me feel any better. When I'm held up, I'm polite an' agreeable. I'm paid to bring the stage an' passengers in . . . not to get killed for the freight. You sittin' there, itchin' to meet trouble, gets me jumpy. I'm too damned near you. You're all right as a sheriff, Cass . . . young as you are . . . but today I wish you was sheriffin' a long ways from my drivin' seat."

Cass Maxton threw back his head and laughed. Just past his middle twenties, Cass was hard, tanned, and broad-shouldered. His short mustache made him look older, and there was a serious set to his face in repose. Grinning, Cass said: "It won't be long now, Perry. Six more miles."

The stage rocked slowly up the ribbon of road on the other side of the limestone cliff. The outside drop went down, far down to the raw white alkali patches on the bleached range below. On the inside, toward the top of the grade, gashes in the rock zigzagged back and up to the rim rock level. Behind them, over forty miles of bad road, was the Queen Mine, and every mile of the road had been uncertain and dangerous. The last gold shipment, and the two before that, had been taken. Johnson, the mine superintendent, had asked for protection for this shipment.

Cass Maxton was still watchful and alert, but it was a relief to know the trip was about over. A box of gold, two ladies, and three men inside the coach were enough to be responsible for. Then, because Cass was watching so closely, he recognized trouble before Perry Boyle was aware.

The shotgun was up in Cass Maxton's hands when he sighted the first gunman crouching behind a rock in one of the gashes zigzagging back and up from the road. Hat pulled low, face masked by a bandanna, his body shrouded by an old slicker, the man crouched there sighting along a rifle.

Perry Boyle yanked on the reins to stop and plunged down between the wheel horses for what protection they afforded. Cass froze, with his shotgun covering the crouching figure. He sat rigidly for one terrible, breathless moment while he went weak and cold inside with fear. In that moment a shouted order came from the rocky slope above. "You're covered! Throw down that shotgun, lawman!"

Cass looked back and up, and saw the head and shoulders of another masked man. For another long moment Cass hesitated—and then threw his shotgun down into the road.

A voice hoarse with anxiety came from inside the stage. "Maxton, are you letting them take that gold?"

A woman began to whimper. "Oh, dear! I thought we were safe with the sheriff riding up there!"

Cass Maxton spoke hoarsely. "Keep quiet, all of you. Nobody'll get hurt, if you stay quiet." He lifted his voice and spoke to the bandit. "There's still a chance to back outta this. Get on your horses an' drift while you got the chance!"

A third man, dressed as the other two, spoke from the rocks above. "This is our deal, law dog. Everybody down on the road! Turn your faces to the stage, an' don't look around!"

Perry Boyle looked up disgustedly from between the horses. "Well, Maxton, if you're takin' it this way, you might as well climb down an' let 'em have it."

Cass Maxton's hands were shaking as he stepped down. He felt suddenly cold, weak, and sick inside. He knew what Perry Boyle was thinking. He knew without looking around that there was red scornful anger on the face of Johnson, the manager of the Queen Mine, who was making the trip inside the coach.

In the years to come, Cass knew that his throwing that shotgun away would dog him relentlessly. But that didn't matter. Nothing mattered much now, but that frozen, crouching figure behind the rocks that he could have riddled with buckshot with a twist of his finger, and hadn't. Then, with his hands in the air, Cass Maxton walked stiffly toward the man.

A hoarse—"Stay where you are!"—did not stop him.

Thickly Cass said: "Put down that gun! Run to your horse an' get the hell outta here!"

"You want to get shot, mister?"

The man stood up, backed away step by step, covering him with his rifle. And Cass walked toward the rifle muzzle with his hands still up.

"You fool! You damned fool! Get outta here!" Cass gritted.

Cass was an arm's length away from the gun muzzle when the quiet behind him was blasted by the snarling crack of a rifle. A bellow of a shotgun came before the echo of the first shot died. A woman screamed, and Cass turned to look.

66

He saw the stage, and a man pitching forward to the ground, and Perry Boyle fighting with the long reins to hold the horses. Then a blow from behind smashed Cass to the ground, blotting out everything.

That last flash of consciousness, and the import of what he saw was one of the most agonizing moments Cass Maxton had ever known.

Cass opened his eyes and found Perry Boyle kneeling beside him, shaking him. "If you're all right, get up, an' let's get goin'!" Boyle said harshly. "Johnson's dead. The gold's gone. We might as well call it a day."

Unsteadily Cass got to his feet with Boyle's help. The late afternoon sun struck down, hot and glaring, against the cliff and the narrow strip of road. The passengers were huddled in a little knot there in the road. A few feet from them Johnson's body lay face down in the dirt. The stagecoach was gone.

"They run us back down the road an' drove the stage up over the rim rock," said Boyle. He spat against a rock. "I reckon we'll have to walk into Alamo. Which'll be a hell of a fine end to the day."

Cass felt the back of his head as he walked to the road. The scalp was broken, there was some blood in his hair, but the blow had only been hard enough to knock him unconscious for a time.

"Are you sure Johnson's dead?" he muttered.

"Shot through the chest. Tore a hole outta his back big enough to put your fist in," Perry Boyle growled. "Your guns are gone. No use lookin' for 'em. Let's start walkin'. They said to wait half an hour before we showed over the rim rock . . . but I reckon they're dustin' a long ways off by now."

Johnson's body had been pulled over to the side of the road and the shotgun Johnson had recklessly tried to use was gone, also. Cass hardly looked at the uneasy passengers. None of them spoke to him. He felt their antagonism; they had a right, he guessed, to feel that way. They'd been so sure everything was safe while he was up there on the driver's seat beside Perry Boyle.

"Come on," Cass said heavily. "Chances are they didn't take the stage far. No place to go with it but straight ahead to Alamo. That ain't the way they'd be going."

Cass walked ahead. Perry Boyle walked at his side. They were first over the rim rock, and the stage was there a quarter of a mile ahead, off the road a short distance, with the horses grazing.

They found everything in the stage but the box of gold and the guns. When the passengers were once more inside, Perry Boyle sent his whip licking and cracking and headed for Alamo at a full gallop.

They drew up in a whirl of dust before the Boston Hotel. Perry Boyle yelled the news to the spectators who were always there to watch the stage come in.

"Held up again, boys! Somebody get a wagon! There's a body below the rim rock!"

Cass swung down. His head still hurt, but he was himself again. "I want a posse quick!" he called curtly. "Every man that can fork a horse meet in front of my office in ten minutes!"

Cass stopped by the livery barn and ordered his horse saddled. He cut over to his little frame house for a minute, and then went on to his office, got out handcuffs and a rifle and another belt gun.

Men were galloping up to the jail by then. Fourteen armed riders clustered around Cass when he was ready to ride.

When Cass spoke to them, his voice sounded cold and strange to his ears. "As far as we know, there were three men. They'll shoot to kill. They shot Johnson down, an' it's hangin' if they're caught. So don't take any chances. They can't travel fast with the weight of that gold. We've got a chance to catch up before dark!"

They sided him out of town in a cloud of dust and a thunder of hoofs—seventeen grim-faced men by the time they passed the last house. Seventeen men ready to kill, for Johnson had been a man well liked there in town. It had been murder, cold murder—and the *malpais* country to the north and west was spawning too much of this sort of thing.

Cass Maxton knew all that as he rode. The sick feeling inside had gone away, and inside he felt cold and dead. He rode like an automaton, and tried not to think. But he couldn't stop his mind from working, living again that shameful moment when he threw down his shotgun and went to the ground with his hands in the air. He passed once more through those long, ghastly seconds when he had walked toward the unwavering rifle muzzle, trying, with agony in his heart, to stop what was coming.

They found where the stage had stopped. Tracks were there where three men had unloaded the gold box; behind a large boulder they found the box broken open and the gold gone. From there the tracks of three riders cut northeast toward the foothills, and separated, one of the riders taking a led horse.

The posse split into three parts and Cass led five of the men after the led horse and the rider. The sun was at the western horizon when they entered the first piñon trees in the foothills. Not many miles ahead the mountain pines were massing on the rising slopes, and there were a dozen trails that a rider could take leading through the wild, broken, empty country.

They were at the pines when darkness fell. The fleeing outlaw was well ahead of them, riding hard. Cass judged they had not gained much. He spoke soberly to the men with him as he called a halt.

"He's headin' this way into Tumbling Spring Cañon. But my guess is as soon as it's dark he'll cut up outta the cañon . . . an' there's not a chance of followin' him tonight. We'll have to try again tomorrow. Maybe some of the other men had better luck."

Ory Carson, who owned the hardware store, swore luridly. "You know, Cass, how much chance we've got of catchin' up with the son after he's had a full night's start."

"There's no moon tonight," Cass pointed out. "Nobody brought blankets or grub. We'd have to stop here until morning. We'll save time by going back."

"You're the boss," was all that Ory Carson said. But Cass knew that Carson's silence meant more than his words.

They were the first ones back to Alamo, and Alamo was waiting for them. Horses lined the hitch rack in front of the jail, and men were crowded in the sheriff's office as Cass entered.

Gaunt old Judge Clark was sitting at Cass's desk. Dan Powers, the district attorney, was standing by the judge's chair. Powers had been talking to a powerful, black-bearded man who Cass recognized as John Walters, one of the owners of the Queen Mine. With Walters was a small, slight stranger, clean-shaven and mild-looking.

"Gentlemen," said Cass heavily, "I'm sorry to disappoint

you. Darkness stopped us before we caught up with anyone."

Dan Powers sneered slightly under his close-cropped black mustache. He never had been very friendly. His cousin had lost the election for sheriff, and Powers had taken it as a personal affront. He had tried to convince the voters that an older man was needed for sheriff, since old Bill Mackinson had died, and had acted since as if he still believed an older man was needed in the office.

Now Powers was coldly sarcastic. "We've been figuring that's about what would happen, Maxton. Lost the trail, did you?"

"We followed it until night stopped us," Cass said shortly. "By daylight, I'll be on it again. An' I can use as many men as can go along for a few days. I aim to stick to the trail as far as it goes."

Powers sneered again. "I reckon not. The trail you're following, Maxton, leads right back to one of your cells. Don't move! The court has ordered you taken into custody. These men are here to see that it's carried out."

Cass felt the two gun muzzles nudge into his back.

II

Cass stood still. "What's behind this, Powers?"

Walters, of the Queen Mine, spoke harshly: "Maxton, where's that gold shipment? Johnson's dead, and that can be laid at your door. But I'm warning you, we aim to get that gold back!"

"I'm trailin' the gold," said Cass curtly.

Powers sneered a third time. "I reckon you could find it,

Maxton. We've got a pretty clear picture of what happened. Boyle told us how you made a bluff with that shotgun, and then threw it down in the road. Then you walked up to one of the bandits to trade words with him."

Cass nodded. "I did that. I was tryin' to talk some sense into him."

Back in the crowd a man laughed, and Judge Clark spoke stiffly: "You had a shotgun to talk sense with . . . and your oath of office to back it up, Maxton. That was all you needed. You were elected sheriff. You had the trust of the people behind you, and you sold them out. You sold us all out, Maxton . . . and Johnson's dead body is there in the undertaking parlor to bear witness against you. Perhaps you didn't shoot Johnson. But"—Judge Clark spoke in the grim voice he used to pronounce sentence from the bench—"you killed Johnson as surely as if you had put a gun against his head."

Cass saw men in the small hot room who had been his friends, but they were not his friends now. His eyes wandered around, and he saw that he stood alone among them.

Cass wet his lips. His throat was dry, so that his answer was harsh. "That's stretchin' it pretty far, Judge. I had to use my judgment . . . an' I used it for the best. If Johnson hadn't opened up with that shotgun, I might 'a' saved the gold."

"What's the use?" said Walters disgustedly. "We know everything, Maxton. We know you must have had a hand in taking that gold. The way you held your fire proves it."

"It don't prove a damn' thing," Cass snapped.

Dan Powers said: "All the proof we need, Maxton, is the fact that the man you edged up to talk with was your kid brother, Jim. He had on an old slicker of yours that carried a patch in front that the preacher's wife recognized. And she saw the way his little finger was crooked. She bound that finger up when he was a youngster . . . and she didn't make any mistake about it now."

Cass felt as if his face were gray; his shoulders slumped. He looked around once more for a friend, and failed to find one. "That's all the proof you need." He nodded. "I saw that patched slicker, an' I saw that little finger . . . an' my shotgun was on him an' I was squeezing the trigger to shoot. I didn't." Cass looked around again, and his voice was thick in the quick, tense silence that had followed. "How many of your men would have put a load of buckshot into the kid brother you had raised?"

No man answered him for a moment. Then the quiet, meek-looking little man standing next to Walters said softly: "I would have, Sheriff, before I'd have let the rest happen."

"Who are *you?*" asked Cass.

"Reingold's the name. I'm with the Pinkerton Detective Agency," said the other mildly.

Cass saw then that Reingold's eyes were an ice-blue, and his meekness was like the watchful quietness of a coiled rattler. He knew that he looked at a killer who would have been an outlaw if he hadn't been a detective. Cass jerked his eyes away from the Pinkerton man. He looked around the room, and he spoke with an effort to every man there.

"Jim didn't know where I'd gone today. Jim didn't know I was on that stage. He's been wild . . . but I never thought he'd try a thing like that. Most of you men know Jim. Some of you know I've had him alone with me since Jim's mother died when he was nine an' I was sixteen. I promised our mother five minutes before she died that I'd look out for him, an' I tried to do it. Some of you know how Jim grew up, always laughing his way through everything. Life was too easy for him, an' I couldn't make Jim see different. The world was his oyster, an' Jim was hell-bent on having a good time opening it. I tried to keep him away from bad company, but Jim didn't see much harm in it. An' today when I saw him down the barrel of my shotgun, I knew Jim had gotten out of hand. But buckshot wasn't the right medicine, men. Jim was too frightened to know what he was doing when he saw me there on the stage. I could 'a' talked him out of it, gotten him away from there with no harm done . . . but Johnson cut loose with his shotgun, an' it was too late then."

Dan Powers broke the silence. "It's a nice story, Maxton. But you were sheriff. Johnson was murdered. Your brother is as guilty as hell, even if he didn't fire the shot."

"I know it," agreed Cass bleakly. "And I took a posse an' went after him." Cass swallowed. "I went after my kid brother," he said huskily, "an' gave the posse orders to shoot to kill. What more could I have done?"

"Found him . . . an' brought him back over your saddle," a voice said over at the side of the room.

Cass wheeled to face the spot, and found the speaker with his eye.

"You needn't have said that, Tom Stevens," he said bitterly. "I came back to get another posse an' take the trail again. My oath of office means something to me. Jim has blood guilt on his hands. I'm ready to go after him."

Dryly Judge Clark said: "That won't be necessary. There may be a lot of truth in what you say, Maxton. It can come out in court later. There seems to be too much evidence that you might have had an understanding with your brother about that gold . . . since no one but Johnson and yourself knew the gold was to be shipped. We have the driver's word for that."

"Damn you, Judge," said Cass thickly. "That's a lie. You know it's a lie. I never was a thief."

Dan Powers said: "That'll all come out after while. We'll lock you up and let your deputy carry on in your place . . . and, if it isn't all legal, you can do something about it later. Here, hold his hands, men. I think he'd better be handcuffed."

Slim Henderson was the deputy. Cass had appointed Slim, and Slim was ashamed as he stood before the bars an hour later.

"Anything I can get you, Cass?" Slim questioned.

Cass had been sitting on the edge of the cot, staring at the handcuffs on his wrists. He looked up, shook his head.

"Nothing, Slim."

"I hate this like hell, Cass. But there's nothin' I can do. Judge Clark an' Dan Powers an' some of the others run things pretty much, an' they're in the saddle."

"I know, Slim. Where's that Pinkerton man?"

"Out gettin' him a bite to eat. He came in hungry from Central City, where Walters wired for a man to come on the next train."

"What's he aim to do?"

"He don't talk," said Slim.

"He's a killer."

"Uhn-huh . . . tell that to look at him close."

Cass stared at the floor. "Reingold's going after those three men. After Jim. No doubt of it. Funny, Slim, I'd rather bring Jim back or shoot it out with him. He'd understand. I'd make him understand. But Reingold'll go after him like a snake striking out from a patch of grass. It's my place to go after Jim, Slim. I raised him . . . an' it's up to me to bring him back."

"That ain't a job I'd want," said Slim bluntly. "An' there

don't seem to be any chance of your gettin' outta here to do it. Better take it easy. Call me if you want anything. I'll hang around in the office there."

"How about the posse?"

"Reingold says there ain't any use wastin' time followin' them tracks by morning. Everybody's sorta waitin' for the rest of your men to come back in."

Slim went back into the office, where voices could be heard talking. Other voices outside in front of the jail drifted through the open window.

In less than a quarter of an hour a group of riders galloped up. Shortly after that another bunch arrived.

Slim stepped back and confided that the other two parts of the posse had turned back from the tracks they were following when it got too dark to see.

One of the bandits had gone west, off the rim rock into *malpais* country; the other had gone on north toward the Dry Bone Hills. By morning an Apache tracker would hardly be able to catch up with them.

Gradually the crowd before the jail began to drift away. After a time there were a few yips and a shot or two down the street, and Cass knew that some of the men were getting liquored up by way of tapering off the day's excitement.

Awkwardly Cass was able to roll cigarettes and get them lighted with his handcuffed hands. He paced the cell, thinking. They hadn't taken his sheriff's badge away. He rubbed his hand over it and grinned bitterly. He'd been proud of that badge the day he took office, and prouder of it every day since. Too proud, maybe, and too intent on making a good sheriff, to pay as much attention to Jim as he should have.

No need to wonder why Jim had brought all this to pass. Jim never thought hard about anything. When Jim wanted to do something, he did it with a grin and a laugh. Now Jim, twenty, with a mop of curly hair, laughing eyes, and a smattering of freckles over his cheek bones, was riding hard away from a murder charge.

Then Cass thought about Reingold, the quiet little Pinkerton man, and his face seamed in grim lines and he came to a decision. He lay down on the cot and closed his eyes and was asleep in five minutes, as he had always been able to do. He waked up at the time he'd determined to, at two hours after midnight.

Alamo was quiet now. Most of the lights were out. No voices were audible in the sheriff's office, beyond the heavy connecting door. But a thread of light showed under the keyhole, and, after gazing restlessly about the cell for a few minutes, Cass heard a chair creak and steps cross the outer room. After he sat down on the edge of the cot and called, the door opened and Slim stepped in, yawning.

"Couldn't you sleep any more, Cass?"

"Too much on my mind," Cass said gruffly. "Bring me some water, Slim."

"Sure," said Slim. "I've got a sack of sandwiches in there, too, Cass. Sent for 'em before midnight. I thought you might be hungry. I didn't want to wake you up."

"Thanks, Slim. I reckon I'm hungry as hell, too. I didn't think about it before."

Slim was back in a few minutes with a bulging paper bag and a glass of water. He sat the glass down on the floor and unlocked the barred door and stepped in.

"Here you are, Cass. Anything else?"

With a quick outthrust of his handcuffed hands, Cass got Slim's gun and flicked the muzzle against Slim's side.

Slim stood still. "Drop the sandwiches, Slim." The bag

fell to the floor with a soft thud. "Slim, I hate like hell to do this."

"Yeah," said Slim calmly, holding the glass of water, "I reckon."

"Get your keys, slow an' easy, Slim. Unlock these handcuffs. An' don't make a hasty move. I aim to go outta here ahead of you."

Carefully Slim unlocked the handcuffs and raised his hands above his head.

"Stand right there." Cass's voice was husky. "God, Slim, I hate this. You trusted me. You're a square shooter. But I've got a job to do. I've got to get outta here and do it."

"You're goin' after Jim?" asked Slim quietly.

"Yeah. You know that. Nothin' else'd make me pull a trick like this, Slim."

"You got the drop on me. I can't stop you. Maybe you know best," said Slim without looking around. "But don't get yourself shot, Cass. One of your hosses is out at the hitch rack. There wasn't anybody around the last time I looked out. An' what you do now is up to you, Cass. God help you."

Cass put a hand on Slim's shoulder for a moment, and then backed away, caught the bag of sandwiches off the floor, and locked the cell door behind him.

In the front office, Cass moved quickly, getting another gun, a rifle, extra boxes of cartridges, and out of the small iron safe he took a money belt that was his personal property. Then quietly Cass stepped outside into the starlit night. A horse snorted at the hitch rack.

The steps of the walking horse were muffled in the dry dust of the street as Cass rode out of Alamo, headed toward the rim rock and Lonesome Creek and the *malpais* country to the west.

There was a lump in his throat and a dead feeling deep down inside, and the last thing Cass did as he passed out of town was to unpin his sheriff's badge, and finger it for a moment, and then put it away in a pocket of his money belt. That night Cass Maxton vanished from the world.

III

A week later a gaunt, careless stranger rode the Fire River country far to the southwest of the Alamo *malpais*. It was a vast and lonely land through which he rode, too poor for cattle in most places, too dry for sheep part of the year. Alkali patches lay white the year around. Prickly pear sprawled over the ground in thorny beds, and stiff stalks of cholla cactus grew out of gravelly soil. At times a man could ride endlessly through the deceptive green of low greasewood bushes, and get nowhere. Beyond the grim barren mountains scattered about the horizon was other country just as bad. The ranches here were poor and far apart, Mexican sheep ranches for the most part.

There were other travelers in the Fire River country. Now and then in the distance a rider would drift off in another direction to avoid contact, and not be seen again. There were close-mouthed, watchful men on the trails who scanned a stranger carefully, and said little, and went their way on their own secret business. Now and then at night a small campfire made a flickering point of light against the backdrop of the night.

Two weeks later the stranger rode up to one such campfire. He came singing, and there was one man standing back from the fire to greet him. The stranger twisted in the saddle. The stubble of brown beard on his face parted with a grin as he said: "I saw the light an' thought I'd drop over to chin a little. Any objections?"

"Anybody with you, stranger?"

"Nope. I wouldn't need any chinnin' then."

"Light," said the bearded man by the fire. As the stranger dismounted, two other men walked out of the night where they had been watching. One of the men had a long scar on his chin. One of his hands was bandaged and his voice was surly as he stepped up to the fire.

"Damned if I didn't think it was that singin' fool we met on the road last week. Your voice sounded just like his. Live around here, stranger?"

"Driftin' through." The stranger grinned. "The name is Denver. An' if your singing friend is heading toward the border, maybe I better keep off his trail. I might get hung for some of his work."

"Don't go over by Wild Horse Valley then," Scarface grunted. "Because there was three of them an' they looked gaunted out an' on short rations. But their guns was prime. You're liable to find a Mex sheepherder strung up by his toes over there an' every Mex in a hundred miles layin' for that damned gun-slingin' Singin' Kid."

"Thanks," said Denver, squatting by the fire and rolling a cigarette. "That the handle he goes by, the Singing Kid?"

"It's as good as any," Scarface growled. "He was singin' when we met 'em, an' singin' the last we heard of him."

The bearded man who had waited by the fire chuckled. "You wasn't singin', Cliff. You was a bellerin' an' cussin' an' a-thirstin' for his gore."

"I'll get him yet," said Cliff viciously.

"You'll hightail fast when you see him comin'," chuckled the speaker. He explained across the campfire to

80

Denver. "Cliff here took a fancy to the kid's rifle an' pulled his gun an' allowed he'd borry it until they met again. An' this Singin' Kid laughed an' shot Cliff's gun outta his hand before any of us knowed what was happening. Greased lightning, he was. Never seen his beat. An' he sat there, whistlin' while Cliff tried to stop the blood, an' laughed an' promised Cliff the next time he'd take out Cliff's back teeth to make a necklace for his next girl."

Scarface spat into the fire and scowled. Denver eyed him speculatively, smiled.

Half an hour later Denver rode away, careful to keep his face to the campfire until the night closed in around him. He also was carrying a good rifle. But Denver's face was grim as he rode half the night before stopping by a chamois thicket and making a dry camp until daylight. There was a sheep ranch and a water hole some miles ahead that he'd hit before he ate again.

Three days later in Wild Horse Valley, Denver crossed the trail of the Singing Kid. And he found a grave.

A flat-faced Dutchman by the name of Kudner ran a shabby saloon and store out there on the flats of Wild Horse Valley. The next liquor was a day's ride away. The Dutchman's was a stopping point for anyone in that territory and Denver started pumping him for information.

The Dutchman was still profane about it. "Saturday night," he spluttered across his rough-plank bar, "dere vas eight customers spendin' plenty. Dot Singin' Kid rides up with two other boys and one dollar. I tell you . . . one dollar! In one hour he win two hundred dollar from my customer, laughin' all the time. An' when dis Mike say he don't lose honest, de Kid laugh an' throw the cards in Mike's face. When Mike draws his gun quick, dis damn'

81

kid an' his frients shoot up the place."

"What happened to Mike?" asked Denver.

"I haf to pay a Mex to dig a hole for that Mike," complained the Dutchman. "Two more was wounded. An' that damn' Kid haf take every *centavo* in de place, all the guns, an' runs off all the horses before he rides away singin'. So I haf to give free drinks. *Dunder,* vot a night!"

"The Singing Kid was busted, huh?" said Denver thoughtfully.

"Not when he left," groaned the Dutchman.

"Who were your customers?"

"Questions," said the Dutchman evasively, "ain't asked here, *mein* frient. You buy . . . I sell."

"I reckon that's healthy." Denver nodded. "Get my grub together. I'm ridin' on."

The trail followed by a gaunt and sober man who called himself Denver was not a straight one, but it never ended. West into the Gila country the trail led, following information Denver picked up in bars and stores and around lonely campfires. There were no tracks to follow, because the Singing Kid and the two riders who sided him changed to fresh horses more than once. They did not buy horses.

A deputy sheriff recognized a brand on a stolen horse, and was shot in the leg and disarmed when he tried to make an arrest. Then the rumors were stronger, for the print of the Singing Kid grew heavier on the country through which he passed.

West of the Gila four men held up a stage. The bandit leader joked with the victims, and was singing when he rode away. Four men—and then there were five.

A posse north of Tucson was held at bay for hours in a running fight by the uncanny marksmanship of the bandit who lagged behind his men with a spare horse and harried the posse.

In Yuma, a month after that, a laughing young gunman with a blond mustache, sided by six riders, took the main street apart for ten minutes, and then vanished south over the border into the bleak brown coastal deserts of Sonora. The gaunt man called Denver found a sheriff's Reward notice in Yuma.

$1000 REWARD
DEAD OR ALIVE!

Jim Maxton, twenty years old, about five feet nine, blond hair naturally curly. Little finger of left hand crooked at second joint. Wanted for murder and hold-up. Dead shot, six-gun or rifle.

The Reward notice had been issued by the sheriff's office of Alamo. But Yuma held no Reward notice for Cass Maxton, one-time sheriff of Alamo. No one in Yuma was looking for the sheriff of Alamo County, nor did anyone in Yuma seem to connect the Singing Kid, as the border country was now calling him, with Jim Maxton of Alamo.

The man called Denver filled his saddlebags with hardtack and bacon, bought another water bottle, and rode south from Yuma, his grim quest far from finished.

Already the Arizona deserts had burned Denver black. He was lean and worn down to bone and muscle. His short beard covered somber lines that were biting deeply into his face. Those lines grew deeper in his cheeks as he drifted down into Sonora, heading south and east, toward the high, broken country of fabulous mines and great *haciendas* on the flanks of the Sierra Madres. The Yaqui Indians held those mountains—the fighting Yaquis, proud, cruel, disdainful of even the hard-riding, hard-fighting Rurales.

But even here rumor crept along the trails, into the hot, dirty little *cantinas,* and about the dusty, lazy little plazas. They told of a handsome young *gringo* who laughed, sang, and danced, loved and killed like the right hand of the devil himself. *El sinsonte,* his name began to be spoken. *El sinsonte*—the Mockingbird who never stopped on his mysterious, night-shrouded travels.

With a relentless, inexorable patience, the man called Denver followed the trail. Again it became clearer as the days and weeks dragged by.

El sinsonte had led his men in a daring raid on the San Jacinto Mine. Then he had attended the *fiesta* of San Miguel in Margarito, and danced half the night in the plaza with the prettiest girls. He had bought tequila for *el jefe* himself before it was known who he was.

El sinsonte had dashed from ambush and captured the pompous Colonel Chavez. A week later the *coronel,* in person, had led a detachment of soldiers on the trail of the young *gringo* and his followers. But *el sinsonte* was waiting for his pursuers. He shaved *el coronel*'s head and left him afoot on the road between Hermosillo and Guaymas, with a canteen of water and no pants. Chavez had sworn a blood feud to end only with death because of that insult.

Then for a day and a night the rich Hacienda del Plata had been held as the personal property of *el sinsonte* and his men while they rested their horses and themselves and entertained *Don* Tomás Carolo y Seville and his daughter with lavish hospitality and politeness—in the *don*'s own house.

Don Tomás, so rumor had it, was so enraged by the mistiness in his daughter's eyes when *el sinsonte* rode off singing, that he was resolved to confine his daughter in a convent until she was of age. But that last was the talk of the *cantinas*. A more sober fact was that *Don* Tomás Carolo y Seville was the brother of the military governor of Sonora. *El sinsonte* was to be hunted to the death for that escapade.

The man called Denver heard all that in Guaymas, where the mountains encircled the cobalt blue water of the harbor and the gossip of the hinterland filtered in over a score of roads and trails. From the Hacienda del Plata, *el sinsonte* and his men rode east into the mountains. Where they might be, no one knew. Perhaps on the way overland toward Chihuahua or El Paso, fleeing from the wrath of the Sevilles.

That night in a *cantina* down near the waterfront, the man called Denver looked over his glass of warm beer into the mirror, and saw a face glance through the doorway, then it vanished. Without looking around, Denver finished his beer, and walked past the end of the bar, out the back way into a black alley. There he flattened himself against the adobe wall and waited in the darkness.

Three minutes Denver waited, gun in hand—and then the back door creaked and a man stepped softly out. Denver's gun jabbed forward. Denver's hard hand grabbed the man's shoulder. His cold voice rasped: "Well, Reingold, you found me. An' I'm saying it's the worst mistake you ever made."

IV

Reingold, the mild, quiet little Pinkerton man, froze in his tracks. Then a soft laugh came from him. "I've been close

85

since you walked out of the Alamo jail, Maxton. I could have taken you twenty times. Put up that gun. You don't have to worry about me."

Cass Maxton scowled in the darkness. "Sounds like you've been following me all the way."

Reingold laughed again. "How do you think you got out of that Alamo jail so easy? I wanted you out, Maxton."

"I'll be damned," said Cass slowly. "Figuring I'd join Jim, huh? An' take you along?"

"Sorta," admitted Reingold. "But I figured wrong, Maxton. I'll take an oath now you didn't have anything to do with that hold-up. I've watched you trying to catch up with your brother week after week. You'd have been there long ago if you two were in cahoots."

"You can head back to the border then, Reingold, now that you know the truth. Jim's my business. I'll take care of him."

"I don't turn back when I start after a man," said Reingold mildly. That soft reply out of the darkness made Cass Maxton once more think of a snake slithering steadily and stealthily after its prey. Reingold said: "Have you found out what happened to that Queen Mine gold?"

"Nope. But Jim wasn't spending it."

Reingold said: "A letter came to you at Alamo from your brother. It was opened. He wrote he was sorry about the gold, and he'd buried it on the west side of the Big Rock, for you to dig up and return. He said he didn't aim to find himself an outlaw, but, as long as he was one, he'd keep going and have a good time at it. He doesn't know you're after him."

"The Big Rock is down the creek two miles from our old ranch house," Cass said slowly. "Jim and I used to play around it when we were kids. You can find it easy enough. Go back an' get the gold, Reingold. I'm going on."

"Before long your brother'll be the most notorious outlaw along the border," said Reingold.

"I'll catch up with him before that," said Cass heavily. "I taught Jim to shoot. I let him get outta hand. I'll bring him back my prisoner, as sheriff of Alamo County."

"You're not the sheriff now, Maxton."

"I'm still packing my badge. That's good enough for me."

Reingold was silent for a moment. "If he wasn't your brother, I'd believe you," said Reingold softly. "But you didn't kill him once . . . and you won't the next time. He's a killer now. He's *el sinsonte,* the bandit. He knows he'll hang if he's caught. You ain't the man to go after him for that, Maxton. Not your brother."

Huskily Cass said: "There's some things bigger than being brothers. I put my hand on the Bible when I took office an' swore to do my duty. Jim knew all that. Jim knew what was right an' wrong . . . but he wouldn't stop to think. There were two more with him. They've all got to answer for it."

"No one knows yet who those two others were," said Reingold. "When you catch up with them, it'll be brother against brother . . . and guns the only way to settle it. What do you think's going to happen?"

"Damn you," said Cass harshly, "I don't know. And you won't be there to see. Good bye, Reingold."

The Pinkerton man went to the ground under the downswinging revolver barrel without a sound. Cass knelt for a moment to make sure Reingold would live, and then walked out of the alley and headed for the stable where he had left his horse.

★ ★ ★ ★ ★

Band music was playing for the promenading crowd in the Guaymas plaza that evening when Cass rode east through the low mountains. He moved fast now. Jim was a killer—but a more dangerous killer would quickly be following. Reingold was deceptive, for in addition to his meekness and deadliness, the man was as stubborn as fate. Reingold would make no more mistakes. But following *el sinsonte* and his men was like trailing the will-o'-the-wisp. They had gone into the mountains, into the fringe of the Yaqui country. After a gun battle with a band of Yaquis they had turned south.

In the little foothill *placitas* Cass heard rumors. A woodcutter had seen a score of heavily armed men led by a young *caballero* in the silver-studded costume of a grandee, riding up an isolated valley trail. Two women coming from a tiny village had heard the voice of an angel echoing in a foreign song through the rocky defile of a deep barranca as the sun went down.

Then in the last hour of daylight Cass rode into a tiny village back in the mountains and struck the broad, fresh trail he had been looking for. A charcoal burner three hours back had told him of this little *placita* of Torilla, where a man might buy tequila and get the gossip of the district.

Cass was riding into the tiny plaza before he saw that it was half filled with armed soldiers in uniform, some on foot, some lounging in the saddles. A dozen men saw him at once, and almost that many riders spurred toward him, bringing up their guns.

Cass reined in while they gathered around him, covering him with their guns, hurling questions at him. Who was he? Where was he from? What was he doing here—dog of a *gringo!* A young officer galloped up, forced his horse

88

through to Cass, waved aside Cass's remark, and ordered the men to disarm the prisoner and bring him to the *cantina*.

The *cantina* at the other end of the little plaza was a long, low building of flat stones mortared with adobe. A line of army horses filled the hitch rack. Two sentries stood guard at the door, and ten or twelve men were inside when Cass was brought in.

At one end of the room two men were seated at a table that held bottles and glasses. One of the men was Reingold, the Pinkerton man. A thin smile spread across Reingold's face.

"I wasn't expecting you to show up around here, Maxton," said Reingold without malice.

Cass had to grin himself. "Got the Mexican army to protect you?" he asked.

Reingold pushed a glass across the table. "Pour yourself a drink," he said. "I'm helping them and they're helping me. This is *Coronel* Chavez, who's been sent out by General Seville, the governor of Sonora, to get *el sinsonte* dead or alive." Reingold chuckled. "And after the trick your brother played on Chavez a few weeks ago, Chavez isn't interested in taking him alive. He swears he'll take *el sinsonte*'s head back in a sack. And I guess he'll do it."

"An' you'll help him, Reingold?"

"This ain't my party now," said Reingold. "But my orders were to get him dead or alive. I never had much idea of getting him back alive from this far south of the border, with that bunch backing him."

Coronel Chavez, on the other side of the table, listened with a scowl on his swarthy face. A thick-chested man, with a broad face and bulging middle, Chavez looked like a man who had not been used to long rides for some time.

He broke in irritably in Spanish: "Who is this *gringo?*"

Reingold answered him in fluent Spanish. "*Señor* Maxton is the name, *mi Coronel*. He is a sheriff from New Mexico . . . a man also looking for this *el sinsonte*. A long time he has been on the trail. A man most deadly, *mi Coronel.*"

"Ahhh!" said Chavez. The scowl left his face. He waved a genial hand to the chair. "*Señor,* be seated. You will have the honor of watching me cut off the head of this so-cursed outlaw."

"*¿Sí?*" said Cass briefly as he sat down.

"*¡Sí!*" said Chavez in high good humor. He pounded the table and bellowed at the bar, where a soldier was serving. "Another bottle, son-of-a-goat! Must I ask for everything I want?" Chavez drained the clear tequila in the glass he had been holding in his thick fingers and beamed at Cass. "Even a wolf must go to a den sometime, *señor*. This *el sinsonte* has made the mistake of finding a den for a few days. My Yanqui scouts have brought in the dog who has seen them there."

Chavez nodded toward a ragged native standing at the bar between two broad-faced Yaquis armed with knives, belt guns, and rifles.

Reingold was smiling again as he spoke to Cass in English. "*El sinsonte* made a mistake where he tangled with the Yaquis. His men killed three of them. They'll help hunt him to hell an' gone."

"Where," Cass asked the officer in Spanish, "is this *el sinsonte?*"

"A night's ride, at the *placita* of San José," said Chavez expansively. "We will rest a little and ride on tonight, and at the light of day we will attack. There are only two ways out of San José, and we will close them both." Chavez filled his glass again. "*Señor,*" he promised, "before breakfast you will laugh to see this hand of mine cut off the head of *el sinsonte.* I have taken an oath that only my sword shall do it." He drank deeply.

Wooden-faced, Cass looked at Reingold, and Reingold shrugged slightly. "This ain't our business," Reingold said in English. "We're in Mexico now." And in Spanish Reingold spoke dryly to Chavez: "I'll be there to help see that *el sinsonte* does not escape. But perhaps *Señor* Maxton would rather stay here. You see, *mi Coronel* . . . this is the brother of *el sinsonte.*"

Chavez did not move for a moment. "*¿El hermano?*" he said gutturally.

In the same dry voice Reingold explained: "*Señor* Maxton has followed *el sinsonte* to arrest him. The law is like that, *mi Coronel*. It does not matter, this being a brother, if one carries the law after a killer."

Chavez emptied his glass again. A slow smile spread across his swarthy face.

"So?" he said. "So? The *Yanqui* law is like that? *¡Bravo!* This man of the law shall go with us to see how glorious is the justice of Mexico." Chavez sighed and shook his head. "But *Señor* Maxton, until the head of *el sinsonte* rolls on the ground, I grieve to keep you by my side as a prisoner. One does not know the heart of a brother . . . *verdad?*"

Chavez barked an order and guns covered the prisoner.

Grim, pale, Cass looked at Reingold. "Damn you, Reingold. I'll never forget you for this."

"I'm sorry," said Reingold regretfully. Then he added calmly: "You asked for it, Maxton. Now you've got to face it."

V

The full moon rested on the shoulder of the mountain across the valley when Cass Maxton rode out on the last stretch of the long trail. The Yaqui scouts went ahead of the column, and near the front rode Chavez and Reingold. Cass was farther back, near the middle of the column, unarmed, with his wrists lashed together and his legs bound tightly to the stirrup straps and his ankles connected by rawhide thongs that ran under the horse's belly. He could ride with a fair degree of comfort, but he could not leave the saddle, and he was unarmed. Half a dozen soldiers had been ordered to watch him.

The Sierra Madres reared, wild and rugged, on all sides. They had not been on the trail half an hour when the eerie howl of a wolf cut through the low murmur of sound that hung over their advance. The road was little better than a trail now, wide enough for the occasional use of a wagon or cart.

Cass rode silently, his chin sunk on his breast. The full bitterness of the long grim chase had closed in. A dozen times as he moved through stretches of shadow, Cass tried to loosen the rawhide thongs around his wrists. But his struggles only drew them tighter, so that his wrists began to swell.

Twice when the column paused for rest, the nearest soldier reined close and leaned over to feel and inspect the wrist lashings. In the moonlight he was a surly, officious fellow who hated *gringos,* and especially this man who all now knew was the brother of *el sinsonte.*

"Ha," he said, so that Cass could hear, "this *gringo* will have a face to see when his brother's head is kicked before him."

San José was a night's ride away, but a slow ride evidently, for they did not hurry. Five times before midnight they forded brawling mountain streams. The water in the last stream reached to the leather tapaderos of the stirrups, and on the other side in a grassy flat Chavez gave an order. The column fell out and dismounted to water the horses and men. Chavez was one of the first out of the saddle.

"Tell the *coronel* I want to drink from the river and stretch my legs," Cass snapped to the guards who remained with him.

His legs were untied. Four men with rifles ready marched with him to the riverbank and watched him kneel and drink.

Cass plunged his wrists into the cold water to soak the rawhide as much as possible. The surly soldier who was watching him so closely jerked up his arms up with an oath.

"See the *gringo*'s trick? He tries to wet the rawhide so it stretches. But Gregorio Cabezon is too clever for him."

The men laughed, and Cass cursed the fellow silently as his wrists were examined carefully after he stood up.

Reingold's amused voice spoke in Spanish a few feet away: "Don't you like the *coronel*'s hospitality, *amigo?*"

Cass said thickly: "I'm tryin' not to make up my mind to kill you, when I get free, Reingold."

"So you would kill me?" Reingold chuckled, then in the same amused tone he shifted to English: "I've just stopped by your horse, Maxton. Feel down in front between the saddle and the pad. What you do is up to you. This is Chavez's party. I'm only along. And dragging a man along to watch his brother get butchered is more than I can stomach. Better turn back. You'll get butchered yourself if you get in the way. Good luck." Reingold turned away, shifting again into Spanish with another chuckle: "San José is not far away now, *amigo*. Wait patiently."

The guards and the men near who heard thought that funny. The laughter was led by the officious Gregorio.

The smoldering fury against Reingold left Cass as he was led back to his horse. Blood was hammering in Cass's veins, although he was cool and alert as he swung back into the saddle and sat there while his legs were tied in place once more.

The reins of the horse had been dropped to the ground. Two mounted men, one of them the officious Gregorio, were considered enough to watch him, and they were not watching too closely as they bantered with their comrades. Cass shifted his position, felt under the front of the saddle, and touched the handle of a hunting knife that had been slipped blade first under there out of sight.

Cass had the knife cradled under his wrists a moment later. Then, with all malice toward Reingold gone, Cass wedged the knife firmly under one thigh and sawed the rawhide thongs against the keen blade. In a minute or so his wrists were free. He held them there and flexed his fingers and wrist muscles to get the stiffness out. When the surly Gregorio rode close to look at the wrist thongs once more, Cass struck him behind the ear with the heavy bone handle of the knife, then snatched rifle and six-gun as the dazed man reeled in the saddle. His horse was plunging down the road before anyone knew what had happened.

Cass's legs were still tied to the stirrup straps and under the horse's belly. He leaned low, raking the spurs hard. He had jammed the rifle down in the empty saddle boot, but he held the six-gun cocked. The lunging horse was half a dozen steps away before a shout broke out behind him and slugs hummed about his head.

Horses and men were all about. The sudden boil of excitement brought confusion to the men who did not know what was happening. The flat was in an uproar as guns blasted, men shouted, and horses plunged, rearing. Cass's maddened horse raced through the confusion to the back of the flat, where the trail curved up a sharp rise of ground into sheltering trees. Twice his horse knocked other horses out of the way. He rode down one scrambling man, and the whiplash crack of a bullet passed close to his head. Then Cass was moving fast through the faint moonlight.

Abruptly the last men were behind him, the trees were just ahead, and a rider galloped out of the shadows to see what was wrong. It was one of the Yaqui scouts. Cass saw the man bring up a rifle. Cass fired two shots from the heavy army revolver. The Yaqui dropped his rifle and fell forward across his horse's neck. He clung there as the beast bolted off the other side of the trail.

The grade was up for a mile through trees that cast heavy shadows. At the top Cass reined up, feeling with relief the blood flow back into his feet and ankles after he'd cut the thongs. Far down the grade the low, ominous thunder of galloping hoofs rolled up through the night.

They were coming—and they'd keep coming. More than fifty of them Cass had counted as they had started the night's ride. Chavez would drive them to the end now. There would be no lessening of the fury of that pompous officer, faced at the last moment with the frustration of his revenge. Both Jim and Cass now were marked for death.

Cass lifted the reins and put his horse once more into a gallop. Reingold had given him his chance. There was no one to look to now but Cass Maxton. San José and *el sinsonte* were hours away.

Higher the trail led, in the moonlight silver spreading over a vast rampart of black rocks off to the left. The pursuit thinned out as the best riders drew ahead of the others. But each time Cass stopped to breathe his horse, he heard the drive of hoofs echoing faintly through the night behind him.

An hour later the trail led over a rickety bridge spanning a deep, narrow ravine. There were no sides to the bridge. Water brawled ominously over rocks far below. Cass walked his panting horse gingerly across and into a winding upgrade between great rocks. He stopped in the shelter of the first rock and dismounted and took the rifle.

He was steady and his horse was breathing easier when shadowy figures raced through the moonlight to the ravine. Three of them strung out in a bunch, and a fourth one was not far behind. The first man yanked his horse to a walk when he saw the bridge. The four of them bunched up, talking excitedly. Then one man started across.

Cass covered the man with the front rifle sight and let him get a fourth of the way across the dizzy drop before he squeezed the trigger. The horse reared with a scream of fright and spun half around.

The rider was yelling with terror and trying to slide from the saddle as the front hoofs of the horse plunged down over the side into space. Horse and rider were turning over and over as they vanished from sight. One more awful yell of terror came up from the black void, and a dull *thud* far below was the last sound.

The second rider had been staring over the bridge. He slid back over the rump of his horse and bolted to firm ground. The others sat for a moment as if frozen by the spectacle.

Cass's shout in Spanish rolled through the night. "Tell *Coronel* Chavez I am waiting here for him!"

His voice broke the spell. The riders wheeled around and galloped madly back from that spot of death. Cass fired a shot after them. They were out of sight a moment later.

Quietly Cass led his horse for fifty yards, until there was no chance he would be seen from the other side of the bridge. He forked the saddle and walked the horse for a quarter of a mile before breaking it into another run.

It would be some time before *Coronel* Chavez could drive men across that bridge to make sure whether or not the hidden gunman was waiting on the other side. They would not come so fast after they were over. They would not be sure until daylight what ambush another mile might bring. He'd have an hour's start.

Twice Cass rode past rock hovels beside the trail where dogs ran out and barked. He forded other streams and rode through trees that muffled the drum of pounding hoofs. When he stopped to rest his horse, the back trail was quiet.

The moon went down and the night was like pitch for a time, and only the uncanny sense of the horse kept the way. Cass had no way of knowing whether there were forks in the road. He was riding slower now, saving the tiring horse and waiting for the dawn. Slowly light seeped in from the east against Cass's haggard face.

Then, when the blush of the rising sun was striking across the sky, Cass rode out of the trees on a rocky crest and heard the distant voice of an angel echoing in song from cliff to cliff. There was San José before him, and Jim was down there somewhere by the shallow creek. Jim might have been a kid, back home at Alamo, on the old ranch, singing again as he washed up in the morning.

For a moment, Cass Maxton sat spellbound with his

heart in his throat, paying no attention to the armed rider coming up the trail toward him.

VI

Long ago, San José had been a mining town, perhaps when the Jesuit *padres* pushed into the innermost heart of the Sonora Mountains and worked mines to build their churches and missions. Here the rocky streambed curved in toward a vast and frowning semicircle of cliff. In the half circle of the cliff, the little tumble-down rock houses were huddled; the stream came past a rocky drop at the top of one cliff and brawled past another drop at the opposite cliff. Two trails led down from San José across the water. That was the only way out for many miles.

Chavez had been right. This was a dangerous den, for men could be bottled up in the semicircle of those frowning walls of rock and be picked off at leisure by rifle fire as they tried to escape.

The bearded stranger, riding up the winding trail toward the rocks and the trees at the top, was evidently a guard coming to replace a night guard. Cass studied him. He rode, hunched and yawning, and did not look up ahead. A moment later Cass was out of sight and out of the saddle, waiting for him.

A great rock lay beside the trail. Cass crawled to the top and crouched, gun in hand. Jim's singing had stopped. The *click-click* of the walking horse approached the rock. The horse snorted, bucked a little. The man cursed, yanked his head up. They came under the rock. Cass jumped, clubbing his gun.

Cass and his victim fell off the bolting horse, and landed hard. The horse bucked on along the trail. The bearded man moved weakly. Cass strapped his arms behind him with his belt, gagged him with a bandanna, and then took his guns and sombrero.

"A bunch of Mexican *soldados* are due this way any minute," Cass said curtly. "When you can get on your feet, you better take my horse an' hunt cover. An' don't come into San José looking for me, for I'll kill you on sight."

Cass rode back along the trail and caught the fresh horse that had stopped with reins dragging. Wearing the guard's sombrero in place of the hat he had lost, and riding the guard's horse, Cass rode down to the creek and up into San José.

A native looked from a doorway and turned hurriedly back inside. Most of the houses were in ruins, roofless stone walls gaping to the sky. *El sinsonte*'s men seemed to be sleeping. An armed guard stepped around a house some distance away, and seemed to recognize the horse and rider for he paid no attention.

Somewhere off to the right a man started singing again. Cass turned at the corner of the next house and rode through the labyrinth of old stone walls toward the sound. He came to the back of a house, where a saddled horse stood waiting and the door was ajar a few inches.

Cass dismounted, drew his gun, and pushed open the door and entered.

Jim said sharply: "I thought you went on guard, Jackson."

Cass said grimly: "I've come for you, Jim."

Jim had been putting on the last of his clothes, buckling on his gun belt. Jim's blond hair, curly and damp, had not changed. But Jim had changed. It wasn't the tight Mexican trousers and the jacket with the silver buttons, or the dark-ening of Jim's skin. That was all the same Jim. But Jim had aged years in months; he was assured and confident, a man now, for all his singing and ready smiles, a man who had killed men, who was deadly, unafraid.

Jim's hand made an involuntary movement toward his silver-mounted pistol. It stopped at the twitch of Cass's gun. For an unsmiling moment Jim looked stricken. Then Jim smiled. "Where'd you come from, Cass?"

"All the way," said Cass. "From Alamo to the Dutch-man's in Wild Horse Valley, through Yuma an' down this side of the border. You knew I'd come after you, Jim."

Slowly Jim nodded. "I kinda thought so, Cass. That's why I kept going, an' headed south of the line where you wouldn't have me on your mind any more."

"You can't leave murder on the other side of a line that easy, Jim."

"I left it," said Jim defiantly.

"I brought it with me."

Jim smiled crookedly. "Many a night I've dreamed you was bringin' it after me, Cass. I knew how serious you took your sheriff's job. But now you're here, put your gun up an' take it easy. I've got eighteen men here, an' you haven't got a chance."

"I've got you, Jim," said Cass heavily. "Stand quiet while I get that Forty-Five." Cass stepped back with the gun. "We're gonna ride outta here quick, Jim. Chavez, the army officer you turned loose in the road without his pants, is half a jump back along the trail with better than fifty sol-diers. He's sworn to take your head back in a sack . . . an' mine'll go, too, if he catches me here with you. I tangled his plans by bulling on ahead. An' there's a Pinkerton man with him who's after you, too. The reward says dead or alive.

You've got to go back with me an' stand trial. Who were the other two men in the Alamo hold-up?"

"One's dead. The other's here an' you don't need to know his name," said Jim. "That was a kind of prank, Cass. We figured the gold was about due on the stage an' laid for it. But after you bein' on the stage, I collected all the gold from the other two when I joined 'em again, and buried it an' wrote a letter back to you about it."

"I heard," said Cass. "They buried the dead man, too."

"I didn't kill him."

"You had a hand in it." Cass's face worked. "Damn you, kid," he gulped. "Why didn't you listen to me? Why did you have to do this to both of us? Why didn't you learn while there was time that you had to mind the rules or you'd suffer? All your helling around since you was a kid, all your tricks since you left Alamo, these fancy clothes an' these gunmen you're heading are cheating on life."

Jim grinned. "It's been fun."

"An' now," said Cass somberly, "the bill has come in."

Jim's face grew bleak. "It's too late, Cass."

"It's never too late to start paying," said Cass huskily. "You're going back with me an' stand trial. Soon as you're in the Alamo jail, I'll turn in my badge an' try to get you off with a term in the pen."

"I don't aim to go, Cass."

"Dead or alive, Jim."

Eye to eye they stood. Cass was haggard, pale, and pallor spread over Jim's face. A shadow of unbelief and fright came there.

"You'd shoot me, Cass?" asked Jim in a thick voice.

"Dead or alive, Jim, you're going back. Hurry up. Chavez'll be here. He'll take both our heads if he can."

"Damn your stiff-necked ideas!" Jim flared with anger.

"From now on you get treated like any other lawman. An' if it takes a bullet to settle you, you get the bullet."

Jim's right hand flirted at his side. There was a barking explosion and Cass's hand went numb. The gun spun from his fingers before he realized what was happening.

Jim snatched his rifle from the wall and stood scowling with a tiny Derringer in one hand. "That's a handy little trick you never taught me," Jim sneered. "I never dress without it harnessed up my sleeve."

The shot brought men running, some of them half dressed.

"Run this damned lawman out with his hands in the air an' get ready to ride!" Jim barked. "The Mex soldiers are comin'!"

"Lawman?" the second man through the doorway snarled. "Where'd he come from? Why don't you plug him an' let it go at that?"

"Damn him, let the Mexicans take care of him!" Jim swore. "From what he says, they're lookin' for him! Run him down to the trail an' get ready to ride an' fight!"

But a rattle of gunfire broke out on the outskirts of San José. Jim was cursing as he ran out the doorway, past Cass and the man who guarded him.

"You're a damn' Jonah!" Jim threw angrily at Cass. "I hope you get what you deserve!"

VII

Cass thought the guard was going to shoot him as the man drove him at a stumbling run toward the edge of the houses. By that time the high rock cliff was echoing to the smash and crash of dozens of guns. Bullets were whining and screaming into rock walls, ricocheting off with vicious buzzes. When they looked past the last houses, across the stream to the slopes beyond, the soldiers were closing in on both trails, hugging every bit of cover and firing at any movement visible among the houses.

The outlaws were fighting back from cover along the fringe of houses. In the little square of open space amid the houses that served for a plaza, horses were being hastily saddled.

Jim came dodging around the corner of a house with a rifle. He surveyed the scene for a moment, came to a decision, called in two men who ran up to join him.

"Now's the time to get out! If we try to fight 'em off, they've got enough men to rush the place or get up on top of the cliff an' pick us off from above. They've been ridin' all night. Their hosses are beat out. Ours are fresh. If we can get outta here, we can leave 'em behind. Get that box of dynamite that Mex was usin' back in the old mine. Cut short fuses an' we'll bust out the south trail, scatterin' dynamite as we go. They won't be lookin' for it. Most of us'll get through."

Cass's guard called: "What about this damn' lawman?"

Jim scowled and shrugged. "Let him loose as soon as we're ready to ride. If there's an extra hoss by that time, he can take his chances on bustin' through without a gun. I'd give a dog that chance." Jim started to stalk away, then he turned, speaking harshly. "But if you get through, an' I catch you sneakin' after me, I'll kill you on sight, damn you! What I said stands. Be damned to you from now on!"

"I heard you," said Cass woodenly.

The outlaws worked fast. They had a box of dynamite, caps, and fuse. Half the men held the outer fringe of houses while the others got ready in the tiny plaza. Cigarettes were lit to fire the fuses, and a shout called the outer men from their posts.

Two were dead and their saddles waited empty. Jim, sitting in the saddle with three sticks of dynamite thrust under his belt with the fuses hanging out, was grim and cool under his high-crowned Mexican sombrero.

"Get a hoss, Cass," he snapped. "An' don't try to hang back to sneak a gun. I don't trust you. Hit the trail with us, an' be damned to you after we start. First gun anyone sees in your hand, you get plugged. All set, boys? Let's go!"

They erupted out of the cluster of stone houses without warning, yelling their defiance as they plunged down the steep trail to the water crossing.

Then a shout went up from the soldiers who barred the way; soldiers popped up from cover near the trail to aim better. But they dived down again as the shouting avalanche of outlaws swept toward them.

The first stick of dynamite arched far over into the rocks and exploded a moment later with a dull boom that scattered dust and rocks all around. Other sticks of dynamite shook the earth and raised a dust haze as they blasted at the men who had crept nearest the trail. But farther up the slope and back, covering the other exit from San José, were riflemen who could sight and shoot with safety. An outlaw sprawled out of the saddle. A horse stumbled and fell and its rider lay among the stones where he struck.

Cass heard lead screaming closely as he rode, leaning low over the horse's neck. A bullet burned across his shoulder and he hardly knew it. The bandanna he had wrapped around his wounded hand was wet with blood and he had forgotten it. Then his horse was hit and plunged to earth. Cass reeled up dazedly. His left ankle buckled and the step he tried was hardly more than a hop. His horse was kicking on the ground. The last of the outlaws were thundering past, ignoring him. Dynamite explosions were shattering the air, and the dust haze was drifting low like a pall of death.

Cass saw that he was done for. He couldn't even make a run for it on foot. He didn't even have a gun to fight.

Perhaps 100 yards ahead an outlaw lay sprawled on the ground. Bullets were whining and screaming over him as soldiers saw his plight. Cass shook his fist up the slope and started a hobbling, reeling walk toward that dead outlaw and the gun that should be there among the rocks. He'd go down fighting. Then Cass's red-rimmed eyes saw a sight that brought a sob into his throat. Back through the dust pall a lone rider was galloping, heedless of the singing bullets and the death to which he was returning.

It was Jim, with his high-crowned Mexican sombrero hanging back on his shoulders and his curly hair flaunting above a stricken face. Beyond Jim the outlaws were rallying for an indecisive moment to cover Jim's retreat, but they could not stop the storm of lead that swept down at Jim.

Cass saw Jim's six-gun fall to the ground, and Jim's right arm hung limply from a bullet as Jim brought his horse back on its haunches and swung it around.

"Climb up, Cass!" Jim yelled, kicking his foot out of the stirrup.

And then Jim flinched and reeled in the saddle, and Cass swung up behind him, reaching around and grabbing the reins just in time to keep Jim from falling.

Cass's spurs drove the horse ahead. Jim was fighting to keep his place. Blood began to seep through his jacket under the armpit. A bullet seared the horse's flank and it broke into a frenzied gallop with its heavy load.

The outlaws closed in behind them and the retreat swept on. Another rider fell out of the saddle. A man caught the reins of the horse and brought him along. The trail turned and the dwindling ranks of the outlaws had a short respite from the gunfire behind.

"How bad are you hit, Jim?" Cass asked.

"Bad," replied Jim with an effort.

"You shouldn't have come back after me," Cass said huskily.

"Couldn't have left you there like that," Jim said. "You're my brother."

"Yeah . . . I understand." Cass tightened his arms about Jim.

"Get on that extra horse an' ride for it, Cass," Jim said. "I'll come along."

"We'll keep on goin' like we are," said Cass gruffly.

Several times the riders ahead slacked up and waited for them. From a rocky ridge they caught a glimpse of distant pursuit. They came to another small bridge spanning a deep ravine, and Cass's shout stopped the outlaws on the other side.

Cass had a stick of dynamite he had pulled from Jim's belt. "Take this an' any more dynamite you've got an' blow up the bridge from this end," Cass said. "That'll hold 'em back some."

A scowling man spoke gruffly: "Are we gonna have to hang back all day waitin' for you two?"

"No use waitin' for me," said Jim painfully. "I'm holed through the middle an' can't last."

"Shut up, Jim," said Cass.

"Jim's right. He's done for," said another man. "Stick with us as long as you can, Jim."

The bridge went up with a thunder of sound, and a half an hour later, Jim gasped: "I can't stick it much longer,

Cass. I'm on fire inside. Put me down an' ride on."

Cass had been expecting it. He stopped the horse. The outlaws stopped and drew up in a circle.

"Jim an' I are turnin' off here!" Cass called.

The nearest man lifted his voice. "Boys, are we gonna leave Jim here with this lawman?"

"He's my brother," Jim gasped. "There ain't any better man to leave me with."

Silently the outlaws watched the double-laden horse leave the trail and climb the steep slope into the trees. Then the drum of retreating hoofs started again, and faded away.

The morning wind sighed through the trees, and the hoofs of the walking horse snapped dead branches underfoot. Jim was gasping heavily with each breath and spitting bloody froth off his lips. Cass's arm was wet with the blood soaking Jim's side.

A long time later they came out on a high rocky slope gashed with small ravines. The world fell away below them and the sun drenched the open.

"I got to stop, Cass," gasped Jim weakly.

A little later, when Jim was lying on the ground with his head pillowed on Cass's coat, Jim groped out and caught Cass's hand.

"I understand, Cass. You had to come after me. I was wrong. An' . . . I reckon . . . the bill's here . . . to pay."

"Keep quiet an' save your strength, Jim."

Jim gripped the hand. "I'm glad you're here, Cass. Don't feel too bad about it after it's over. I'd rather have it this way than a noose."

"Shut up!"

Jim struggled for breath, and then lay with his eyes closed like a dead man. Presently Jim's eyes opened. A grin struggled across his pinched face.

"You damn stiff-necked lawman," Jim whispered, clinging to Cass's hand. "So long . . . brother."

Cass found a cleft in the rocky ground close by. He put Jim there, and hobbled to the nearest trees and brought branches to cover him, and piled rocks for hours until Jim was safe.

The sun was high overhead and Cass was standing somberly by the spot when the horse pricked its ears down the slope. Cass was waiting with his rifle when Reingold, the little Pinkerton man, rode out of the trees.

Reingold was alone. He called as he approached: "Chavez and his men have gone on after the bunch!" Reingold dismounted and explained: "I figured you two couldn't get far on that horse, an', when I saw the buzzards gatherin', I cut up this way toward the spot."

"You're too late, Reingold," Cass said thickly. "Jim's under the rocks there. He got it from tryin' to save me."

Reingold nodded. "I saw it. I reckon it's best. Isn't there something in the Bible about . . . 'I will lay down my life for my brother?' "

"If there isn't," said Cass, "there oughta be." Cass fumbled under his shirt, in his money belt, and handed Reingold a nickeled badge. "It was dead or alive, Reingold. Turn in my badge an' tell 'em the case is closed."

Reingold's fists doubled. "You damn' fool, Cass." His voice sounded strangely choked. "You've kept that badge cleaner than any other man would have done. I'll take you back if I have to myself. You'll be wearing that badge when we ride into town together, and, when I tell them that you're the whitest, gamest lawman I ever saw. . . ."

Reingold couldn't go on just then, but Cass's arm was about his shoulder as they slowly walked together toward their horses.

King of the Río Gunmen

This was the fourteenth story T. T. Flynn wrote in 1935. He titled it in his notebook "Gil Magee Western". It was purchased upon submission by *Star Western* for $350 and given the title "King of the Río Gunmen" upon publication in the issue dated November, 1935. It was subsequently reprinted in *Big-Book Western* (11/53), another Popular Publications magazine, under the title "No Man's Guns".

I

Gunman Gil Magee stood in the thorny mesquite thicket and watched the stranger dying, the pallid face, deep-etched with pain, and the blood blackening where bullets had smashed the man's chest and stomach. Death was nothing, Gil knew. He'd seen men die before. But this man with hate in his dark eyes was puzzling.

The man had tried to kill him on sight. Only a dying man's unsteady hand had made the bullet miss. Only a quick lunge forward and a kick that knocked the gun aside had turned the second shot. A snatch had torn the weapon from the stranger's weak grip. Gil Magee wondered what it was all about.

"Stranger," he said, "could you use a smoke?"

The stranger's throat rattled as a thin, bloody froth

stained his lips. But his answer was a harsh whisper: "Damn you, no. I tell you I don't want nothin' from you."

A water bottle lay on the sandy ground. Gil Magee had brought it from his saddle, knelt, and offered it, and a convulsive blow had struck it from his hand. Gil Magee shook his head.

Already, high overhead in the vast blue depths of the sky, two buzzards were wheeling in slow, majestic circles. At the edge of the mesquite, the stranger's big bay horse lay dead, with four bullet wounds in its hide. It was catching sight of the dead horse that turned Gil from the trail. You didn't ignore such matters in this dry waste of the Chufletero Sink, where every mystery carried a warning—and a lesson.

Speaking bluntly, Gil Magee said: "Mister, I'd do somethin' if I could. If you've got any messages, I'll be pleased to deliver them."

He had to kneel down to get the weak, slurred reply. "If there's a tally time in hell, I'll see you counted. Damn you."

A few moments later Gil Magee stood up. The buzzards were swinging closer.

Slowly Gil Magee built a cigarette, lighted it. The silence was like a hot, oppressive mantle.

If men lurked nearby, they were staying under cover. They had not come to see whether their victim was dead. They must have feared an ambush or were certain their bullets had done the work.

Looking through the mesquite, Gil Magee could see in the loose sandy soil where the stranger had fallen hard out of the saddle, and had dragged himself into cover. A rifle lay nearby with sand clogging the barrel. He had been too weak to keep the muzzle up.

Looking up at the circling buzzards, Gil Magee swore softly. He had only his hands and the rifle barrel with which to dig, but the dry soil was loose. On his knees, sweating, grinding away the tough skin on his fingertips, Gil Magee scooped out a long, shallow hole.

Before putting the body in, he went through the pockets, piling the contents on the ground. Tobacco, matches, a few coins, some keys, a Barlow knife—nothing in the lot to identify the stranger. Then, under the coat and shirt, he found a fat leather money belt. Inside, he found gold and bills totaling over $3,000. He strapped the money belt under his own shirt, above another, not so fat with wealth.

A little later, Gil Magee turned away from the sandy mound and studied the ground at the edge of the mesquite. Swinging on his horse, Gil Magee backtracked the bay. The trail led out into the open, and suddenly turned to the right and became the lighter prints of a walking horse. Here the stranger had been riding leisurely. Here, just at the turn, the first shots had found him, and he had swung his horse sharply for the shelter of the mesquite. The shots had struck the stranger from the front. Warily Gil Magee rode on, in the direction the stranger would have gone.

He came to a steep-banked wash and in its bed found the sign for which he searched. Three horsemen had come riding into the wash. They had dismounted and scrambled into hidden positions directly in the path of the approaching stranger. The empty rifle shells were still scattered about. They must have kept up a running fire until the stranger had reached the shelter of the mesquite. Then they had left, riding back up the wash. They had killed, and left—without making an effort to get that fat money belt.

Turning in the saddle, Gil Magee squeezed through the sun glare toward those low hills. Heat waves shimmered over the dry slopes. Scattered stands of green cholla cactus stood motionlessly. Nothing moved. No ray of light glinted off a shifting gun barrel.

Gil Magee rode on his way. Someone else would have to settle this mystery. In Santa Cruz, where he was going, he would make inquiries, and turn the dead man's money over to any rightful heirs. Loot from a dying man did not interest Gil Magee.

The following afternoon, near sundown, Gil Magee rode along a narrow, dirt road that led to Santa Cruz, the wild new boom town, when a buggy coming out from Santa Cruz pulled up, and a familiar voice hailed Gil.

Squinting against the sun, Gil recognized Big Lace Kincaid, who had been dealing faro in a small El Paso joint not many months before. Kincaid looked prosperous. His curling black mustache had a flare that matched his flashing diamond ring and a massive gold watch chain.

Gil grinned. "Looks like you hit pay dirt, Kincaid. Who's your young partner? Had a hard day, ain't he?"

Beside Big Lace Kincaid a good-looking young fellow slumped in the buggy seat, his mouth open and his eyes closed. Kincaid looked at him and chuckled.

"Friend of mine. He took a few snorts too many today. I'm takin' him out to his ranch. I ain't minin'." Kincaid winked. "There's more money on top of the ground than under it."

Kincaid looked ahead suddenly over his team. Gil saw a buckboard approaching at a smart pace. The buckboard swung across the road, blocking Kincaid's path, and the driver leaped out.

Big Lace Kincaid spoke in an undertone from the buggy seat: "I ain't got a gun. Watch this fellow, Gil."

The man was young, almost as large as Kincaid, but Gil

Magee gave him only a glance. The girl who sat on the buckboard seat, pale and quiet under the brim of a small white Stetson hat, was more interesting. Gil Magee decided he had seen girls almost as pretty before. She was small, slender, young, and her pale, set face showed a smoldering anger that made her even prettier. Gil rather liked her.

The stranger spoke harshly. "Damn you, Kincaid. You were warned about this. And you've been at it again."

Big Lace Kincaid grinned derisively. "You don't say? Bob's man enough to run hisself. When he offers to buy a drink, his friends ain't turning their backs. If you want to take him on home, he's yours. It'll save me drivin'."

The reply was clipped. "We'll take him home. But you had your warnin'. I'll pay off here in the road. Climb outta that buggy."

"Damn you, Elliot." Big Lace Kincaid lost his temper. "Take Bob if you want him. But don't bother me if you aim to stay healthy."

"Are you comin' down off that seat?" Elliot rasped.

"Go to hell."

"I'll bring you down." Elliot's hand shot over the seat and caught Kincaid's wrist. At the same moment he drew his gun.

With a careless motion, Gil flipped out a pistol. "Put up your gun, mister. Kincaid ain't armed today."

"And who the devil are *you?*" Elliot said.

"Me?" Gil's mouth twisted in a grin. "A friend of Kincaid's. That's enough. He ain't packin' a gun . . . so don't draw on him if you want to stay healthy."

Big Lace Kincaid wrenched his arm free. "Watch the girl, Gil!" he said suddenly.

Gil saw the girl on the ground, covering him with a rifle.

"Put up your gun and keep out of this," she said with an

113

unsteady edge to her voice. Color stained her smooth cheeks now, angry color, and she seemed to Gil prettier than ever.

"Give her any back talk, mister," Elliot's angry voice cut at him, "an' I'll kill you myself."

Gil put up his gun and said meekly: "Ain't much I can do against the two of you. Sorry, Kincaid. I did the best I could."

Kincaid found his voice indignantly. "Gil, you can. . . ."

"I did the best I could for you. It's your scratch match now. Handle it any way you can."

"You're like the rest of them," Elliot said to Gil contemptuously. "You'll eat dirt when you ain't callin' the game yourself. Sit there an' see what I'm giving this crooked, fancy dandy friend of yours."

Elliot caught Big Lace Kincaid's coat lapel, and, despite his weight, brought him flying out of the buggy.

Staggering on the ground, Big Lace bawled: "If you didn't have that gun, I'd . . . !"

Elliot tossed the gun aside, cutting the words off with a smashing blow. Kincaid reeled back, spitting a broken tooth, lowered his head, and charged back, bawling threats. The young cowman was tough, strong, fast. Kincaid's blows did little damage when they landed—yet Elliot's smashing fists drew grunts of pain each time. He beat Kincaid back, and back. Big Lace rushed close and grappled. Elliot broke the hold with sheer strength, kicked a leg out from under Kincaid, and knocked him flat on the road.

Kincaid stayed there, covering his face with his arms.

"Get up an' get some more of it," Elliot panted bitterly.

But Kincaid was through.

Elliot waited a moment, swung on a heel, picked his gun out of the dust, and turned to the buggy. The young man had slumbered through it all. Elliot roughly pulled him off the seat, carried him to the buckboard, and dumped him in the back. Now the girl, who had stood there covering Gil with the rifle, backed toward the buckboard.

Gil watched her go. "You don't need that rifle now, ma'am," he said, grinning.

The color had left her cheeks while the two men fought. Now it rushed back. "Your kind doesn't fight at all . . . unless someone's back is turned. I hope this is warning enough for you."

"It better be . . . for *both* of them," Elliot snapped. He took the rifle from her, climbed on the buckboard seat, and sat watchfully while she took her place beside him, picked up the reins, swung the horses around, and whipped them into a run back down the road.

The gambler, Kincaid, staggered to the buggy, dabbing a bloody handkerchief over his face. One eye was closing fast, his bleeding nose was knocked askew, and his pulped lips were puffing badly.

Big Lace peered at Gil from one good eye. "You could 'a' stopped him," he said. "That damn girl an' her rifle never bothered you. Ain't I seen you . . . ?"

"Shut up, Kincaid," Gil said. "I don't like the sound of your voice right now. He whipped you fair . . . an', if you weren't man enough to stand up to him, don't whine to me. Reckon you can see to drive back in to town? If you can see, look me up when you get to town, and I'll buy you a drink. *Adiós*."

Gil rode on toward Santa Cruz, leaving Big Lace Kincaid mumbling through his swollen lips. With him Gil took the memory of a flushed, angry face and scornful eyes. Her hair had been black. He wondered what color her eyes were.

II

It was dusk when Gil rode along the short length of the
noisy street of Santa Cruz lined on both sides by sketchy
adobe and wooden buildings that had been hastily thrown
up. Windows were already showing lights. In spots oil
torches flickered and blazed over merchandise counters
hastily erected in the open. The sidewalks were filled with
jostling crowds. Saddle horses, teams, oxen, wagons, buck-
boards, here and there a buggy, lined and jammed the sides
of the streets. Saloons were running wide open. The crowd
was boisterous. Boom wildness filled the air like an intoxi-
cating draught.

Jigger Gunn's Ace-Deuce saloon was the biggest and
wildest of the lot. It had been one of the first to go up and
housed gambling, dancing, and drinking. The hitch rack in
front was full. Gil rode on to the first vacant spot, racked
his horse, and pushed through the crowd into the Ace-
Deuce. He found a vacant space at the bar, ordered
whiskey, drank it, tossed half a dollar on the bar, and spoke
to the bartender who swept it up.

"Where's Jigger Gunn?"

"Back in his office, I guess. By the arch back there."

Hilarious couples were dancing to music from two gui-
tars, a fiddle, and a tinny piano. Some of the girls were
pretty. Gil walked back along the bar toward the back of the
room.

Gambling was going on beyond a low open archway,
and, just beyond the arch, **OFFICE** was painted on a door.
Gil opened the door and stepped into a small room beyond.

116

The air was thick with tobacco smoke. Two men were in there, talking to Jigger Gunn.

When he saw who had entered, Jigger Gunn smiled. "I'll see you boys later," he stated hurriedly, and rushed with an outstretched hand. "Damned if I ain't glad to see you, Gil!"

The two men cast curious looks at Gil as they walked out. They wore sombreros and colored scarfs. Guns were under their coats. They looked like Mexicans. But after one quick look Gil decided their faces had been burnt dark by the sun.

"I just got in," Gil said. "I was about busted when I got your letter, so I started riding. Plenty of easy money sounded good to me. Who do you want killed?"

"Nobody right now," he replied. "Whiskey?"

"Nope. I just bought one at your bar."

"Huh? You paid money over my bar? What's the idea? Everything's on the house for you."

Jigger Gunn was a strange-looking man, a wizened, frail body, topped with an over-size head. He was not good-looking, but he was cunning and shrewd. He always succeeded. His thin, long, sensitive hands could handle a six-gun with flashing dexterity.

Now he stood there with the whiskey bottle, and repeated: "Your money ain't any good in the Ace-Deuce, Gil. Not while Jigger Gunn is running the place."

With a slight smile on his lips, Gil answered as bluntly. "I don't drink on the house until I work for the house, Jigger. I never aim to have any favors to pay back. What's on your mind?"

Jigger Gunn downed a drink, put his back against the table edge, and his manner grew brisk with business. "Easy money for you, Gil. I sent for you because I don't know any other man I can trust who'll be able to do the job. Maybe you'll have to use your gun. Maybe not. I hope not. I'm a man of peace."

Gil grinned crookedly at that.

"I've got my eye on a ranch, Gil. One of the biggest ranches in this part of the country. It's been in the same family for some sixty years. It's worth plenty now, but it'll be worth plenty more in the next few years. Cattle prices are on the way up."

Jigger Gunn indicated the noisy saloon beyond the small hot office. "There's money in this, too. But how long will the town last? I've got it straight that no big money'll be made out of these mines. A few months more and the crowd'll be on the way out. Easy money'll be over. Right?"

"Sounds straight."

"I'm smart," said Jigger Gunn, nodding his big head wisely. "When the crowd goes out, I go, too, if I can't sell first. I'm sick of this business anyway."

Jigger Gunn took another drink. Gil waited in silence.

"I'm ready to grab that ranch. But I need you, Gil. You savvy running a ranch. Hell, I'll give you a share."

Gil grinned. "Better get the ranch first."

"I make sure of what I go after," Jigger Gunn said with a shrewd grin. "The owner is a proud old fool who oughta been dead long ago. His grandson really runs the place. The old gent is crazy about him. The boy has lost plenty gambling here in Ace-Deuce. He's drinking heavy, too. I've lent him money an' taken his notes. We're pretty good friends. He hired a foreman I recommended. The foreman damn' near runs the place. All the men he's hired are taking orders from me."

"Big Lace take orders from you too?"

Jigger Gunn nodded. "Why?"

"You didn't happen to tell him to take this young fellow

118

out to his ranch this evening, did you?"

"You must 'a' met them."

"Happens I did. A girl an' a fellow came along in a buck-board. The fellow messed Kincaid's face up with his fists, an' they took the young man back with 'em."

Jigger Gunn swore softly. "That's Bob Hanson's sister, Mollie. She's a spitfire. She must 'a' brought a cowhand named Tom Elliot along. He's in bad with Bob Hanson, from speaking out too plain, or he'd have made more trouble than he has. He'll have to be steadied down."

"The old man owns the ranch?"

"Everything. But he won't live forever. He won't need to. Cattle are going to start leaving that ranch in a hurry, Gil. With the boom on here in Santa Cruz, an' strange men all over the country, anyone could be to blame. I've made a dicker to handle them across the border. When I need 'em back, they'll be ready to come back . . . onto *my* land." Gunn tossed off his drink, and set the glass down hard. "I want you to haze those cattle over the border, Gil. I know you never bust your word. You're the only man I can trust. I ain't even sure that Skinner, my foreman at the ranch, will play straight with me. Go out to the ranch tomorrow. Skinner'll hire you and turn you loose. Spend a few days lookin' the ranch over. Figure out how you'll want to handle the cattle. I'll give you men. Make two or three drags an' clean the ranch off. I'll do the rest."

"I'm not drawing any pay from a ranch I'm going to clean out, Jigger."

Gunn shrugged. "You don't have to. Tell 'em you're ridin' the grub line. Skinner'll give you a little riding to do to make up for the grub. You'll be even."

"This Mollie Hanson is a pretty kid," Gil said slowly. "I kinda hate to go after her cattle."

"Hell, Gil, never knew a pretty face to hobble you before. It ain't her ranch or her cattle. She's just living there. She'd be the first one to turn you over to hang if the law came after her. She ain't our kind, Gil."

Gil grinned crookedly as he thought of the girl's scorn. "I'll take it," he decided. "And a cut of the ranch. Half shares."

A spasm crossed Jigger Gunn's face. "A quarter."

"Half."

They looked at each other for a moment.

"Half it is," Jigger assented glumly. "At least I'll know you'll go through with it." For one moment Jigger Gunn's look smoldered. "You'd better," he said softly. "I've got my heart set on this."

That was a statement and a warning. Jigger Gunn was a bad man to cross. He could outthink most people, he had no scruples, and his memory was long.

"You'll get it," Gil said. "Where is this ranch?"

"They run the Sunrise brand. Half a sun coming up, with six rays spreading out above it. Starts about ten miles south of here, runs back to the edge of the Chufletero Sink, and south toward the border. The headquarters is about sixteen miles from here, on Indian Creek. I'll give you a letter to Skinner."

"Speaking of the Chufletero Sink," Gil remembered. "D'you know any reason why a man should 'a' been dry-gulched out there yesterday by three men?"

"Dry-gulched? Who was he?"

"Never saw him before. The dirty sons killed his horse, filled him full of lead an' left him in the mesquite to die. I'd have killed 'em myself if I could 'a' caught 'em. Three of them . . . an' they never gave him a chance. I've done my share of killin' but I never drew on a man unless he had the same chance I did."

Jigger Gunn shrugged. "I'm with you there, Gil. If I hear who they were, I'll let you know. Wait, I'll fix that letter."

"I'll get it later," Gil said, turning to the door. "I want to get cleaned up, fix my horse, take on some chuck, an' turn in. I've hit the trail hard getting here."

"Don't forget. Your money ain't any good in the Ace-Deuce now, Gil. We're partners."

"Partners," Gil agreed with a nod as he went out.

The late noon sun next day was hot again as Gil Magee, clean, rested, jaunty, rode up to the Sunrise Ranch. He had left Santa Cruz early and circled out of his way to see some of the ranch land. It was a place a man could hold with pride—if he was willing to fight when necessary. Gil's lip curled as he thought of the owner, old, soft, careless, and the weak-featured young fellow in the drunken stupor who Big Lace Kincaid had been hauling home. Two men—and they didn't make a real man between them. A girl and a cowhand had to show some spirit for them.

Men were saddling horses at a corral beyond the buildings. Gil rode to them, called to the nearest man.

"Who's the foreman?"

"Skinner. Comin' from the bunkhouse there."

Skinner looked like a hard-working foreman. His face was expressionless as Gil swung down and faced him.

"You Skinner?" Gil asked.

The other nodded.

Skinner read the letter without comment, tore it into bits, and shoved them into his pocket.

"All right, Magee," he said briefly. "Go over to the cook house an' see if the cook'll scare you up some grub. We've et."

Gil was almost to the adobe cook house when the back

121

door of the main house opened and Mollie Hanson and her brother Bob came out. Mollie Hanson wore the same white Stetson. A leather quirt hung from her wrist. Her brother, taller than she, was dressed elegantly and carefully, as if he might again be going to town.

Mollie Hanson glanced toward the cook house, stared for a moment, and abruptly left her brother and came to meet the newcomer. Her small, oval face was flushed with displeasure as she drew near.

"I thought I recognized you," she said coldly. "What are you doing here?"

Gil looked at her with a faint smile. "I hit Santa Cruz busted last night, ma'am. I'm not a mining man. So the first thing today I made for the nearest cows. The foreman says I can ride a few days for my grub."

"I don't believe you," she said bluntly, while her glance went over him scornfully. "That gambler Kincaid and his friends will feed you."

"He's no great friend of mine, ma'am. I hardly know him."

"You seemed to know him well enough," she reminded him coldly. "At any rate I don't want you on the ranch."

"Do you own the ranch, ma'am?"

She turned. "Bob, come here!" she called imperiously. Yes, she was pretty, proud, scornful, and contemptuous. Hard antagonism leaped in Gil to meet it.

Bob Hanson was frowning with irritation as he joined them. Today he showed the effects of his drinking bout. His face was weak where strength should have been.

"This is the man who drew a gun on Tom yesterday, Bob. Skinner is letting him ride a few days for his food. He can't do it."

Antagonism already lay between them. She had said the

wrong thing. Bob Hanson said with sullen irritation: "I've had my say about Tom. I'm sick of you two minding my business. If this man wants to ride for his grub, it's all right with me. Tell your grandfather if you don't like it."

Her reply was stormy. "You know he thinks everything you do is right!"

"Then this man can stay. Come on, if you're going riding, Mollie."

Brother and sister. Pride and anger. Mollie Hanson gave Gil Magee a furious look as she went on with her brother. It warned him that she would not forget. Gil grinned ironically. That stiff pride of hers was due for a jolt before long.

Before supper other men rode in. Tom Elliot trailed after them with Mollie Hanson riding beside him. She must have gone out to meet him.

Elliot's actions proved that. Straight from the corral, he came to Gil. His face was hard and determined.

"I hear your name's Magee, an' you have the nerve to come here an' get a bunk."

Gil grinned provokingly. "Heard a lot in a short time, didn't you?"

"You ain't wanted here, Magee. I warned Kincaid. I'm warnin' you . . . little man or big, you'll get the same."

Gil stopped smiling. His blue eyes shaded to a wintery hardness. His reply had a smooth, soft chill, deceptive, unless a man had an inkling of what lay behind it.

"I watched you manhandle Kincaid yesterday, an' didn't give a damn. But lift a hand to me . . . an' I kill you. If my talk don't suit, go for your gun."

Gil held his hands away from the holsters, giving the bigger man all the advantage.

Tom Elliot wore a gun. He looked like a man who knew

how to use it. But he ignored the dare. A faintly puzzled look came into his eyes.

"You talk like a killer. By God, you *look* like a killer now," he said with slow surprise. "You're a two-gun man, an' too little to talk this way if you ain't sure you can back it up."

"I'm waitin' for you to make your move," Gil said coldly.

Tom Elliot stared for a moment more. Then the ghost of a smile came on his lips.

"I'll fool you, Magee," he said quietly. "My hands are in the clear . . . see? I'll leave my gun in the bunkhouse after this until I savvy why you're hankerin' to drop me." He walked away.

The icy look faded from Gil's eyes. It had been instinctive. You got that way when you carried a price on your head. Tom Elliot would be dangerous now. But somehow he couldn't dislike the man for it.

That evening Gil kept to himself and sized up the other hands. With no effort Gil picked up the six men who had been on the ranch before Skinner came as foreman. They kept to themselves. Those who Skinner had hired were quiet, hard-faced, taciturn. They threw a chill over the bunkhouse. There was no good-natured chaffing, no horseplay.

The older hands seemed to resent Skinner's men, and Skinner's men to have little use for them and content to keep to themselves. It made a queer situation, but understandable when you knew about Skinner and the kind of men he was hiring—and with Jigger Gunn in the background.

Dawn turned them out in the morning. Skinner gave curt orders to Gil before everyone. "Ride over toward

Chufletero breaks an' throw back any beef you find over there. We're working them south."

That order gave the whole day and a fresh horse to ride free and unnoticed over the eastern side of the ranch. Gil came in dog-tired well after dark, with a working knowledge of the range in that direction.

The next day he went west; the next he took blankets, grub, and rode to the south line fence, quartering back and forth through the broken hilly country, and then going on south toward the border.

In five days of hard riding Gil saw that Skinner had been drifting most of the Sunrise cattle south into the broken, somewhat higher country. They were bunched more closely than they should have been. Good men could throw them together and haze them over the border with little trouble. In a few trips the Sunrise brand could be stripped down to culls. The border was not over 100 miles away, and Skinner would keep the men he could not trust away from that part of the ranch. Only a doddering old fool and a drunken young idiot would let a ranch be rigged so.

When he got back to the Indian Creek headquarters, he found that Tom Elliot lay in the big house, with a broken leg. A horse had fallen on the leg. The accident called for little regret. With Elliot out of the way, there was not much to worry about. Two more days Gil rode with the Sunrise hands, lest a sudden departure after his five-day swing seem suspicious.

The second afternoon he met Mollie Hanson coming down a narrow trail from a long, high bluff. Gil expected to be ignored. Instead, Mollie Hanson reined in and stared at him evenly. "What do you want on this ranch?" she said.

"Grub, ma'am. Didn't I say?" Gil asked, smiling.

"Your kind doesn't go hungry. It's something else."

125

Gil knew he should grin and shrug it off. She didn't matter in this game that Jigger Gunn and he were playing. But his face reddened. Resentment flared.

"What do you mean, my kind?"

Mollie Hanson looked at him for a long moment. "I think you're a gunman and a troublemaker," she said quietly. "We're not. You'll be more at home in Santa Cruz, with men like Kincaid, than on our land."

Gil grinned then. "If it'll make you feel any better, I'll leave tonight, ma'am," he promised. He chuckled inwardly at her puzzled look as he rode on.

That evening Gil Magee faced Jigger Gunn in the latter's crude office.

"I'm ready," Gil said shortly. "I want half a dozen men. Skinner'll have five or six scattered along his south wire to help throw the critters together. It'll take two weeks anyway."

Jigger Gunn's squinting eyes were bright with satisfaction. "You'll be fast to do it in two weeks. You'll have to go well south of the border to an old *hacienda* I've rented. Two of the men will guide you. Joe O'Leary and Jack Samson. I could have them do all this job, but I don't trust them. When you're done, leave the men there, ride by the ranch, and tell Skinner, and then come on here. Sound good?"

"Smooth," Gil assented. "Trot out a drink."

III

In the past Gil Magee had rustled many times but never so openly. The days and nights of hard work were once more like wine. This was living, this was life, when a man's blood sang through his veins with the surge of reckless adventure. The long miles dropped behind—the border fell back of them, and they pushed the drive hard into old Mexico. Then they came to the mountains and the valley, the cañon, the inner valley where water rippled in a swift little stream, and ungrazed grass grew high, and the fire-scorched ruins of the old *hacienda* buildings lay among a rank tangle of old flowers and vines gone wild since a bandit raid years before had wiped out the owners.

Joe O'Leary rolled a brown paper cigarette and spoke to Gil and four others who had gone on ahead with him.

"I was with Diego Morales when he raided this place about eleven years ago. An old *caballero* named *Don* Felipe Serrano owned it. He was of the blood . . . in a straight line from the *hidalgos*. White as a white man an' proud as a splinter of hell. When the outbuildings were burning and that north wing of the house was on fire, *Don* Felipe called that he would come out himself with his gold if Morales would swear by all he held holy that the women would be spared. *Don* Serrano pitched out a cross wrapped in a towel. Morales took it and swore by the Virgin, the Son, and the saints that all he wanted was gold for his patriotic *soldados* who were starving. Old *Don* Felipe marched out with his white hair flying and four peóns staggering after him with a chest of gold coins they could hardly keep off the ground. Fresh dirt was still on it, from where they had dug it up inside the house."

O'Leary fell silent, smiling reminiscently to himself.

"And then?" Gil prompted with a soft edge to his voice.

"And then," said O'Leary, "Morales had *Don* Felipe nailed to a door, and stood it up against that old tree back of the house while the women were brought out. Four daughters, white as the old man. God, I'll never forget them. They were white . . . all over.”

Gil looked sick as he spurred his horse to O’Leary, dragged the man half out of his saddle, and smashed a gun barrel across his face.

“I oughta kill you for bein’ alive to tell it!” Gil cried.

O’Leary screamed with the pain and pawed for his gun. Gil shot it out of his hand, and struck with the smoking gun barrel again—again battering O’Leary’s features horribly. Panting, he let the limp form fall heavily to the ground between the horses.

“Anybody got anything to say?” he said.

“My God, no!” one of the men gulped.

“He should ’a’ been hung eleven years ago. Two of you drag him to the well over there and fix him up. He an’ his pardner’ll stay here while we make the next trip. I won’t ride with them.”

Jack Samson was on the other side of the valley when it happened. He said nothing when he came in, but Gil knew that, if O’Leary recovered, both men would be ready to kill for that beating.

But that day Gil and the rest of the men left. Jigger Gunn’s money had made certain that Mexican law would not bother the Sunrise cattle. In the valley they were safe. Gil and his men rode back for the rest, if Skinner had covered up as he should.

Skinner had. Three men waited with the cattle. They rode south with Gil, his men, and almost the last of the Sunrise beef. The big ranch had been stripped of its wealth in two easy forays. Gil himself would not have thought it possible. He knew he could never have done it without the cunning moves of Jigger Gunn.

Once more they crossed the border, and came again to the ruined *hacienda*. The first herd was growing sleek and fat on the tall grass. O'Leary was riding again, his face a mass of livid, half-healed scars, his right hand swathed in dirty bandages.

They met in front of the men. Gil wasted no words. "Is it war, O'Leary?" he asked curtly.

O'Leary held up his bandaged right hand. He had to speak from the corner of a mouth that would never be straight again, so badly had one side been torn. "How can I fight with a hand like this? But in a week, when the hand is good, Magee . . . by God . . . !" O'Leary suddenly screamed in frantic passion from his twisted mouth. "Son-of-a-bitch . . . I won't forget! Never! I'll drop hot stones in your open belly! I'll stake you out on an ant hill! I'll peel your skin off in strips! I'll . . . I'll. . . ." O'Leary became incoherent and began to curse wildly in Spanish and English.

Gil laughed at him. "Watch out you don't bite yourself an' pass out from your own poison. You're bein' mighty hard for a one-fisted fellow who's got to wait. I'm leavin' you today an' riding north again. But I'll certainly be back." Gil smiled crookedly as O'Leary quieted. "I'll be back," he repeated. "Drop me with the first bullet, O'Leary. Because I'm right pleased with my hide an' I don't aim to lose even one strip."

Days later Gil rode over an empty sweep of the Sunrise range. The deserted range cried all too plainly how well the rustling had been planned and carried out. But as he rode this afternoon, Gil found himself thinking of O'Leary, of Diego Morales, the bandit, of the *caballero*, *Don* Felipe Serrano and his women, and of Mollie Hanson. They raised a troublesome problem. Gil groped for the answer as he rode north and the sun began to set. He had ridden far this last day. With luck he would get to the Indian Creek ranch house sometime after dark, tell Skinner the work was finished, and go on to Santa Cruz and Jigger Gunn.

Mollie Hanson would be at the ranch house. Gil wondered whether he would see her cool scorn again. He suddenly hoped not. The idea made worse the problem on his mind. Gil wondered if Mollie Hanson thought of him as an O'Leary, a Morales. Gil had always thought his own ways good enough, his guns, his luck all he needed. But tonight, as the stars began to glitter and the wild howl of a border country wolf quivered on the wind, something was lacking. Something that two guns and the luck of the devil had never been able to find.

Gil was still pondering it when he reached the buildings north of Indian Creek. Lamps were lighted in the bunkhouse, men were standing outside. Strangely quiet, queerly tense, they eyed Gil as he rode up and spoke from the saddle.

"Where's Skinner?" Gil asked them.

"He ain't here."

One of the men drifted off into the darkness.

Gil looked for Skinner's men. They were gone, too. From narrowed eyes he watched for some move toward a gun. All the men were armed tonight. But no one moved a hand. Carefully Gil said: "Where did Skinner go?"

"Santa Cruz."

"Where's the other men?"

"Santa Cruz."

"How come they went to Santa Cruz?"

"They quit."

The feel of danger hung in the air. The men stood stiffly, not looking at anything in particular, but waiting.

Gil looked over his shoulder. He caught one fleeting glimpse of a black, snake-like coil flying past over his head.

He threw up an arm and dodged, but he was too late. With a whispering *hiss* the riata loop slapped down past his arm and jerked tightly around his body, pinioning the other arm. A mighty yank toppled Gil from the saddle.

He hit the ground, staggering. Another yank jerked him off balance, and the waiting men jumped him. A gun barrel skidded over his head, dazing him. They held him and disarmed him.

Tom Elliot limped up.

"So you had the nerve to come back?" he snapped. "I reckon we'll find where our beef went now!"

Gil grinned faintly and said nothing.

The big cowhand balled a fist, and his voice shook with rage. "I sent Baldy out to ride the ranch. He got back at sundown with news that we were cleaned out. Skinner couldn't lie to me. We killed two of his men before the rest got away. And now you come ridin' in just in time to guide us."

"I'm heading for Santa Cruz," Gil retorted curtly. "Don't ask me to mix in your troubles."

"Search him, boys."

They found the money belts. Tom Elliot inspected the bushwhacked stranger's money belt in the light from the bunkhouse doorway. "It's jammed full of money! An' he was ridin' the grub line, boys! Maybe the major'll listen to this."

They shoved Gil into a huge, low-ceilinged living room, brightly lighted with lamps. There, for the first time, Gil saw the owner. He was old, seventy, eighty—one couldn't be sure, for the old fellow stood from his chair, tall and straight under the age-darkened ceiling beams. His face was serene and peaceful, and he was smiling faintly, smiling, when he was a ruined man.

Mollie Hanson was beside the chair, unsmiling, pale. Her bitter glance accused Gil.

Tom Elliot spoke with quiet deference. "This man helped get our cattle, sir. All the men Skinner took on were crooked. Bob's foolishness is behind all of this."

A shadow crossed the serene old face. "Bob has been sowing a few wild oats, Tom. But I can't believe he's as bad as you and Mollie claim."

"This man came here pretendin' he was broke, sir. We found this money belt on him crammed with bills. It can't be anything but his cut from your beef."

"Guess again," Gil said coolly. "That money doesn't belong to me. I'm just carrying it until I find who it does belong to."

"He sounds like he's speaking the truth, Tom. What does he look like, Mollie?" The old man's unwinking stare turned to Gil.

The truth hit Gil like a blow. Gil Magee had been rustling cattle from a blind man.

Mollie Hanson caught the money belt from Tom Elliot's hand and looked at it closely. Her voice broke as she said: "This is Uncle Bert's belt. Three years ago I saw him cut these little notches in the strap. A month ago I wrote Uncle Bert to come here quickly, and help me. I haven't heard from him. This . . . this man Magee killed him!"

"Did you tell your brother your uncle was coming here?" Gil asked her bleakly.

"Yes. I . . . I hope they hang you for this!" Mollie Hanson cried fiercely.

Heavily the old man sat down, looking older now, his sightless eyes staring into space. "You're going after the cattle, Tom?"

"Yes, sir. This man'll guide us."

The old man sighed. "I'm sorry Bob had to be in Santa Cruz today. Bob will straighten all this out." He sighed. "If I could only see. . . ."

Mollie Hanson put a hand on his shoulder in a quick gesture of reassurance. The men shuffled uneasily, ready to go.

Behind the chair was the side wall of the room, and a window. The men holding Gil had relaxed their vigil, and, with a savage twist, he freed his arms, dove past Mollie Hanson, and hurled himself, headfirst, through the window glass, with his arms across his face.

A gun blasted through the noise, but the bullet missed. Gil hit the porch hard, reeled to his feet groggily, and lunged off, around the end of the house, and back to the bunkhouse. His horse still stood there. He was in the saddle before the pursuit got out into the open after him, and spurred off into the night with lead singing closely.

The horse was lathered and spent when Gil reached Santa Cruz. A wagon lot on the outskirts served as a livery stable, and Gil rode in among the wagons that jammed its yard.

"Who's the boss here?" he asked a black-mustached man who came to meet him.

"I am, at night, mister."

"Fellow named Bob Hanson, from Sunset Ranch, got a horse here?"

"Yep. Bay hoss. Been here all day."

"Saddle it an' put my saddle on a fresh horse. Bring them to the back of the Ace-Deuce quick. Jigger Gunn will settle the bill."

Gil entered the Ace-Deuce from the back. Men crowded the gambling tables, lined the bar. The dancing floor was full. Jigger Gunn, standing behind the back end of the bar, stepped out quickly and led the way into the office.

"What's wrong with your head, Gil?"

Gil grinned coldly. "I had some trouble at the Hanson ranch. Get me two guns, two rifles, and a sack of ammunition. A man from the livery yard will be here with a fresh horse I asked for. OK it for me."

"Hell certainly busted loose at the ranch," Jigger Gunn said. "Skinner come helling in here to say the lid had blown off, and Elliot was on the warpath."

Gil had put down two drinks from a bottle on the table when Jigger Gunn returned with two Colts, two rifles, and a flour sack bulging in the bottom with boxes of cartridges.

"What happened to Skinner?" Gil said.

"He and his men are waiting around to see if there'll be any trouble."

"There will be."

Jigger Gunn swore softly. "We've got their beef. They can't get it back."

"Elliot'll track it down."

"I'll send Skinner and his men over the border, too. When the boys get through with Elliot and his men, they won't bother us any more."

"That'll only leave the old man, the girl, and her brother."

"I'm keeping the brother ory-eyed. The old man ain't anything to worry about. And the girl never was."

"Where's the brother now?"

"Upstairs, asleep. I give him a room to use while he's in town."

Gil reached for the bottle and took another drink. "He's starting to the border with me tonight."

"It's as good a way as any to get rid of him I guess. Want me to go with you?"

★ ★ ★ ★ ★

No one paid any attention to Gil as he limped up the stairs to the balcony. The door to Bob's room was unlocked. The room was dark and Gil lit a lamp.

Bob Hanson lay face down on the bed in his clothes, breathing noisily. Five minutes later he was unsteady, but sober, backed into a corner, staring at a gun in Gil's hand.

Gil spoke to him savagely. "Do you want a bullet in that dirty, worthless belly along with the whiskey you've been lappin' up?"

"What's the matter with you, Magee?" Hanson's face was pasty, puffy, and his hands shook.

"You're coming downstairs with me, Hanson."

"I d-don't understand."

"You don't have to. Get downstairs."

Bob Hanson walked downstairs. Gil herded him into Jigger Gunn's office. Jigger was waiting. "The horses are out back," he said.

Bob Hanson burst out: "Do you know what this man is doing, Jigger?"

"Shut up! Get over in the corner there!" Gil commanded.

Bob Hanson backed into a far corner. Gil turned the key in the door lock, stepped back to the table, and put both the pistols on it, side by side, and stepped to Jigger's side.

"Now, you dirty son-of-a-bitch, I'll get it off my mind," he said to the saloon owner. "You lied to me about that fellow who was dry-gulched out in the Chufletero. I don't have to be a damn' fool to know you ordered that. If I'd known it before, I wouldn't have touched your dirty ideas with a prod pole. We're quits. Jump for a gun if you've got any arguments."

Jigger Gunn looked at the table where the two guns lay

135

side by side. Slowly his big head turned. "I'm not a gun-fighter, Gil. Pick up your guns an' get out. We'll forget it."

"A yellow-bellied snake like you never forgets," Gil retorted. He stepped to the table and without warning flashed into action. His body was already turning back as his right hand swept a gun off the table.

The sudden move caught Jigger Gunn with a tiny Derringer half out of his coat. Gil whipped the gun under his left arm and fired without completing the turn.

Gunn bent in the middle convulsively. The little hole was hardly visible. But the Derringer dropped. Still bent over, Jigger pressed his hands over the bullet hole.

"Damn you, Gil!"

Gil grinned crookedly. "I've heard about that Derringer, Jigger. That poor devil out in the Chufletero will be glad to see you coming." Swinging to Bob Hanson, he snapped: "Get out that window. Take these rifles. They're empty now. I'll be right back of you. Don't try anything."

Jigger Gunn was on the floor and fists were banging on the locked door when Gil followed Bob Hanson out the window. They found the horses, swung into the saddles.

"Keep the rifles," Gil ordered. "Stay close to me and ride, damn you! Ride!"

IV

Four days later the low dark mountains in Mexico loomed ahead under the golden wash of the afternoon sun. Gil and Bob Hanson were unshaven, gaunt from hard riding and little food. But the puffiness was out of Bob Hanson's face, the whiskey out of his system. The long, hard miles behind him had worn and sweated him into a new man, who his sister would hardly have recognized. His weary, sullen face had new lines, hard lines that had never been there before. Angry red weals girdled his wrists where Gil had tied him up in the brief halts to snatch sleep. He still carried the empty rifles. Gil had the sack of cartridges.

"How much farther are you taking me?" Bob Hanson said.

Gil pointed with his chin at the mountains ahead. "There."

"And then what?" Bob Hanson demanded.

"And then we'll see how tough you are."

"Damn you!" Bob Hanson choked. He had said the same thing many times before in the last four days, never so violently as now. "Give me a gun and a fair chance, and settle it like a man!"

Gil grinned. "You ain't a man, Hanson. You're just a pup who figured he could drink himself man-size. Your cattle are ahead there where we're going. Skinner and his men are coming. Tom Elliot and a few soft-bellied riders are tracking the cattle down to try to get 'em back. They'll be wiped out. I've got you, and I'll get your ranch. Your sister is the only one who'll be left to hold it."

A spasm crossed Bob Hanson's face. For a moment he looked wild, desperate. Gil dropped a hand to a gun. He removed it only when Bob Hanson shivered and looked away.

The rest of the afternoon Bob Hanson rode in stony silence. Long purple shadows in the first valley were about them when the sun vanished. They had been trailing the Sunrise cattle; the turn of those thousands of tracks into the side cañon was plain.

When darkness closed down, Gil roped his prisoner and rode behind him through the cañon toward the inner valley.

Near the cañon end a voice challenged from the rocks beside the trail. A guard had been posted.

"It's Magee!" Gil called. "Anyone come yet?"

"Nary a one," was the short answer.

"O'Leary still here?"

The man was none too friendly. "O'Leary ain't left. Who's that with you?"

"Bob Hanson. Kill him if he makes a break to get out."

"Don't worry. It was a damn' fool idea to bring him."

"Maybe so," Gil said, and rode on.

Starlight lay, pale and bright, over the inner valley. The Sunrise cattle grazed all about. Ahead, among the ruined *hacienda* buildings, a large fire blazed in the open.

Gil dismounted his prisoner under a tree beyond the brawling little creek. With the rope he lashed Bob Hanson's elbows and wrists behind, and ran the rope down to a loose hobble between the ankles, so that Bob could shuffle clumsily, but not run.

Tying the horses to a tree, taking the rifles and ammunition, Gil conducted his awkwardly hobbling prisoner past the shadowy *hacienda* buildings to the fire behind it. The men were lounging about the fire, smoking, talking. One of them looked around to see who was coming. Gil dropped the rifles and ammunition, and called: "It's Magee! Where's O'Leary?" In the same moment he tripped Bob Hanson and ran lightly forward.

The men on the ground came to their feet, scattering from one man who had scrambled up with an oath, drawing his gun.

It was Jack Samson, O'Leary's partner. O'Leary was not visible. Gil was still running forward as Samson's gun came out—running, while his two hands flashed down, and up.

The crossfire of shots crashed to the stars as Gil closed in, shooting.

Jack Samson lurched into the fire, kicking up a swirling cloud of sparks. In the brighter light from the sparks he reeled away two steps, falling as he went. He did not move after he crumpled to the ground.

Whirling, Gil scanned the men. "Where's O'Leary?" he demanded again.

They looked at the body, at him. None of the glances was friendly. The answer he got from one of the men was short.

"O'Leary rode south to get some liquor. He'll be back tomorrow. He wasn't lookin' for you so quick."

Two more men had run out of the old house. Gil counted them all—eight men here, Samson dead, O'Leary gone, one man guarding the cañon. He backed off, putting them all in front of him.

"Jigger Gunn's dead," he told them. "I killed him. I'm running things now. Anybody got a different idea?"

Startled, they stared back. Their faint hostility became open antagonism. One man put it into words with a sneer. "How come you'll run things now? I reckon we'll all have something to say about it."

The others backed him up.

Gil continued to grin at them. "When I rode here, I figured you'd all get greedy . . . even if you had to get me. I'll call your cards, boys. Reach high . . . or start shooting!"

They were eight, and Samson's body lay by the fire as a warning. Gil's guns waited for a move. Hands shot up. Scowling faces waited for some man to make a move, but no one started it.

Grinning coldly, Gil lined them up before him, backs to him, and dropped their gun belts and guns in a pile at his feet. His order brought Bob Hanson shuffling to him. With one hand Gil untied the rope.

"Take a couple of these guns, an' pump lead into the first man who moves," he told Bob Hanson. "If you don't, you won't have a chance. If you go for me, they'll probably get you, too. I'll be back in a little while."

Half an hour later, when Gil returned with the man who had been watching the cañon, Bob Hanson was still guarding the sullen prisoners. Gil lined the new man up with them, tossed wood on the fire, and lay down on the ground behind Bob Hanson.

"I'll sleep until daylight," he said. "Don't close your eyes, Hanson. They'll get you. Keep 'em up on their feet. They won't feel so frisky by morning."

Bob Hanson cursed him and stood there with the guns.

When Gil awoke, shivering in the dawn, Bob Hanson was pacing back and forth, haggard, dead-beat, and cursing his prisoners, who were as badly off as he was.

Gil went to the well and washed. The horses were in an old corral. He turned them out. Rifles, six-guns, and cartridge belts he carried into a front room of the house. And then collecting all the extra ropes, he marched the prisoners one by one into the same front room and hog-tied each man expertly.

Gil stood up from the last man to find Bob Hanson standing behind him, glaring from bloodshot eyes, ready to open fire.

"Damn you, Magee. You outthought yourself," Bob Hanson said hoarsely. "I'm the man now."

Gil gave him a crooked smile. "And then what?" he asked. "I ran all the horses off. You won't get one easy.

Skinner and his men'll be along any time. O'Leary is due back. They'll kill you on sight. There ain't enough water outside this valley to get far on foot. You've got a tiger by the tail, an' you'll get clawed if you let loose. Better get some sleep an' let me watch. One of these jaspers is likely to work himself loose. There's some grub in the back room."

Bob Hanson cursed him again. "You're a lunatic, Magee. What's on your mind?"

"Ants, hot stones in my belly, strips off my hide, an' Skinner an' O'Leary." Gil chuckled. "Hellfire is going to be popping around here soon. Better get that sleep."

"I know you're crazy now," Bob Hanson mumbled. And he plodded out of the room and returned shortly, wolfing the last of a strip of jerky, threw himself down on the floor, and was snoring almost instantly.

The hot, mid-morning sun was striking into the roofless room when Gil made out a scattered group of horsemen emerging from the cañon mouth and trotting across the valley. Picking up a rifle, he stepped through a gaping window opening and took his stand in front of the house.

When they drew near enough to be recognizable, Gil sent a warning shot over their heads. Horses were reined in. The men stared. Skinner wheeled his horse around and addressed the bunch, waving his arms.

But another man opened fire, throwing shot after shot at Gil as fast as he could pump in the shells. The whiplash scream of bullets passing closely ended in dull impacts as they struck the crumbling adobe wall. Even at that distance Gil could make out the scarred, raging face of O'Leary, who had met up with Skinner's party. The other men spread out and opened fire as Gil dodged back to the window and vaulted through. Two bullets struck beside the window, a third passed through and slapped into the back wall of the roofless room.

Bob Hanson was on his feet. Gun in hand, yawning from the drunken fatigue that still gripped him, he stuttered: "Wh-what's matter?"

"Skinner and his men," Gil said, grinning coldly. "They'll fill you full of lead quicker'n a bunch of Yaqui Indians would. Better grab a gun an' see how much of a man you are. Here they come!"

Kneeling before the window as he spoke, Gil began to shoot. Out across the valley the riders had scattered still more and started at a gallop toward the house. Gil threw shots at them, but the running targets were hard to hit. He dropped the empty rifle and snatched another off the floor.

Bob Hanson was firing out the next window. One rider tumbled out of the saddle. Another swerved around, dropping his rifle, and retreated, holding the saddle horn with both hands as he lay across it.

Part of the men, led by Skinner, swung away from the house and galloped to the left, up the valley; the others bolted the opposite way, down the valley.

Bob Hanson emptied his rifle after them and turned from the window with relief.

"That stopped them!" he exclaimed.

Gil leaned out and watched for a few moments, and then swung around, chuckling grimly as he dumped boxes of cartridges out of the cloth sack, and began filling his pockets.

"They're circling around behind these buildings, where the old fruit trees are. They'll work in from the back where they've got some cover. You never were so near dead as you are right now, *hombre*. Reload some of those guns an' get out back if you aim to live a little longer. Those rannihans have got their teeth in a heap of money, and they won't let go. And one of them would rather have blood than gold."

The prisoners were all awake. One of them jeered: "When O'Leary gets you, Magee, God help you!"

"All he's got to do is get me," Gil retorted. "Bring your guns, Hanson!"

They ran out of the room together. Bob Hanson demanded wildly: "What are you up to, Magee? You rustled our cattle and brought me over the border with a gun in my back. Now you give me guns to fight the men who helped you. Don't figure I'm helping you get away with my own cattle."

Gil threw the answer at him harshly. "Your life ain't worth a bent nickel. Mine ain't worth that. Try to save your skin if you're half a man. Get over to the other corner of the house. Keep moving from window to window. They'll get as far as those old buildings beyond the back garden. Maybe we can hold 'em there. If they get in the house here, get back into that front room an' drop as many as you can. Your sister'll have that many less to worry about."

"My sister." Bob Hanson groaned.

An agony of remembrance was in his bloodshot eyes, his haggard, exhausted face. Mollie Hanson would not have known the savage look on her brother's face as he ran to his post. Major Hanson would have smiled with pride if his sightless eyes could have seen it.

Gil had no time to think about it. Death was too close. Behind the sprawling ruins of the old *hacienda* building, beyond the ruined adobe huts where the *peón* servants once had lived, beyond the jungle-like tangle of long-neglected gardens and trees, Skinner, O'Leary, and the men were closing in.

They were audible before they could be seen. Then only glimpses could be caught. Gil opened fire with a rifle; a moment later he heard Bob Hanson's gun barking. Distant voices shouted back in the trees; the riders left their horses and advanced.

Gil began to dodge from window to window, throwing a shot at the glimpse of a head, a glint of sun on a gun barrel.

A bawling threat from O'Leary crossed the open: "I'll get you this time, Magee!"

Gil answered with a bullet that chipped dirt from the side of the window where O'Leary spoke. A storm of lead drove him to the next room.

Skinner's men began to spread out. Shots beyond the front of the house drew Gil there. The instant he showed himself at a window, two guns spoke from the shelter of the creekbank. One bullet ripped a furrow through Gil's shoulder.

Bob Hanson's handguns opened wildly, meeting a storm of gunfire behind the house. Gil ran to the back. Bob Hanson had stopped shooting by then. A thin, running line of dodging figures had almost reached the house, was already past the ashes of the fire and the stiff body of Jack Samson.

With roaring guns, Gil dropped one of them, and then retreated to the front room. Bob Hanson was already there. A flying splinter of wood had cut a bad gash in his cheek. "Now what?" Bob Hanson demanded.

"Get over in that front corner with half of these guns. I'll take the rest into the other corner," Gil snapped, scooping up gun belts and rifles and making for the corner as he spoke.

The yells of Skinner's men were already echoing through the house. They were searching the rooms, moving to the front as they found no one. They reached the adjoining room, to the rear. From the corner where he crouched, Gil emptied a gun through the door leading into that room. A yell of pain marked a hit. A moment later Skinner's men were shooting through a hall door and through the door of the next room; outside, men were firing through the gaping windows. From all sides lead was sweeping the room.

Gil motioned Bob Hanson down on the floor, and dropped down himself. One of the prisoners on the floor yelled wildly as a bullet splintered through a heavy hall door and struck him. The other prisoners began to shout and swear. The guns went silent.

Gil raised his voice. "I've got nine of the boys tied up on the floor, Skinner! You've hit one already!"

Skinner's cold, angry voice answered: "You dirty double-crossing skunk, Magee! What are you up to?"

"I've taken over the Sunrise cattle from Jigger Gunn," Gil answered from the floor. "You men are butting in where you ain't wanted. Get back over the border an' stay healthy. I can hold this room till hell cools off."

A chorus of hoots and yells answered that. O'Leary's raging voice was loudest. "Are you going to let that sawed-off little runt bluff you thataway?"

"I'm waitin' for you, O'Leary," Gil invited.

One of the prisoners shouted hoarsely: "Don't shoot in here! You'll hit us!"

O'Leary raged back at him. "You fools should 'a' had better sense than to let him get you! Keep low!" And O'Leary started to shoot through the door again.

The other men followed his lead. The gunfire rose to a deafening crescendo as shots poured in through both doors and the windows, raking the room from all angles. Mud plaster from the walls sifted down on the floor, and the rank fumes of burning powder grew strong.

Men had crept up just outside the windows. A hand

thrust in the side window and emptied a gun toward the corner where Gil lay. He smashed the hand with a careful shot.

Bob Hanson was firing at the doors and through the front windows. Risking the flying lead, he flattened himself beside one of the windows, waited a moment, and fired twice. His voice rang out as he dropped back to the floor. "I got that one!"

Bob Hanson had forgotten fatigue. The fire of battle was running through his veins.

The firing beyond the doors and windows died away. Skinner's men could be heard running toward the front of the house.

Skinner's angry voice rang out: "That's Tom Elliot riding in front! He's got ten or fifteen men! Get back to the horses, boys! If they trap us in here, away from our horses, we're done for! We could 'a' held 'em off at the cañon . . . but not now! *¡Vamos!*"

They ran back through the house. Gil stood up and climbed through one of the front windows, and, as he appeared in the open, a gun roared by the front door. A bullet struck Gil's shoulder.

He saw O'Leary standing there, waiting to settle the score. His second shot struck Gil's left arm. His third, lower, hit the leg; his fourth missed as Gil fell to the ground. He held his last two shots while he ran forward, taunting: "Where do you want it, Magee? In the head?"

Gil was lying on his right arm. He could move only the wrist and the gun in his right hand. He flipped the gun up and fired once, and, as O'Leary started to fall, Bob Hanson shot him, also, from the window. O'Leary pitched forward on Gil's legs, rolled off, and lay still.

"Dammit, Magee, I hated to see that happen," Bob

Hanson said thickly. "How bad did he hit you?"

"I reckon I'll live," Gil said, grinning.

Part of Tom Elliot's men galloped up to them; the rest thundered on around the house after the fleeing rustlers. Big Tom Elliot was among the men who leaped from their saddles and gathered around that spot in front of the house.

"Good Lord!" Tom Elliot cried in astonishment. "It's Bob! Where'd you come from, Bob? We thought you were dead or. . . ." He broke off awkwardly, and covered it up by snapping: "What are you doing here with this rustler?"

Gil looked up, grinning faintly. "Bob rode along with me to help get his cattle back," he said. "Robbing blind men an' dry-gulching relatives never was in my line. Bob said he'd ride here an' give me a hand in making some of my dirt right. You fellows never would have got through that cañon with the men watching it, so Bob an' I rode down ahead of you an' tied the boys up. They're in the house. It was close, but we made it. This Bob is a two-gun, fightin' he-man. I couldn't have done it without him."

Tom Elliot looked dazed as he stared at Bob Hanson's blood-streaked face.

"You've got eyes, ain't you?" Gil snapped. "Make sure Skinner an' his men are run off, an' then start your beef back toward the border while you've got a chance. Bob'll give you orders. I guess he's ready to run his ranch now."

Bob Hanson's bloody, stubble-covered face worked oddly for a moment. But when he spoke, his voice was strong. "That's right, Tom. Round up the cattle and start them north. Magee here is an awful liar, but I'm running the ranch now." Bob Hanson's arm tightened about the bloody shoulder he supported. "I've just found out what makes a man," he said in that same husky voice. "Magee is too good a man to lose. I want him close."

Gil Magee, gunman and outlaw at twenty-two, said nothing. His throat was too tight. From Bob Hanson's lips he had just discovered why two guns and the luck of the devil had never been enough.

Noose of Fate

T. T. Flynn was living in Albuquerque, New Mexico, in his Chrysler Airstream trailer with which he traveled extensively, when he completed this short novel. Street & Smith's *Western Story* customarily featured a short novel at the beginning of each weekly issue. This story was purchased by Jack Burr, editor of the magazine, on May 31, 1941. The author was paid $310.50 at the general rate of 1½¢ a word. It appeared under the title "Help or Hang!" in *Western Story* (9/13/41).

I

The sun was a molten disk pushing up into the cloudless eastern sky when Breck Coleman got back from the scout to Stinking Lakes. The herd was already strung out from the dry bed ground, and the fine alkali dust was a sinister haze over the gaunt, dry animals that plodded into the north. It was Gunsight and Steve Coleman, Breck's father and oldest brother, who came galloping toward that distant rider they had spotted in the dawn. It was Gunsight Coleman's shout that covered the last ground before they met.

"What'd you find, boy? What'd you find?"

"Water!" Breck called back.

"Ya-hooooo!" Steve yelled in a burst of exultation that

made Breck smile grimly through the soggy weariness.

Even Gunsight, tall, gaunt, and worn, like the herd in the distance behind him, was smiling as he reined up. "Say it again, Son. There never was a sweeter word."

"Water," Breck repeated, grinning as he relaxed to roll a cigarette. "Two of the lakes are dry. But there's enough in the third one to hold us a couple of days. Maybe a little more. There's about enough grass around to hold 'em that long, too."

"Two days rest'll shape 'em up fine to make it to the Río Puerco," said Gunsight. "And Pete Huxtle's ranch'll be easy to reach from then on. The drought ain't been near so bad north of the Puerco."

"Reckon Pete'll take them all?" Steve asked.

"Pete'll have the cash waiting," declared his father without hesitation.

He pushed his sombrero back on his head and turned to face the border, two days behind them, beyond the low hazy mountains off in the south. The spasm that crossed his face, the big fist he shook toward the far hazy distance, was the first glimpse Breck had of the passions that had stirred and seethed inside his father's broad chest.

"Ten years," Gunsight said. "Ten years of Yaquis and rustlers. Ten years of crooked politicos and ridin' and fightin' and trying to stay top dog. We licked it. And now we'll stay north in God's country, where your mother wanted to stay all the time."

He choked a little on the last, reined his horse around, and rode back toward his cattle. Breck and Steve followed him silently, each thinking of the past years when they had grown into hard-riding, trouble-filled manhood. Steve was the oldest, Sam was the middle brother, and Breck, long, rangy, and lean, the youngest. Their mother was back there across the border in a grave, killed by bandit bullets, for which the Coleman men had taken a terrible toll. That had started the final troubles, which had come to a head when the grass began to burn up and the water gave out. Gunsight had announced his decision abruptly.

"Boys, I've seen this coming. Pete Huxtle writes me he's bought a new ranch that needs stocking. He'll pay cash for a thousand head of prime stuff or go halves on anything over that we trail north to him. Bring everything in an' get the wagons loaded. We're pullin' out."

Better than 3,000 head had trailed out of the Rancho del Oro. The slow-plodding herd would do good now to tally 1,200. His excellency, General Maximilio Pindales, governor of the district, had culled out 1,000 head the first day for taxes and fines, which, Pindales had said suavely, had not been mentioned before as a matter of delicacy and friendship.

The Coleman *vaqueros* had been helpless before the troop of armed soldiers backing Pindales. Cursing, Gunsight had been forced to watch 1,000 of the best beefs culled and turned back.

An Indian raid that stampeded the cattle had cost them hundreds more and four dead *vaqueros* before the cattle were thrown back into a herd and headed north again.

Then the drought-weakened culls had started to go as the trail grew dryer, the grass scantier. Drought had struck even more fiercely along the border. Yesterday Gunsight had received Sam's report of the country ahead with grim fatalism: "First time I ever heard of it happening, boys. I counted on water here. Maybe we can make it to the Stinking Lakes. Can't turn back, anyway. There ain't anything back there. Breck, take a couple of horses, kill 'em if you have to, but get to the Stinking Lakes an' see what's there. If they're dried up, we're sunk. We'll do good to get the wagons on through to the Puerco."

Breck had left one dead-beat horse at the Stinking Lakes. But he had seen the water, had buried his face in the warm clear shallows, and then rolled out in the water and wallowed there, clothes and all, grinning at the news he had to take back.

"Better crawl in a wagon and sleep some," Steve told him now. "You look tuckered out."

"Might be a good idea," admitted Breck.

Back of the dust haze that hung over the dregs he tossed his saddle in the bedroll wagon and climbed in under the dirty gray, weathered wagon sheet. Ramón, the young driver, turned on the seat and grinned through the alkali dust that powdered his dark-skinned face.

"The Holy Mother listened and saved water," he said in Spanish. "We have no more trouble now, no?"

"Looks like we're in the clear," Breck agreed. "I'm gonna sleep a week."

Ramón's voice was the next thing Breck heard—sharp, urgent through the loud creaks of the lurching wagon.

"*Señor* Breck! Trouble I think! *¡Señor!*"

Breck scrambled out, snatching the rifle he had taken from the saddle boot and put at arm's reach from habit. He had slept until midday. The sun glare was blinding; the heat came off the parched ground like flame from an invisible fire.

A butte and a distant rock spire beyond indicated that they were better than halfway to the Stinking Lakes. The drive had plodded steadily, was still strung out in a bawling line that crawled toward the distant horizon where water meant life instead of death in the shimmering heat haze.

"What's wrong?" Breck asked, and then he saw the thing Ramón was pointing at from the seat beside him.

Dust a mile away marked riders coming fast. More than a dozen of them, Breck counted at a glance.

"It is another cattle drive, I think," said Ramón in Spanish.

Eyes clearing in the sun glare picked out what Ramón saw far back beyond the riders. The faint dust haze hanging, low and motionless, could only come from more plodding cattle, heading north, too, and bearing toward the Stinking Lakes.

"There ain't enough water for two drives!" Breck jerked out, and went over the wheel of the big ox-drawn wagon with a jump that carried him running toward the nearest *vaquero*. "Here!" he shouted. "Give me that horse!"

Leaving the *vaquero* afoot, he spurred toward the front of the drive where the strange riders were heading.

II

The other three Colemans were already riding out to meet the strangers. Breck fell in at his father's right. Gunsight again was gaunt and grim.

"Let me do the talking," was all he said.

They were four abreast, waiting, when the strangers galloped up. Thirteen of them, Breck counted, unshaven, trail-worn, dusty, but hardcases, too, heavily armed. The horses were branded Circle S. The man who reined up before Gunsight was lanky, flat-faced, and curt as he came to the point.

"Headin' for Stinkin' Lakes, I make it."

"That's right, mister," said Gunsight, curt himself. "No you ain't."

Gunsight looked toward the dust, off in the distance. He seemed thoughtful. "We aim to," he said. "We're closer. The cattle have dried out all the way across the border. If they don't make this water, they're done for."

The flat-faced man had a loose, crooked mouth under the tobacco-stained mustache when he grinned. "Mex outfit, huh?" he said. "Well, you ain't dealin' with Mexes now. I'm Clem Springer, ramroddin' for Hardy Young's Circle S. We're movin' north to grass an' water . . . and we aim to get there. Hardy Young don't take excuses."

"We're closer to the water," said Gunsight again, and his gaunt face showed lines to match the metallic quietness of his voice.

Springer chewed his tobacco for a moment. Then he spat deliberately, grinning again. "You ain't closer to the water. You're so far from it that you'll never git there by night. Take it or leave it, mister. What's your play?"

Gunsight looked again toward the dust haze in the west. Then he looked at Breck. "How much water is there?"

"Not enough for two drives."

Gunsight nodded as if he had already accepted that fact. "There ain't any place to go but on to the lakes," he decided. "That's our play, Springer, an' all we can do."

Clem Springer spat again, grinning. "It ain't all *we* can do. Better get to work, boys."

His men had been waiting for the order. They knew what they were to do. Springer led them himself, spurring hard around the Colemans and galloping toward the first plodding cattle.

Sam's furious cry cut through the dust and departing drum of hoofs. "They're scattering the drive an' turning it back!" He rode after them, jerking out his rifle.

Breck had never heard his father cry in so terrible a voice: "Sam, come back here!"

But Sam was either out of earshot or refused to listen.

"They're too many for us!" Gunsight shouted. "Stop Sam!"

Breck knew what his father meant. Nine of the Mexican hands had crossed the border with them. Four were driving wagons. But the Mexicans were not gun hands. Not here north of the border, out of their own country, against fighting *gringos*.

Salazar, riding point, pulled up his horse and stared uneasily at the thunderbolt of riders bearing down on him. The lead cattle stopped, heads coming up with newly frightened life as they stared. Then a volley of six-shooters crashed. Yelling, whooping, the Circle S riders came at them and cattle turned tail and bolted and the stampede was on.

Sam, always headstrong and full of temper, brought up his rifle, fired, and a Circle S rider pitched from the saddle. Gunsight had known it would happen. He had tried to head off Sam's recklessness that would bring hardcase guns blazing back. As they did now.

Half the Circle S riders saw their man go down. They must have had their orders about this, too. They wheeled back through the dust as one man, guns blazing.

Sam's horse fell heavily, throwing his rider in a rolling heap. The Circle S men raced toward him. Sam staggered up—and then went forward on his face, arms flailing out helplessly.

Breck caught a glimpse of his father, looking like a gaunt fury as he worked his rifle. The other Circle S riders had turned back through the wall of dust lifting behind the stampede. Breck knocked a man out of the saddle with his second shot. Another one went down in a tally for Steve or Gunsight. Then as Breck's rifle sights covered another man, his horse collapsed under him.

He saw the ground, felt himself slam violently, helplessly against dirt, small stones, and scattered rocks. After that everything blotted out.

Pancho, the squat, scar-faced horse wrangler, was the one who was shaking him, dribbling canteen water in his face, when the glaring, cloudless sky registered again.

"¡Gracias á Dios!" cried Pancho, unashamed tears in his eyes. "Those cabrónes don' keel him, Don Steve!"

Pancho's long, ape-like arm helped Breck sit up. Steve was there on his horse, ghastly pale. The sun was a full hour farther over in the sky. The dust had settled. The gunshots, the pound of hoofs, the roll of stampeding cattle, had left only dry, hot quiet that hung about the spot like a shroud.

Half a mile away the wagons and yoked oxen waited alone. Four of the vaqueros were digging in the ground not far off. Dead horses lay in sight. A thin scattering of cattle was visible miles away.

"Sam . . . Gunsight?" Breck asked thickly.

Steve pointed to canvas-covered objects on the ground where the vaqueros were digging. "Dead," he said harshly. "They got Salazar, Lopez, and Citriano. Shot my left leg up. I can't get down an' walk on it. That Clem Springer left word we started the fight, an', if we crossed their trail again, they'd finish it."

Breck gulped the last water in the canteen. Pancho helped him up, handed his sombrero off the ground, stood somberly waiting. "God's country," he said bitterly. "And they did this to us. Damn them! If I live long enough, I'll face that Springer again."

"That won't help now," said Steve in the same harsh voice. "We can get some of them cattle back together this afternoon. It'll be tomorrow before we can get them to Stinking Lakes. Maybe there'll be a little water left. Can't stay here. Ain't nothing to do but go on to the Puerco."

Three days later a few hundred stumbling, thirst-maddened cattle and two of the wagons reached the meandering shallows of the Puerco. All else that the Colemans had brought out of Mexico was back there on the death trail past the Stinking Lakes, now only sun-cracked mud and a few hoof-churned skims of soupy moisture, ringed with bloating carcasses.

Steve was in one of the wagons, burning with fever from the wounded leg, but able to grin when Breck brought him fresh water.

"We'll make it now," said Steve.

"Water and enough grass from here on," Breck agreed, grinning back. "We're tough, *hombre, que no?*"

"*Si.*" Breck nodded.

"You never was one to say much," Steve said. "But I can read you, kid. You're tough. You're fast with a gun. You don't forget. That Circle S *segundo* has been as good as dead from the time you hit the ground back there beyond the lakes. *Que no?*"

"I ain't said," Breck evaded.

Steve's eyes were bright with fever, but clear and shrewd. "You'll hunt him down, Breck. You'll kill him . . . an' most likely get killed. He don't ride alone. It ain't worth it. It never got us anything down below the border. It never got us anything when Sam cut loose the other day. All of us gone now but you."

"And you," Breck said roughly.

"You ain't a fool," Steve said calmly. "Most likely, even if there was a doctor handy, which there ain't, I wouldn't make it. The poison's in my blood now. I can feel it taking hold. Promise me you won't go gun huntin', Breck. Get you a wife somewhere an' a little spread an' settle down peaceful."

"I ain't lookin' for a wife, Steve."

"You're lookin' for trouble. Ain't I your brother? Don't I know you? Let that curly wolf get his gun pay from someone else. It'll happen. Promise me you'll dodge trouble an' settle down. There'll be a girl someday that'll be worth fightin' for if she needs it. Nothing else *is* worth it. There's gold in that old leather trunk. Plenty for you to get settled an' start over for yourself."

"There ain't any girl and I ain't ready to settle, Steve."

"I'm asking you for a promise," Steve said huskily. "No gunfightin' out of the past. No trouble if you can dodge it. Gunsight an' Mother'd want that promise. It's all I'm asking from you, kid. It'd make me feel a heap better . . . about everything."

"All right . . . I promise."

"Gimme your hand on it."

Steve's hand felt as though it was on fire. Breck's throat was tight when he walked away from the wagon. Steve was going, too. They both knew it now.

They buried Steve two days later beside a rocky spine that was like a marker for the grave. The country was higher and rolling. Grass was getting better. Far to the northeast the first high green mountains were piling up over the horizon. Another few days would bring the bony, trail-worn dregs of the drive to Pete Huxtle's place.

Breck called the *vaqueros* together. Good men. Loyal. Everyone had been with the Colemans for years. And of them all, Pancho, the scar-faced, the ape-like, was the best.

"You're the *segundo*," Breck told Pancho in front of the others. "Take everything on to Pete Huxtle's ranch. I'll give you a letter telling Huxtle to pay you all off and store what's in the wagons until I see him."

Pancho's black eyes were intent. "W'at you do, *señor?*"

Breck's gesture included the cattle, the two wagons, the grave, the long trail back across the border. "Nothing. It's finished. I'll take a ride and think it over."

"Perhaps ees better," said Pancho simply.

III

Breck holstered and drew his gun fast for each shot at the old pine beside the mountain stream. A rock beyond the water caught his eye. With the same fast draw, he emptied the gun in a ripping, roaring blast of lead at the new target. As silence fell, a sharp order snapped from the edge of the clearing behind him.

"Drop it an' reach!"

When Breck dropped the empty gun, he was ordered to turn around. The man had come noiselessly on the matted pine needles. Now, as he stepped into the clearing with rifle ready, he was a stumpy, bowlegged, threatening little man.

"Who was you shootin' at?"

Breck grinned. "That pine and that rock across the creek. Take a look if it'll make you feel any better."

"Keep them paws up!" The bowlegged man sidled over to the splintered pine knot, ordered Breck to wade the creek ahead of him, and inspected the raw, plain bullet marks on the rock. "Guess I figured wrong," he admitted. "I got a pardner around here on the mountain somewhere an' I figured you was cuttin' down on him. Who you ridin' for?"

"Just riding through. I hit here last night and camped."

Pack saddle, tarp, blankets were in sight over in the clearing. They seemed to convince the stranger. "Lookin' for a job?"

"Might keep me busy. I kind of fancy the country through here."

"You got a job. Foller the trail down to the T Slash an' tell Ory Shotwell that Link Tucker sent you."

"Who owns the T Slash?"

"Shotwell. I got to be movin' on. See you later."

When Tucker was gone, Breck rolled a cigarette and started for his two horses. Something about these high peaks and broad valleys appealed to him. Trees, brush, and grass were lush green, with plenty of water brawling down the slopes.

Even the solitude was different from the dry, broad stretches of the border country. The wind in the high pines had a soothing softness. Birds flashing from sunshine to shadow called and sang. Here was peace where a man might forget the past.

The valley ahead was green and smiling to the next upsurge of mountains, and the sun was canting past noon when Breck followed the little-used trail down through foothills. He topped a last rise and saw a ranch house, outbuildings, and corrals ahead and below. A great draw sloped away to the south and east, and the ranch road to the valley ran out that way. Drifting dust on the road marked a wagon coming to the ranch.

When Breck rode in, a plunging horse was trying to throw a man in one of the corrals. Six men were outside the corral, watching. One of them was Link Tucker. He grinned at Breck's surprise.

"I came down fast on a short cut. Shotwell says you're hired."

Ory Shotwell was a big man, gray coat open over his broad chest, trousers outside his riding boots, eyes coldly direct in a hard, forceful face.

"You're on the pay already," he told Breck. "What's the name?"

"Coleman."

"Tucker says you're handy with a gun."

"Average."

"Tucker says you'll be better than average when trouble breaks. Baldy Catton, the foreman, will be in after a while and line you out on the job. Rustle some grub in the cook shack if you're hungry." Shotwell turned to look in the corral, where the lathered horse was standing and blowing.

"You're talking trouble, Shotwell," Breck said. "What are you hiring, me or my gun?"

"Both," said Shotwell, turning.

"I'm not looking for trouble. My guns aren't for hire."

The quick silence was suddenly hostile. A raw-boned, sandy young man at Tucker's left grinned unpleasantly and drawled: "He don't want trouble. Let's git him on his way."

Breck started back to his saddle horse and pack horse. A gun blasted behind him. Lead spewed dirt up against his right leg. Another gunshot smashed dirt against the left leg. Shotwell's loud voice stopped it.

"Put up them guns! Here comes the sheriff!"

Breck had already turned. He saw that Link Tucker had

161

been watching the fun with a crooked grin. The buckboard coming around the ranch house was the one that had been on the valley road.

The driver was a lanky young man, somewhat of a dandy. The older man beside him had white hair and mustache, and age lines deep in his face.

"Howdy, Bradshaw!" Shotwell called. "Off your range some, aren't you?"

The old sheriff limped a little as he came around the front of the team. His reply was dry. "That's one way of lookin' at it, Shotwell. But I sort o' figure the whole Tampiano district is my range."

Seen closer and on his feet, he looked even older, a little shrunken inside the coat, as if age was pressing heavily. But his look was cool as it ran over the men.

"I've got a warrant here for one of your crew, Shotwell."

"Makin' a joke, Bradshaw?"

"I don't drive twenty miles to make a joke, Shotwell. Before Ben Jordan was shot the other night, he got a look at one of the men who was firing his place. Wasn't until last night he pulled through enough to talk." The sheriff turned to his companion, still on the buckboard seat. "Cully, which one's this Link Tucker?"

Link Tucker's voice answered behind the sheriff. "Here! You man enough to take me?" He pulled his holstered gun as he spoke.

"Look out, Sheriff!" Breck called sharply.

A younger lawman might have been quick enough. Probably not. The old man's hand went up his coat like a veteran gunfighter. But he turned too slowly. Tucker shot him.

Breck swore as the sheriff staggered. It was murder. Bradshaw dropped his gun. He was a stumbling target for the second shot Tucker's grinning hate had ready. Breck's bullet smashed Tucker's arm and drove the second shot wild. Breck stepped back, covering the others.

"Get 'em up. You too, Shotwell. Keep your men quiet. That one in the corral, too."

The sheriff had pawed his gun off the ground with his left hand, but he was still dazed.

"There he is," said Breck, nodding at Tucker. "He was set to dry-gulch you when you rode up. Kill him if you like."

"I don't like," old Bradshaw snapped painfully. "The law'll settle this bowlaiged turkey. Cully, gimme your handcuffs."

"I'll handle him, Andy. How bad you hurt?"

"Not bad enough for a dirty, yellow-bellied skunk like you, Cully Carnes. You never made a move when he pulled that gun. I ain't a fool. I sharpened my teeth on skunks like you when they was still hangin' out your diapers. Shuck off that badge an' gimme them cuffs. Shotwell, get us fixed to travel."

Cully Carnes, the deputy, looked sullen and uneasy as he surrendered badge and handcuffs. Ory Shotwell was scowling as he shouted an order that brought the cook out of his shack with water and towels.

Breck's gun covered them as they got the sheriff's coat and shirt off. The bullet had entered under the shoulder, and the wound was not bleeding much as strips of towel were tied over it.

Tucker's arm had been holed cleanly. He was in good shape after he was bandaged and climbed on the buckboard. But the sheriff weaved slightly as he turned to follow.

"Sheriff, you ain't going to make it," Breck decided. "This bunch smells dirty enough to run a sandy on you down the road. Shotwell, let's help 'em get to town. You drive an' I'll leave my pack horse here an' ride behind with the sheriff."

"Gettin' that old baboon to town ain't any of my business," said Shotwell flatly. "I don't like his guts an' he don't like mine."

"And I don't want trouble . . . an' I bet I'm gettin' it so fast you'll be surprised," said Breck. He was lean, loose-jointed, almost Indian-brown under the old sombrero pushed back on his head. His grin had a wolfish edge that made the big rancher bite back what he was going to say.

Breck tied his saddle horse to the buckboard and tossed Shotwell's .45 to the ground before the rancher gathered the reins to drive off.

"Baldy Catton'll know what to do!" Shotwell called to his men.

"That makes Catton an' me know what we're doing," Breck added to the men. "Tell Catton not to make any mistake about headin' us off from town. I don't want trouble . . . but Shotwell won't like it if Catton gets ideas about his boss' little *pasear*."

Breck looked back as the buckboard took the long road into the valley. None of the T Slash men was trailing them.

"How's the shoulder, Sheriff?" he asked the lawman.

"Tore up inside. There ain't any blood in my mouth. I'll be all right."

Breck doubted that. The old man was tough—but he *was* an old man. By his voice he was worse than he admitted. He began to sag more and more on the jolting seat. When he spoke again, his voice was weaker.

"What's your name?"

"Breck Coleman."

"One of Shotwell's men?"

"I ain't done anything to get greased with that," said Breck, grinning. "I stopped by for a job and was ready to move on when you drove up."

"Want a job?"

"I had one in mind."

"I like your style, son. I'm gonna make you my deputy. Raise your right hand."

"Can't use it, mister. I'm peaceable. Trouble's the last thing I want."

Breck had to lean close to hear the reply. The sheriff was getting weaker.

"I ain't askin' you questions, young feller. I'm tellin' you. Got to get the prisoner locked up. I ain't gonna make it. The law's got to be in charge here when I go down. I know what I'm doing. I been a peace officer forty years. Raise your right hand."

Breck was smiling crookedly as he obeyed. He could humor an old man who might be dying. He had to go to town anyway, and he might as well wear the law badge and take the jail keys old Bradshaw handed him.

Link Tucker turned on the front seat and snarled: "Gittin' in with the law now, huh? Wisht I'd shot the stuffin's out o' you when I had the chance."

"That's the way the preacher felt when he bet the collection on a bobtailed flush." Breck grinned. "Ride on, you maggoty little bait. I'm gonna lock you up in a jail cell before I move on, an' I hope your poison chokes you."

Andy Bradshaw was unconscious before they reached the valley town of Tampiano. Breck eyed the place with interest as the racing buckboard whirled past the first scattered adobe houses and came out on a wide, rutted main street.

Brick buildings were mixed in with frame and adobe buildings. Mines back in the mountains would account for a string of empty ore wagons. But the town looked like a cow center for the whole valley region. A doctor's sign was on a small frame building where Ory Shotwell stopped the buckboard. **DR. TAYLOR.**

There was no lack of help to get the sheriff inside. Breck stopped the crowd that would have pushed in after them. They could see the sheriff's badge. One of the men Breck blocked in the doorway slyly asked: "You got Ory Shotwell under arrest?"

Shotwell heard it and blared angry denial. "I came along to get Bradshaw to the doctor!"

"Where's Cully Carnes?" another man called.

"Bradshaw acted like a drunken fool and fired Carnes," Shotwell answered angrily. "Bradshaw came out to the ranch, claiming Tucker here helped fire the Jordan place . . . as if it ain't known who was behind that. When the old man pulled his gun like he meant a killing, Tucker shot first. And then Bradshaw got sore because Cully Carnes didn't start shooting. He gave the deputy's badge to this saddle tramp, who rode into my place and mixed in the matter with his gun."

"I'm still mixed," said Breck calmly. "Shotwell, you're a lowdown liar on top of everything else. You watched Tucker go for his gun when the sheriff's back was turned, an' you never made a move. Now shut up while I close the door."

The men outside didn't know him. Some of them were Shotwell's friends. But they weren't sure what had happened. For the first time in his life Breck had the experience of law power at his shoulder. The crowd cleared the doorway obediently. The men who had helped carry old

Andy Bradshaw into the back room went out, and no man protested the door closing in their faces.

Doc Taylor was a brisk, wiry little man in shirt sleeves, short mustache iron-gray, and a hurried coolness that suggested he was used to this sort of thing. In a few minutes he had the sheriff bare to the waist on a table in the back room.

"Andy was shot in the back like you say," he stated over his shoulder. "He's too old for this sort of thing."

"He asked for it," growled Tucker.

"And you asked for the jail cell you're getting," Breck said. "Might as well lock you up now. Shotwell, I don't rightly know what the law can pin on you. Rattle your hocks an' stay out of my way while I'm wearing this badge. I don't want any trouble. ¡Vamos!"

"You're ridin' high for a little with that gun and badge," sneered Shotwell as he stepped to the door. "It won't last long."

"Nobody said it would. But I'm dealin' the law now. Tucker, get going."

Shotwell pushed through the crowd ahead of them, speaking angrily to men he knew. "It's time we had a real sheriff. We've had enough of this."

Although Breck met plenty of scowls, no one tried to stop him as he followed his prisoner up on the buckboard. But as he started to sit down, a sudden flat silence in the crowd held him standing, watching four riders coming from a hitch rack down and across the street.

Ory Shotwell had been on the point of moving away with friends. Now he wheeled back, waiting. Breck saw one of the men pass him a gun.

The silence was ominous, laced with the tight, rising threat of trouble. Standing there on the buckboard, Breck studied the four men who were causing it. Three of them he marked off for gun hands who had no more than wary watchfulness in what was happening. But the man who walked his big bay horse in front sat straight and challenging.

IV

You couldn't miss a man used to giving orders and having his own way. There was something about this man that reminded Breck of his father. Not as old, not as tall, or as gaunt as Gunsight had been the last year. But both men had the lean, hard, purposeful look, the same cold-eyed challenging way of going into trouble. Gunsight would have been as curt as this stranger in the black suit, Stetson, with saddle gun, and belt gun under his open coat.

"What's this I hear about Andy Bradshaw being shot?"

He asked the question of the crowd in general, while his look ran over them. He reined his horse over beside the buckboard as Breck gave him the reply.

"That's right. Bradshaw was shot. He's in there with the doc. I'm lockin' up the man who did it."

"Who are you?"

"I'm the new deputy."

"Andy Bradshaw went out to the T Slash to get a man." The bay horse obeyed the reins and moved ahead toward Ory Shotwell. The curt voice spoke to Shotwell. "Bradshaw wasn't gunned at your place, was he, Shotwell?"

Men began to edge away from Shotwell, who stood blackly scowling. But Shotwell wasn't alone. Breck marked a dozen guns that would be drawn when trouble started, if his guess was right. Shotwell knew it. His sneer gave back as much challenge as he got.

"Bradshaw came looking for trouble . . . an' he got it. He's about run his bolt in this Tampiano country. We're lookin' for a new deal from the law. If we don't get it one way, we'll get it another."

"Did you shoot him?"

Ory Shotwell jerked his head at the buckboard. "That maverick deputy's got the man who shot him. Nobody's stopping the arrest. If you want to hear more about it, ride in when court sets an' hear what the jury decides."

"I don't have to sit in court to guess what the jury'll decide if it touches my interests," the other man said. "There's only one kind of law you and your friends want, Shotwell . . . and it ain't the kind of law that suits me."

"There's the law now . . . a no-account saddle tramp."

"If he suits Andy Bradshaw, he suits me."

"We figured that."

Breck drove the buckboard between the two men. "The law right now doesn't care about who it suits. But it's heard enough talk about itself. That goes for you, Shotwell, an' you, too, mister . . . whoever you are."

Surprisingly the stranger on the bay horse did not resent the order. He chuckled. "That's the kind of talk I like to hear. I'm Hardy Young, of the Circle S . . . and I'm agreeable. I'll drop in and see how Andy Bradshaw is and let you handle the law."

"Hardy Young . . . Circle S," Breck said. He was half off the seat, hand going to his gun before he remembered Steve and the promise. "Get in and see Bradshaw then," he said huskily, and slashed the rein ends across the team and headed for the jail.

"I was gettin' ready to duck," said Link Tucker on the seat beside him. "You sure fanned up a hate when he allowed he was Hardy Young. Thought you was gonna cut down on him an' start all hell poppin' there in the street, with me right in the middle. What'd he ever do to you, Coleman?"

"Nobody said he did anything. Here's the jail an' in you go."

The small brick jail had an office in front and three cells in the back. Link Tucker was grinning slyly as Breck used the sheriff's keys and locked him in one of the cells.

"I won't be in here long," Tucker said. "Ory Shotwell'll take care of me. And Ory ain't a fool. He don't bear a grudge if he sees a man is thinkin' right. He seen that little play back there. You listen to Ory next time he talks to you. Maybe he'll be glad to have you packin' that deputy's badge, after all."

The bowlegged little gunman was still grinning when Breck locked the cell door in silence and left him. Old calendars and Reward notices covered the walls of the dusty office. Chairs and a scarred roll-top desk formed a half circle around a sawdust box. Whiskey glasses in the desk suggested a bottle was kept near. Breck found the bottle in a bottom drawer, poured himself a drink—and then another.

His hand was shaking. He was back on the drought trail, watching Sam go down before Circle S guns, watching the dry dirt thud down on the tarp-wrapped bodies of Gunsight and Sam, watching the stampeded cattle drop by scores as the strongest were urged on through the night to the scanty hoof-churned slope that the Circle S drive had left at the Stinking Lakes. And Steve had died and stayed in his lonely grave. All gone—Gunsight, Sam, and Steve—cattle and the high strong future that Gunsight had trailed north to build.

Breck took another drink.

"You shouldn't have made me promise it, Steve," he groaned. "I got him here. That Clem Springer'll be around

170

somewhere, too. This ain't what Gunsight an' Sam'd want
. . . ridin' out an' leavin' them on the fat grass an' water,
laughin' at the way they busted us, and trompin' other folks
that get in their way. You were wrong, Steve. God wouldn't
have put him down there in front of me if it wasn't on the
cards I was to even it up for Gunsight, Sam, an' you.
Lemme take it back, Steve. I didn't know what I was prom-
ising. I got to stay here now."

He jumped as a laughing voice said: "Why do you have
to stay, cowboy? And do you talk to yourself much?"

It wasn't Steve talking. Steve was north of the Puerco in
his dry, lonely grave. This was a girl who had stepped
through the doorway in time to hear his last words. She
wore a riding skirt, small buckskin jacket, and the wind had
been in her copper hair that swirled on a level with Breck's
shoulder. She was young, too, and her laughter was an invi-
tation to friendliness.

Breck was sheepish as he blinked. He wrenched himself
out of the past, and grinned at her. "I forgot that door
wasn't closed. It's a kind of fit I am apt to get 'most any
time. Might even start foaming at the mouth."

"And fall down on the floor and kick?"

"Can't ever tell," said Breck, grinning broadly.

"Couldn't you do it now?" she asked hopefully.

"I only have floor fits in the morning."

Still smiling, she looked puzzled as she eyed the deputy's
badge. "I saw the buckboard in front and thought Cully
Carnes or Andy would be in here. Where are they?"

"Carnes stayed out at the T Slash Ranch," said Breck,
unable to stop staring. Down there across the border where
the *señoritas* were black-haired and dark-eyed, you thought
of girls like this, and never saw them. You planned someday
to ride up north and meet a girl like this—but you never did.

"But Andy came back, didn't he?" she was saying. "And . . . and isn't that Cully's badge?" She was more puzzled, uncertain about him.

"There was a little trouble."

The laughter went from her face. "What happened? Andy wasn't hurt, was he?"

"Sort of. He was shot. I brought him in to Doc Taylor's . . . and he made me deputy for a few hours." The girl's stricken look made Breck ask: "You any kin to him?"

"He's my grandfather. Tell me what happened?"

Breck told her, expecting tears. But she stayed dry-eyed, pale, watching his face.

"So Cully double-crossed him," she said. "I'm not surprised. There was something about Cully I couldn't trust. He must have been working with Shotwell and his friends all the time." She swallowed. "I've got to go to Andy. They'll be needing me to help take care of him. You're going to act as sheriff, aren't you?"

"I aimed to turn back the badge and move on."

"You can't do that," she protested quickly. "Andy must have expected you would stay and help him. Can't you see that's what they want? They want Andy out of the way. They want one of their own men in as sheriff. Andy's helpless. He's trusting you or he wouldn't have sworn you in. We . . . we need you."

"*We,* ma'am?"

She was bitterly urgent. "Don't you see it means a lot to me, too? There'll be trouble if they take the office away from Andy."

Breck moistened his lips. "All right . . . I'll stay."

"I'll tell Andy. He'll feel better," the girl said.

The little office seemed more dusty and drab without her. Breck rolled a cigarette. A small picture back in the cluttered desk caught his eye. It was Andy Bradshaw's granddaughter, standing beside a white horse, cream-colored Stetson hanging back on her shoulders, riding gloves on her hands, laughter once more inviting friendliness. On the framed picture was written: **ANDY, FROM JEAN.**

"Jean," Breck said aloud. He smiled slightly. Jean had been his mother's name. "Steve, you called the turn," he said aloud again. "This one's worth trouble . . . an', if that Circle S bunch is makin' part of the trouble, it ain't my fault."

Breck was sober and calculating as he drove the buckboard and his lead saddle horse to the livery barn down the street. He was a stranger on a strange range, with trouble strange to him seething all about. Breck Coleman— deputy—under oath to uphold the law.

The liveryman was fat, hickory shirt open at the neck, broad face pink and smooth. "You found the right place," he cheerfully agreed. "Andy Bradshaw boards his hosses here. I heard Andy made you his deputy. Coleman's the name, ain't it? I'm Huck Haines. Gonna be with us long?"

"Long as I'm needed."

Good-natured eyes looked Breck over. "It ain't any of my business. But you're kind o' young for the job. You'll have to step fast to fill Andy's shoes. I reckon you know that."

"Plenty of man, is he?"

"Always has been." Something close to pride entered the fat man's voice. "Andy was marshal in Leadville an' Golden, deputy in Denver, an' worked for the Pinkertons. He helped tame some of them hard-rock towns up north when they was woolly and wild. It ain't his fault that trouble has blowed up under him here."

173

"What kind of trouble?" asked Breck curiously.

Huck Haines stopped short with harness over an arm. His jaw sagged. "Say . . . don't you know what you're tackling?"

"I just rode in today." Breck smiled thinly. "I can guess some of the trouble . . . but guesses ain't enough if I'm crowded in a tight."

"Jumpin' Jehoshaphat!" The liveryman wagged his head as he put up the harness. "*If* you're crowded in a tight," he muttered. "And you're Andy Bradshaw's deputy an' tangled already with Ory Shotwell an' Hardy Young."

"I'd like to hear," suggested Breck.

Haines regarded him pityingly as he reached for a plug of tobacco. Biting off a corner, he spoke past the chew. "It ain't any of my business. I got to trade with ev'body. But don't you know about Hardy Young an' the Circle S?"

"I've heard the name," Breck said. He kept a pokerface, but the grit of his feeling must have been in his voice or the fat man had heard talk that made him look keenly. "I don't know much about Young or his ranch," Breck added.

"*Hm-m-m,*" said Huck Haines noncommittally. "Well, Hardy Young's got a dern' sight more land down on the border than he's got around here. Always stayed there most of the time. But he's lost his grass down there. Drought's burned out that border country. So he's been trailin' cattle up here, where he's got water an' grass."

"And he hasn't got enough water and grass," guessed Breck without expression.

"You know that much about him, anyway," Haines said. "He's leased all the land he can get, bought what he could, an' it still ain't enough. He's trailin' in more cattle than a houn' dog has fleas. They're wore down, starved out, an' eatin' everything in sight. They're up in the free land on the mountains, hoggin' the summer grass that other outfits in the valley has been used to gettin'. Hardy Young says it's free grass, an' the beef that walks on it gets it."

Breck nodded, hard-faced at memories. "Been any gun play so far?" he asked.

Huck Haines was started now and voluble. "There's been a little bit of ev'thing. Jerk ropin' that's left cattle with busted necks. Rustlin', gun snipin', hide stealin', hard talk an' threats. So far it ain't a cattle war, you might say. But Ory Shotwell and a bunch of the small outfits is primed for trouble. They don't figure Andy Bradshaw has give 'em a square break." Haines shrugged. "That's what you're buckin'."

"Has Bradshaw played square?" asked Breck bluntly.

Huck Haines shrugged again. "Andy says the law can't keep Circle S cattle off free mountain grass. Claims he ain't been able to catch anybody cold at any dirty work. It's worked hard on Andy. He's always been a square shooter. There's cooler heads that ain't takin' sides so far. Some of them got their money out o' the bank on account of Hardy Young."

"How so?"

Haines spat at the base of a stall post. "Little over a month ago the bank was robbed. Cleaned out one night. It busted the bank as far as cash went. Left folks without money to run on. Hardy Young sent to El Paso for cash and took a bunch of the bank's land notes for it, so's the bank could open again an' pay out."

"And now," guessed Breck shortly, "Hardy Young is squeezing on those notes."

"Not yet," Haines admitted. "But he's got a club over folks that own land he can use. It's powder waitin' for the right spark . . . an' the sheriff is right on top. I ain't takin' sides. Can't afford to . . . but if I was you, mister, and wanted to stay healthy, I'd peel off that badge an' move on."

Breck spat, too. "My health is good. What about this Ben Jordan who was burned out?"

"Jordan lived on Cat Creek, near the Circle S line. Not much of a place. Ben was kind of shiftless. But he was stubborn, too. Hardy Young wanted that Cat Creek water. Ben wouldn't sell. The other night Ben an' his wife got back from town here and caught men firin' his house. Ben was hot-headed enough to start shootin'. Hit one man, he thought. But Ben was drilled, too. His wife got him back here to town. He got clear-headed enough last night to talk to Andy Bradshaw. An' Andy goes out to the T Slash with a warrant, claimin' Ben said one of the men firin' his house was this Link Tucker."

"Wait a minute," said Breck, scowling. "That doesn't make sense. The Circle S wants Cat Creek water . . . but a T Slash man was at the burning. Why should one of Shotwell's men help in a burning that'd likely throw the Cat Creek water to the Circle S?"

"That's been asked around town," Huck Haines admitted cautiously. "Ben Jordan's dead. Andy Bradshaw's shot . . . an' Link Tucker's in your jail. Whittle your own stick on it."

"I'm already whittling," Breck said. "Meanwhile, I'm the law. You might tell folks who ain't got it straight."

V

Sun-washed fiery color was on the mountain crests to the west as Breck left the livery barn. The feel of tension, of gathering trouble, was in the air, sharp, stark as the purple shadows crawling across the dusty street. Horses were at the hitch racks, wagons and buggies waited along the street as if trouble held the owners in town beyond the time they had intended to stay. Men were out in the open, singly and in groups, as Breck walked the street, rifle carelessly over his arm. He could feel himself a stranger among them, marked for trouble.

The hotel was adobe, two stories high. The clerk was a wizened, gray-haired, shrewd man, with a pen stuck behind his ear and steel-framed glasses askew on his nose.

"You don't aim to bunk with Bradshaw, then?" he commented as Breck signed the dog-eared register.

"Bradshaw keeled over before he could ask me."

"Figgerin' on bein' here long with us?"

"Bradshaw can fire me when he says the word." Breck grinned.

"He won't fire you as long as you handle things to suit him."

"He didn't say. How about sending some grub over to the prisoner I locked in the jail?"

The wizened clerk looked disappointed as he nodded, reached for a key, and came out from behind the desk. Breck grinned again as he followed upstairs to the room. Men in the lobby had listened intently, but they had learned little from the clerk's pointed questions.

Alone in the room, Breck stripped to the waist and washed. Then he pulled off his boots, rolled a cigarette, and lay on the bed to think. He was hungry, but he had to try to figure this out. It had happened too fast, had piled in too confusingly. He was the law on Tampiano range while Andy Bradshaw was down. He'd taken the oath, sworn to uphold the law. While he wore the badge, no man would get a crooked deal from the law. Gunsight had drilled honesty into his sons by rule and rod.

From there the facts were tangled. Breck lay, cold and rigid, cigarette forgotten in his fingers as he thought of Hardy Young, of Clem Springer, and the hardcase gun hands who had wiped out the Colemans in an hour's ruthlessness. Like Hardy Young was riding roughshod over smaller ranchers here in the Tampiano. No need to question the fat liveryman's story. Gunsight's body, Sam's body, Steve's lonely grave cried the truth that the Circle S smashed anyone who blocked the plans of Hardy Young.

But Andy Bradshaw was friendly with Young. Out there in the street before the sullen crowd, Hardy Young had branded his approval of Bradshaw on the lawman's new deputy. Andy Bradshaw had gone after one of Shotwell's men. His granddaughter had been bitter about Shotwell and men who thought as Shotwell did.

"She said she was in trouble . . . an' I said I'd help," Breck mused ruefully. "And I never stopped to think she wasn't talking against Hardy Young. She must have thought he was all right, like the sheriff seems to." Breck sat up on the edge on the bed, shaking his head, scowling. "She couldn't. Even if the sheriff sold out to Hardy Young, she wouldn't think it was all right. You could look at her an' know it. No girl like that ever boosted for a cold-blooded killing outfit like the Circle S. I'd know if it was in her. It'd show on her face."

Breck rolled another cigarette. "Steve, I sure played the devil. If I help her, maybe I'll be against men who are fighting Hardy Young."

A knock rattled the door. It was Ory Shotwell, big in the gray suit, gun filling his holster again, and suspicion leaping in his glance as he looked past Breck into the room.

"Thought I heard you talkin' to someone, Coleman."

"Talkin' to myself," said Breck calmly. "Habit of mine. It'll get me in trouble sometime. Come in, Shotwell. I had an idea you'd show up."

Shotwell showed no surprise. He walked to the closet door, opened it, and turned back satisfied that they were alone. He was smiling.

"I thought Hardy Young would have to make a fight of it a while ago. Maybe we got off on the wrong foot, Coleman."

"Not when it comes to cuttin' a man down when his back is turned. That'll get the same foot from me every time."

Shotwell shrugged, hooked a chair over with his foot, and sat down.

"Tucker shouldn't have done it," he admitted. "He's got a mean streak. Soon as Bradshaw called Tucker's name, I knew there'd be trouble. Tucker's not the kind to be roped in on a fake charge. But I thought the sheriff would get his chance to fight back. You saw how quick it happened. I wasn't looking at Tucker when he pulled his gun."

"I was."

"Maybe it was a good thing. You're chasing the law around now. You've got Tucker in jail . . . and maybe you ain't so anxious to keep him there after finding that Hardy Young's behind it."

"I never laid eyes on Young before," said Breck slowly and with convincing truthfulness.

Shotwell leaned forward, studying him closely.

"Maybe you didn't," he agreed. "If you had, you'd have knowed who he was when he rode down the street this afternoon. But you sure as shootin' knew his name. When he said he was Hardy Young of the Circle S, you came as near throwing lead in him as I've ever seen."

Breck, on the bed, said nothing as the big rancher felt him out, watching his face. Ory Shotwell wasn't all bull chest and loud voice. He could be wryly humorous, as now, with a streak of convincing friendliness.

"That was good enough for me," Shotwell said, still leaning forward. "You came in over that Buzzard Rock trail from the west. That ten-gallon hat has got Mex-style silver work on it. Your horse has got a vented Corralled Cross brand. That Corralled Cross brand belonged to Pablo Moya, when he was ridin' high as General Moya, with his own private revolution. The brand was Moya's little joke, after he corralled his first big money by making the churches in his district shell out their gold and silver work and hidden money. Moya claimed he'd corralled all the religion in his district by setting the peóns free to follow him. So he just allowed he'd take the *padre*'s *dinero,* which they wouldn't be needing now. Moya took their cross, too, and put his corral around it for his hide brand. Then he went out an' burned Corralled Cross on everything that had four feet. Claimed the good work had to be supported . . . an' there'd be special blessings for everyone who contributed. An' if they were stubborn about it, Moya claimed they were too sinful to live. Sometimes he gave them a cigarette and an adobe wall, with a guard of honor to fan 'em off in style. Most often one of his *bravos* did it with a shot behind the ear. Moya claimed more'n one bullet was a waste of good lead on sinners."

"You've heard a lot about Pablo Moya," said Breck, pokerfaced.

Ory Shotwell chuckled. "I usta get around some before I settled down on the T Slash. You've been along the border an' south of it, Coleman. Somewhere down there you've tangled hard with the Circle S. Maybe it wasn't Hardy

Young himself, the way you didn't know him. But you've got his number an' a hunk of lead cut to fit him. That's good enough for me. You're on the prod for him. So are we. If you don't know what it's all about, I'll tell you."

"I've heard."

"Heard about this?"

Shotwell drew a folded dodger from his coat pocket and handed it over. "Hardy Young had 'em printed this afternoon an' passed out before he left town a few minutes ago."

WARNING

$1,000 reward for every cow thief, hide thief, cattle killer, and troublemaker caught in a move against Circle S property. $5,000 reward, dead or alive, for the men who robbed the Tampiano Bank. WARNING—Circle S fences and grazing areas are a deadline given in advance to all persons who walk, ride on, or drive cattle on Circle S range. Exceptions apply to Hardy Young for written permission.

Breck looked up bleakly. "This sounds like trouble."

Shotwell stabbed a big finger for emphasis. "It's the way Hardy Young does things. It's worse'n trouble. It closes off Cedro Cañon an' the way out to the railroad by the Cedro Cañon short cut past good grass an' water to the shipping pens at Honeywell siding. The only other way is by the stage road, down through the salt flats to Morgantown, or out by the North Pass and through the Cold Rock country, which is ten days' extra of grief and hard luck for any cattle drive. And to Morgantown, by the salt flats, is mostly through greasewood country, with two dry camps that frizzle tallow off a beef like fire under an iron skillet. Prime stuff gets to Morgantown sorried out and in no shape to be loaded for the trip East. It'll make cow raising on the Tampiano a cold-deck gamble, with Hardy Young dealin' a dead man's hand to any small outfit he wants to break. Figure it out yourself."

"That doesn't need much figuring out," admitted Breck cautiously.

"It's plain as day. Been plain for weeks, ever since the bank was robbed and Young took over his pick of the notes for cash. Look at that bank reward he's got a nerve offering."

Ory Shotwell was flushed and angry as he leaned forward once more and slammed a big fist on his knee for emphasis. "Three men got into the bank. Andy Bradshaw made a half-hearted play, next morning, of riding after them with a posse. The trail split up in the high country east of the Circle S, and the sign faded out. But it didn't take half a guess to know Hardy Young was behind the job, and Andy Bradshaw would cover for him. It gave Young a chance to buy those notes. Now he's got a legal club to use where it'll do him the most good."

"I keep wondering," said Breck slowly, "why Andy Bradshaw should be partial to Hardy Young. Bradshaw is not the breed. You can tell it in five minutes."

Ory Shotwell stared. His astonishment was plain. "Holy smokes, stranger! Ain't you heard they're kin?"

"Kin?" said Breck, gaping himself.

"Hardy Young married Andy Bradshaw's daughter when they all lived up around Denver. She's been dead for years, but Young's girl, Jean, is over there nursing Andy Bradshaw right now. You wouldn't expect Bradshaw to be anything but partial to his own blood kin. Would you? That's what we're fightin' against. That's why we want a new sheriff."

VI

Breck was grinning coldly when he stood up, walked to the window, and stared out into the gathering darkness. Grinning—and inside he felt like a fool. Ory Shotwell was watching him.

"I didn't know it," said Breck.

"That's the way it is," said Shotwell. "And now Hardy Young's called the tune with that warning notice . . . and we don't aim to dance to it. All we're asking is that you don't throw the law to Hardy Young like it's been going."

Breck turned back from the window, deceptively mild again. "Shotwell, everybody will get an even break while I have the say."

"That's good enough for us." Ory Shotwell was satisfied as he stood up. "If you have to use a posse for anything, we'll see that you get one that'll think the same way." A grin spread over the cowman's hard face. "This'll surprise Hardy Young . . . but as long as old Bradshaw is out of the way, there ain't anything he can do about it. Good thing you turned up, after all. From now on you'll have plenty of friends in the Tampiano."

Shotwell was telling the truth about that. Two hours later, after he had eaten down the street, Breck had met a score of men. Most of them were likable—hard-working small ranchers, for the most part, who had heard about the gathering trouble and come to town, and stayed on into the night after the excitement of Andy Bradshaw's shooting and the new deputy who had replaced Cully Carnes. They were angrily grim about the Circle S. Shotwell had passed the word about the new deputy, and they were satisfied and wanted to show it. Breck Coleman met them politely, shook their hands, accepted a drink or two, bought a round himself. No one noticed the tight reserve behind his politeness.

Something was wrong—and Breck couldn't strike the sign. Bitterness had whipped these men to dangerous fighting pitch. But they weren't gunmen, cattle killers, hide thieves. They wouldn't shoot a man in the back; they regretted the bowlegged little gunman's shot that had dropped the sheriff while he was turning. Tucker should have waited until Andy Bradshaw had his chance. But their bitterness convinced them Andy Bradshaw had been covering up for the Circle S's burning of the Jordan place. Had it coming to him, they said, for the way he sided in with his son-in-law. He had been primed for a killing if Tucker resisted arrest, like Shotwell had told them.

Breck turned in at the hotel, trying to sort it out in his mind. But soggy weariness cut his thoughts short with quick sleep.

Hammering on the door woke him. Sun was streaming in the window. The voice of the hotel clerk was outside the door.

"Got a message for you!" When Breck opened the door, the wizened clerk was slyly important behind his spectacles. "Jump Beasely just come by an' said Bradshaw's granddaughter wants you over to the house quick as you can come. Says not to lose no time."

"Bradshaw worse?"

"Nope. I asked. Beasely looked like he knew, but he wouldn't tell me." The clerk's smile was knowing. "Guess they got something up their sleeves." He looked disappointed again as Breck's pokerface told him nothing before the door closed.

Andy Bradshaw's small frame house was two blocks away, on the east edge of town. The picket fence was neatly whitewashed. Flowers bloomed in spaded beds, and Jean Young was pale and worried when she opened the door and stepped out into the early sunlight.

She had one of her father's dodgers in her hand. "Have you seen this?"

"Saw one last night. It's asking for trouble."

Jean nodded. "Dad shouldn't have done it. He won't back off from trouble. And now . . . there's going to be trouble. A man just rode in and said cattle are already being driven toward Cedro Cañon. They want trouble. You've got to stop them before there's shooting."

"Maybe your father'll think twice when he sees they mean business," Breck said unsmilingly.

Gold from the sunlight lay on the curve of the girl's cheek. She had looked too young and friendly last night to be this pale, tense girl of the morning. She had caught the thread of detached hardness in his voice and instinctively resented it.

"It isn't up to him. He's given them fair warning. They could talk to him." She slapped the dodger. "He said in here there would be exceptions if they came to him."

"And did what he wanted."

She was awkwardly drawing away. An angry edge entered her voice. "You talk as if you think Shotwell and his friends are in the right. Can't you see they want to start shooting. With Andy out of the way, they can take the law into their hands. Dad will fight them. The whole valley will be at war. Andy's tried to prevent it. And now he's helpless. He can't do any more, and it's happening just like he was afraid it would. You've got to stop it."

"I don't want to stop it," Breck said, and the hardness

185

came fully into his voice. "It's none of my business. I didn't ride into this valley to get mixed up in this kind of business. I was hoping I could see Bradshaw this morning and give him back his badge."

"You said last night you'd help us."

"I didn't know what I was saying."

Jean had red hair, and temper to go with it. Angry scorn was stormy in her eyes, and she made it clear that she despised him. "Dad talked to me a few minutes before he left yesterday. He said there was something queer about the way you acted when you heard his name. He thought you were going to draw a gun. He wondered if Andy had been right in swearing you in as deputy."

She was Hardy Young's girl—but Breck couldn't hate her. He'd tried when he had heard who she was. She couldn't know about Gunsight or Sam or Steve. About those lonely graves and the dead cattle scattered over the drought-seared plain. But—she was Hardy Young's daughter.

"Looks like your father was right," he said evenly.

Jean's bitterness was almost a cry. "So Andy guessed wrong again! And now he won't even know about it until he wakes up late today. The doctor gave me medicine to make him sleep. When he does wake up, it will be too late. Give me the badge and . . . and get out. I . . . I'll do something about it."

"This isn't business for you to mix in, ma'am," Breck said softly. "Bradshaw gave me the badge. I'll turn it back to him myself. Meanwhile, I'm the law . . . even if it doesn't suit the Circle S. Stay here where you belong."

Her bitterness seemed to follow him off the porch and down the street, as if Hardy Young's Circle S was always a deadline of trouble.

186

★ ★ ★ ★ ★

"Shotwell stay here last night?" Breck asked the hotel clerk.

"Nope."

"Know where he is?"

"Likely to be anywhere."

When Breck came down from his room in a few moments with his rifle, the clerk was bursting with curiosity.

"Ain't anything happened, has there?" he asked, leaning across the desk.

"Nope," Breck said shortly, and strode down the street to the livery stable.

The fat liveryman was puffing and blowing over a bucket of wash water.

"I told that other Hang Noose feller you'd most likely be pullin' out this morning an' stay healthy," he said shrewdly past the grimy towel.

"Other Hang Noose man?" Breck repeated suspiciously.

Huck Haines jerked a thumb upward. Hay rustled up there over their heads. A voice groaned: "*Por diablos . . .* never I sleep weeth soch rats. They poosh me an ron on my face all night. *Buenos días, Don* Breck. Ees nice morning for to ride, no?"

"Come in last night near bedtime, ridin' the same brand you was," said Haines. "Vented Corralled Cross into a Hang Noose. So we powwowed a little on the side afore he crawled up there an' turned in."

Haines watched with interest as Pancho, the scar-faced, came down the ladder with ape-like agility and grinned broadly as he slapped bits of hay off himself.

"You wouldn't be grinning like a monkey if there was any trouble," Breck guessed. "Tie on your saddle. I'll get it out of you after we start. Haines, what's the quickest way to get to Cedro Cañon?"

"You won't stay healthy ridin' that way."

"I'll take a chance. Line it out to me."

The Hang Noose horses carried them out of town with a rush, leaving the fat liveryman no wiser. When they were alone under the bright wash of the early sun, Breck eased his horse and demanded sharply: "Now tell it . . . and it better be good."

Pancho pushed back his sombrero, squinted at the sun, spat, and grinned complacently, answering in Spanish. "Am I a driver of cows when the *señor* rides alone with his guns? 'By the Holy Mother,' I tell my cousin Santiago, 'if one thing of a *centavo*'s value is lost, I, Pancho, will cut your liver and burn candles to the devil for keeping you. And now I follow *Don* Breck, as his father would have wished.' "

Breck swore softly at the squat, ugly Mexican, and his anger was a thing of the lips, as Pancho well knew. "You been following me all the way?"

Pancho grinned, shifted into his broken English. "I t'ink I am pretty good, no? Then I am not so good. *Mil diablos,* w'en I rope these Circle S cow, I t'ink ees troble quick if *Don* Breck so close to thees Circle S. But the troble ees with Pancho w'en the Circle S man find him weeth cow. I tell you, he ees kill me sure right there, for being one strange *Mejicano* looking at hees cow."

"What happened?" asked Breck sharply.

"So I keel him first," Pancho replied cheerfully. His long, ape-like arm made a flashing move—and a keen-bladed bone-handled knife was in his hand as if by magic. Pancho grinned, wiped the blade suggestively on his leg, and slipped the knife down out of sight behind his belt.

Breck groaned. "I know how you handle that knife. An'

I'm the law. When the body's brought in, I'll have to lock you up for the killing."

"I t'ink we wait plenty long," said Pancho comfortably. "I am not one fool to leave heem w'ere they find heem. Maybe all these one beeg lie I tell you."

"Maybe," said Breck dryly. "We'll see what's proved on you. Maybe I won't be deputy by then. Now lemme get this straight. You were back on the mountain, beyond where I camped, an' you roped a Circle S cow an' got caught by a Circle S man?"

"*Sí.*"

"How'd you know he was a Circle S man?"

"Ees Circle S cow," said Pancho. "Who else keel me for rope that cow to look?"

"That's what I'd like to know," said Breck. "How many other Circle S brands did you see?"

"*No mas.* Me, I am too busy for not be keeled myself."

"See any other men?"

Pancho shrugged. "Me, I am leave queeck. I tell you, to mak' no trail."

"The Circle S is ahead of us," said Breck shortly. "Southerly, across this end of the valley. And you found that cow plenty miles away, up north on the mountain line there. Back behind the T Slash range. If there was one, there were more up in there. And there were two T Slash men that I know of up in there about the same time. Savvy?"

Pancho shrugged. "W'ere these Circle S *segundo*? I t'ink he's two-legged cow we want, no?"

"We want a bunch of fools that are set on trouble they think *they* want," said Breck shortly. "And we're a couple of bigger fools to be ridin' after them. *¡Andale!* Maybe we're too late already!"

VII

Huck Haines, the liveryman, had said that a rider who lined from the Bear Claw Creek crossing of Creaky John Hanlon's HJ Ranch road, to the saddlebow in the mountains to the southeast, would cross Cat Creek and find himself cutting the cattle trail near Cedro Cañon. Not a road. Wagons couldn't get through the cut, back up in the cañon. Grub was packed through.

Once more the valley looked green, deceptively peaceful under the climbing sun. But as the miles dropped behind the running horses, Breck's observant eyes noticed too many cattle down here in the swelling foothills. They belonged up on the high slopes, on free summer range, so the valley grass could grow and cure in the first frosts. No need to wonder why the small outfits to the south in the valley weren't pasturing high.

Hardy Young's drought-starved cattle were up there on the free grass like a killing locust plague. Hardy Young's hardcase gun hands were up there, holding free range against the smaller outfits. And now Hardy Young had marked his deadlines, closed the Cedro Cañon trail, and was sitting tight with a creeping strangle hold on the south end of the valley. Edging north steadily as he swallowed the small outfits and took the high free grass for miles ahead of his holdings, closing his grip on the whole Tampiano until he was kingpin. It had been done before on other ranges, and Hardy Young was trying it here. Breck's face was hard as he thought of the Hang Noose brand that had been wiped out in an hour. Gunsight, Sam, Steve, who

190

had died because they had fought back.

Pancho pointed silently to buzzards flopping sluggishly off dead cow carcasses ahead. Here and there they had passed other dead cattle, jerk roped and left with broken necks, each one a hard loss for a small rancher who couldn't afford any loss, each one herding a man closer to the point where he'd be likely to sell or lease on Hardy Young's terms.

"I t'ink we have comp'ny," said Pancho as they topped a rise.

The rider was two, three miles away, galloping across an open flat where scattered cattle grazed, heading as they were heading. In the thin, clear air Breck made out the white hat hanging back on the rider's shoulders, hair loose in the wind. No need to wonder if the fast-running white horse was the one in the picture on Andy Bradshaw's desk. That was Jean Young, riding to the trouble as she had threatened.

"Hardy Young's daughter," Breck told Pancho briefly. "*¡Andale!* Ride her out!"

The cutbank stream channel they crossed would be Cat Creek, Breck guessed. The burned ranch house of Ben Jordan would be somewhere near. Then in the brushy foothills they struck the cattle trail, fresh with sign where cattle and shod horses had recently passed. Jean was out of sight again, but her way was the shortest. Breck sighted the cattle first, bunched up, moving briskly toward the deeper notch just ahead in the mountain saddle back. Not many cattle— and too many riders for an ordinary trail crew.

Then the white horse swept out of a draw between the rising foothills and stopped short in the trail. Jean looked to right and left, seemed to hesitate, and then quirted the white horse uptrail after the cattle.

"*¡Aie!*" said Pancho with admiration. "I t'ink she's ride like one *dulce* she-devil, no?"

"She's got no business out here in this," Breck said angrily. "And I'll tell her so plenty!"

Pancho was spurring to keep beside Breck, but his chuckle was audible. His wide grin met Breck's scowling inquiry, and his big hand indicated the livid scar over cheek, jaw, and part of his neck. "I tell one she-devil plenty, too." Pancho laughed ruefully. "Soch pretty she-devil, too, an' you see w'at happen to Pancho? I t'ink eef I don' crawl under table an' jump out window, she cut me to *niño* size an' t'row rest away. You look out for w'at happen to Pancho, *Don* Breck. Ees not so good fooling with pretty she-devil, sometimes I t'ink."

Breck had to laugh, too. "I'll watch for her knife, *hombre*."

"Ees not knife to watch," Pancho warned. "You look w'at happen to Pancho."

"I see it. You got over it."

"No!" denied Pancho wryly. "I am papa eight times now an' she's still carry knife to show she lof me. You look w'at happen to Pancho . . . an' don't talk so moch w'en one pretty she-devil come along."

"I thought you were talkin' sense," Breck said disgustedly, and gave his attention to the trail ahead where Jean was spurring and quirting her horse toward the small herd.

They saw her coming, and several of the riders turned back to meet her. Jean talked angrily for a few moments with them. Breck saw her gesturing vigorously—and the white horse reared as she quirted it again. The nearest man failed in his grab for the reins and Jean raced on ahead of the cattle.

One rider started to follow her, and then turned back.

Their attention was on the other two riders fast overhauling them. Ory Shotwell was the first man Breck recognized, then several other faces he had met last night. Jubilee Keene, owner of the Bar S Bar—raw-boned young Ken Waters, who had had his small outfit less than two years and was still touch and go whether he'd make it on his own—somber Kyak Jones, brooding and quiet under black brows and drooping, untrimmed mustache. Others that Breck did not know. Eleven of them, he made quick count as they galloped up—and every man heavily armed.

"Should have left word for you to come along!" Ory Shotwell called. "Having the law along is just what we need!" He was grimly jovial, but his look at Pancho was hard and questioning.

"What did Hardy Young's girl want?" Breck asked as he pulled the lathered horse to a stop.

"Wanted us to turn back. Said it was a fool stunt to try an' buck her father this way."

Young Ken Waters was scowling doubtfully. "She said to hold up while she tried to find her old man an' talk to him. Said if the shooting started, there wouldn't be any stopping it an' not to be fools about it."

"More of her old man's tricks," growled a stocky, stubble-faced stranger to Breck. He slapped one of two guns he wore, low and business-like. "Shotwell told her right. Damned right! If there was any shootin' from the Circle S, there sure wouldn't be any stoppin' it. There ain't gonna be any trail blocked through the cañon an' we'll have that laid out an' settled this mornin'."

"Best thing for you to do, Coleman," said Ory Shotwell bluntly, "is to turn us all into a posse. We'll open up this Cedro trail an' keep it open."

Jean had vanished around a turn in the trail. The cattle

were still moving forward and the riders moving with them as the talk passed around. These men welcomed the new deputy; they knew now where his sympathies were. Most of them had been up all night, and they looked raspily grim with weariness and stubborn purpose. Breck was grim, too, as he spoke to them.

"I'm packin' the law around . . . so we'll let the law take hold here. The girl was right. Hell will bust loose if there's any shooting this morning."

"It'll sure bust loose," Shotwell promised in an ugly tone.

"Maybe that's what Hardy Young wants," Breck pointed out. "He's got the law on his side when he says it'll take his permission to cross his land."

"Law, nothing!" said Kyak Jones sullenly. "Ain't you with us? Ory said you was. That's all the law we need."

"I'm not friendly with Hardy Young," said Breck evenly. "But I'm still the law. I'm not a fool, either. Most of you men own land an' cattle. You've got a stake here in the valley. If there's any law busting, let Hardy Young do it. I'll handle him then. Long as I'm deputy, an' can make a move, I'll hold that gun-hiring wolf to the law as quick as I will any of you. But if you give him the deal an' all the cards in the deck, he'll have you where he wants you. It's plain as the trail you're makin', that this'll be a mouthful hard to swallow if you try to push through Circle S land right under their noses. Hold the cattle here an' let me ride on and talk with Young."

"Ride on if you think it'll do any good," Shotwell said angrily. "But we'll keep movin'. The Circle S asked for a showdown with those printed warnings . . . and from now on they'll get it."

"Where's the Circle S headquarters?"

"A trail takes off to the right about a mile ahead, just before you head into Cedro Cañon. Four, five miles of it'll bring you to where Young holes up. He's got a place built out o' heavy logs, like a fort. Who's this fella riding with you?"

"Friend of mine," said Breck shortly, and put his horse into a run again past the small bunch of steers that were gun bait and nothing else.

The rocky slopes here were brush-covered, and the trail was climbing. Ahead of them the steeper mountain slopes rose sharply. When Breck and Pancho rounded the turn in the trail where Jean Young had vanished, they could see not far ahead the narrow gash of a cañon, steep-walled, almost invisible until one rode close.

Pancho's dark scarred face lighted with a brief grin. He called: "I t'ink now you better remember w'at happen to Pancho!"

Jean Young and five riders waited in the trail. Breck's face settled into stony lines, and his voice came out colorless, flat, dead, as he recognized one of the men.

"Let me do the talking," he said to Pancho.

For an instant his mind flashed back to Gunsight, saying the same words as he rode out from the long trail herd to meet this same Clem Springer.

VIII

Their horses were walking as they met the Circle S group. Down the trail, still out of sight, the bawl of a steer lifted faintly through the deceptive quiet. The lanky, flat-faced Clem Springer leaned forward in his saddle and stared with a startled, narrowing look.

"So it's you," he rasped, ugly from his surprise. "From that Mex outfit. Both of you. What are you doin' here on the Tampiano?"

"Not looking for you just now," said Breck evenly. He had steeled himself for a meeting like this. Surprisingly it was not hard. The pull of Steve's promise was not what brought this tight, icy steadiness, different from what he had thought it would be. He had not come here looking for Springer. He was the law on the Tampiano now, under oath, acting as sheriff. The law, backing his moves, had laid hold of him in an impersonal way.

Springer would have his turn to die, as Gunsight and the boys had died. But that could wait. The law, the trouble now, was bigger than Springer, bigger than Hardy Young's devouring cattle and need for land, water, grass. The Tampiano was the trouble—the whole sweep of the valley, seething and ready. Men like young Ken Waters, the brooding Kyak Jones, and fat Huck Haines back at the horse barn would have their part in the explosion, if it came. Each one trying for his own law. Gun law. They didn't know what it would mean to them. Gunsight and Sam could have told them. Steve, with his time to think before he died, could have told them. Ten years of gun law over the border had made Breck able to tell them. But they wouldn't listen, wouldn't believe. The widow of Ben Jordan, the shiftless little rancher, might believe, now that it was too late. Young Ken Waters had a wife, kids, who would know, too, if Waters was buried. Like Breck knew—and Andy Bradshaw and Jean Young had known. More than land and cattle would suffer if gun law swept the Tampiano. The small ranchers had families, hopes, and dreams to lose against Hardy Young's hardcase riders. Jean, too, had sensed it, for all of having Hardy Young for a father.

Breck had been watching the girl as he rode up and reined to a stop. The wind had left her hair like tossed flame. The challenge and defiance were still there on her face, when she should have been laughing and friendly as he had first known her—and something else was there, dark and fearful in Jean's eyes, like a tight sickness that was gathering behind her control. For all of her defiance, she was afraid, Breck saw, and not afraid for herself as she sided her father's men there in the trail. Breck touched the shiny little badge, and touched the law books, the courts and judges, with the same motion, and it didn't seem strange.

"I'm Bradshaw's deputy," he said evenly. "I heard there might be trouble out this way, and I rode over to look."

"Look!" Jean said, and it was wrung from her scathingly.

"Deputy?" Springer repeated. He was astonished and so were the men behind him. Then he split the flat face with a grin. "So you're the guy we heard about? I'll be hanged." Still grinning, Springer spat. "You young fool," he said contemptuously. "Ain't you learned any sense? Get out before we give you some of the same medicine again. That blasted Mex there with you, too. I mind that scar on him now."

Puzzled, Jean demanded: "What are you talking about?"

"Had a little trouble with these two, an' some more in their outfit, when we were comin' up from the border," Springer said carelessly. "I told your father about it. They started some gun play an' we scattered 'em."

"I didn't know. . . ." She said it to Breck, startled uncertainty in the fear behind her eyes.

Clem Springer, turning to his saddle, grinned to take the edge off his bluntness. "Time for you to be gettin' back out of the way, miss. They're comin' 'round the bend down there. This ain't a place for you now. We'll handle this."

"I told you there wasn't to be any trouble until Father

gets here. Let them start through, if it's the only thing you can do. If Curly rides hard and finds Dad, you won't have long to wait."

"Sure," said Clem Springer, humoring her. "Your father don't want trouble either . . . unless they start it."

"Then there's no need for me to leave."

Breck's smile was a twitch of the lips, no deeper, at Springer's discomfiture. But the man saw it and was furious, and met it in his own way.

"Buck, take her horse an' lead him out of sight."

Breck's fleeting smile twitched again. Jean saw it. Pink rushed in her cheeks. She lifted the braided leather quirt that hung by a thong from her right wrist, looking at Buck, a thin-faced, close-eyed young man, black hat pulled low.

"Don't try it!" she warned dangerously.

Buck hesitated. Clem Springer was scowling. The other men watched stolidly, showing no desire to interfere. Breck knew what they were thinking. If it was gun work, they were on the pay for that. But they had no wish to tangle with Hardy Young's girl. No wish to make a move that might bring Hardy Young's wrath on them.

Springer was no better. His black mood shifted to Breck and Pancho. "I told you two to fade out o' here. You been on Circle S land for half a mile. There's a deadline. The lady here read us your brand. You're ridin' point for that bunch of troublemakers an' you'll get the same shift they do."

"Even Hardy Young's not big enough to draw a deadline on the law," Breck said softly, sitting straight, loose-jointed, arm indolent at his side. "You're not scattering a starved-out trail herd now, Springer. I'm here to stop trouble before it starts. That goes for the other bunch, too. Or did you figure on making trouble?"

Springer's reaction to that was a violent jerk on the reins, so that his horse reared back, and spun around. "You boys heard the law speak!" Springer sneered. "I'll let him hear your orders again! No trouble unless that bunch starts it by tryin' to shoot a way through the cañon! Now sit tight an' see what happens!"

Breck considered that. His last words, the almost idle question, had struck Clem Springer into action, reversed his stand, and thrown the deal to Breck himself and the valley men. It wasn't like Clem Springer, when you had watched the cold, vicious smashing of the Hang Noose outfit. It was sign again, if a man could strike the trail. Faint sign—and, as Breck sat there considering, he had the dim conviction that the trail would be like the sign, back behind words and actions, hard to find, harder to read.

The cattle were coming now toward Cedro Cañon, and Ory Shotwell and most of his men were galloping ahead. Shotwell wasted no words as he pulled up; he spoke to Clem Springer almost violently.

"Laying for us, are you?"

"You're on Circle S land," Springer snapped. "Nothin' goes through here until Hardy Young says all right."

Shotwell's gesture indicated the men fanning out around him, rather than the cattle slogging steadily toward them. "This'll be all right with Hardy Young, I take it."

"Ask him. He's coming. Throw them cattle back an' ask him."

"We started an' we'll go through!" Shotwell said loudly. "Ain't that right, men? Clear the trail."

Breck drew his gun. The Circle S men were to his left, the valley men to his right. He was a little to one side, and a touch of his heel moved his horse so that he could see them

199

all. The gun rested almost casually on the saddle horn and his voice was casual.

"Hardy Young's coming. We'll wait an' see what he says. Turn back those steers, Shotwell, until he gets here. No use asking for trouble when you can get around it, is there?"

He saw young Ken Waters and several of the other men wavering. They were at fighting pitch, but they weren't gunmen, killers. They could see reason, and back off from trouble a little, if there was an excuse.

But Shotwell's violent reply had no basis in reason. "Who's asking for trouble? We're after our rights an' we might as well get 'em now as later. Damn Hardy Young. He won't be any better when he gets here than he is now."

Breck had one instant of noting the hard grin on Clem Springer's face, as if Springer were satisfied and enjoying it.

"Don't anyone pull a gun!" Breck warned sharply. "You, there . . . !"

He shot among the valley men, at the truculent, stocky stranger who wore two low-holstered guns. The man had drawn fast, furtively, reining his horse a little so the way would be clear ahead of him.

IX

The bullet knocked the drawn gun, spinning it down against the horse's neck, so that the animal shied hard. The stubble-faced stranger stared with almost stupid amazement at the bloody wreck of his hand as he fought the startled horse.

"Get 'em!" Clem Springer yelled, spurring his horse to

one side. His men did the same, as if by prearranged signal, opening fire as they moved.

Cursing, Breck holstered his gun, used spurs and reins to bring his horse spinning around toward Jean. He acted in a purely automatic way, lashed by fear that had been coiled back in his mind while the tense moments dragged out. One deputy, one gun, could do nothing against this shattering crash of many guns. Hell had finally broken loose on the Tampiano. The first thing to do was get the girl out of the way.

Jean had not believed it would happen. For all her temper and defiance, she had not believed it would happen. She was only a stunned, confused girl as the tense quiet erupted in blazing gunfire about her.

"This way!" Breck shouted, and it cut through her confusion. The lash of her quirt was automatic, too. Their horses bolted side-by-side up the rocky slope into the covering brush. Not until they crashed past a kneeling man levering a fresh cartridge into a rifle did Breck understand what his ears had been trying to read. Most of the gunfire was coming from the brush on both sides of the trail. Clem Springer had men posted in ambush. Many men. Springer and a handful had waited down in the trail so the trouble would break in the middle of the ambush. Springer had meant this to happen all along. He'd given the signal to fire, and had ridden out of the way before a shot had been sent toward his men.

"Keep going!" Breck called to Jean as they broke over the top of the slope, where bullets could not reach. As he turned back, he heard the gunfire slackening into ragged bursts and brush crashing as riders spurred through.

He saw two men racing across the downslope ahead of him, and others were bursting down the opposite slope into

the trail and riding after the valley men, who had come
grimly and heedlessly, and now were riding for their lives.
Those who could still ride. And their steers had stampeded
and were fanning out through the brush in a diminishing
drum thunder of hoofs.

A horse with a broken leg tried to hobble up the slope.
Breck rode close and shot it, before taking tally of this first
round of hell now loosed over the Tampiano. Four men
were sprawled on the trail. Two were moving. One of them
sat up, holding his side, face pale and hair tousled down
over his eyes.

"They was layin' for us," young Ken Waters said in a
thin, strained voice as he sat there holding his side, while
Breck bent over him.

"How bad is it?"

"Bad enough. Saw you tryin' to stop it . . . but they
wouldn't have it thataway, would they?" Waters's face
twisted. "When the folks hear about this, they'll get together an' do somethin'."

"Lie down. Let's see it."

"If it's bleedin' much, it's doing it inside," said Waters.
"Went clean through me. Don't know how bad I'm tore up.
Wish my Mary was here." He was grinning sheepishly as he
lay down, still holding his side. Maybe he would live, maybe
not. Waters knew now, Breck thought bitterly, and Waters's
knowledge was tortured behind the sheepish grin. Waters was
thinking of his wife and kids, not his anger at Hardy Young.

One of the dead men was the stubbled stranger who had
started the trouble. A bullet in the head had dropped him.

"Who is he?" Breck called to Ken Waters.

"Monty was the only name I ever heard. He's one of Ory
Shotwell's men."

"Breck! Breck Coleman!"

That cry from Jean sent Breck riding back up the slope. She was just over the top, kneeling beside Pancho. Blood on Pancho's chest was centered by a bullet hole, where bubbles lifted and broke as the Mexican struggled to breathe.

Pancho's smile was twisted as Breck knelt beside him, too. "Anyway, I keel him, *Don* Breck."

"Who?"

"That *hombre* you shoot. He pool hees other gun to shoot your back . . . and then see me an' shoot me before I keel him."

Breck put a lighted cigarette in Pancho's mouth.

Jean whispered: "Isn't there something . . . ?"

Breck looked at her and she knew. Pancho was smiling past the cigarette when Breck looked down, but a grayness was coming on the dark-brown face. Pancho's voice was a strained mutter when he spoke.

"I t'ink you tell her plenty, *Don* Breck. Ees good, too. Look . . . w'at happen to Pancho. . . ."

The scar made his grin crooked, wistful. A far stare came into his eyes. Then the lids came down slowly, as if Pancho were closing other sights, hard and tight, in his mind. He lay quietly—and bubbles stopped breaking in the bullet hole.

"He's dead," Jean gulped.

They stood up. She saw Breck's face and caught her breath.

"Our men didn't do it." When Breck said nothing, she asked uncertainly: "What happened to Pancho?"

"He thought too much of the Colemans," Breck said. "And once he talked too much . . . and was glad." Breck's weathered hand gestured to her horse. "Ride to your father's house and stay there."

203

"No," Jean refused. "I want to see him here."

Breck shrugged and turned to his horse. Jean, watching him rein back to the trail, understood the oblivion to which he had consigned her. This was not a woman's business. This was death and treachery and raw tragedy unheedingly loosed. Ken Waters was the only one still living.

"We'll get you a doctor soon as Hardy Young comes with help," Breck said.

"I'd 'most rather die than get help from Young."

"You've got to live for your wife," Breck told him. "Hang on to that."

Ken Waters nodded, with despair in his feverish eyes. Probably he'd die—but he'd hang on as long as he could for the wife and kids.

Breck searched the man called Monty and found a money belt next to his skin. Inside the sweat-dampened leather was new money: twenties, fifties, and a handful of gold pieces.

"Where'd he get all this, working for Shotwell?" Breck asked Ken Waters, and had the answer in his mind that Waters gave him.

"The bank lost money like that."

"Remember where I got it," Breck said with steely emphasis. "You're the only one who can back me up on it."

Waters nodded, visibly struggling to assimilate the fact that one of Shotwell's riders had been carrying part of the stolen bank money.

Then Hardy Young came, riding recklessly ahead of three men. Gunsight had often come recklessly like this to meet trouble, Breck thought.

"What happened here?" Young rasped as he came off the horse and looked about. "Where's Clem Springer and his men?"

"Running them back to town like you wanted," Breck said curtly. "He had his men planted out of sight up there in the brush. He didn't give me a chance to hold off trouble until you got here. This was murder, mister."

Hardy Young's denial was furious. "I told Springer not to start anything unless he caught rustlers or strangers damaging Circle S property. His men weren't supposed to be bunched up here. Jean, are you all right?"

She had come down the slope and joined them. She nodded and spoke to her father as though he were a stranger. "Andy saw this coming. He begged you to go slower. So did I. And then I saw Clem Springer start this."

So this had been between them before, Breck thought. Hardy Young brushed her words away angrily.

"You know it's touch and go whether I pull enough beef through to keep from going broke. And these people have been trying to break me. I've bought and leased all the land I could. Played fair with them. I even helped their bank open when it closed. And in return they've rustled and killed my beef, torn down my fences, burned haystacks and line cabins, and shot at my men. So I gave them a deadline, fair and square."

"Fair and square," said Jean and her voice shook. "I *saw* Springer trap them. Kill them when it wasn't necessary." She turned to Breck. "What kind of trouble did you have with Clem Springer?"

"We came up over the border with about fifteen hundred head," Breck explained. "All we had left from ten years down there. They were droughted out an' could just about make the water at Stinking Lakes. We'd have got there first. Maybe there would have been enough water for everybody. But Clem Springer rode over with a bunch of men and stampeded our drive. My brother Sam shot first when he saw what they were doing. They got Sam and my father and some of the men. My brother Steve died later, after we got about three hundred head across the Puerco. Springer told us Hardy Young didn't take excuses . . . so he busted us."

"No wonder you hate Hardy Young . . . and everything that's part of him!" Jean cried. She was swinging blindly on her horse when her father called:

"Jean, come here! Let me talk to you."

She rode hard away from them, toward the ranch house. Young stared after her like a man who was losing what he valued most.

"This man has got to have a doctor," Breck said. "Your place is nearest."

Hardy Young met the problem as though it was welcome. "Latigo, you're the biggest," he ordered. "Curly and Ed can pass him up to you, and side you to the house. I'll send another man for the doctor."

When the three men were started with their burden, Breck said: "Hell is loose now. Before dark every man in the valley who can carry a gun will be on the prod. Your hands can kill a bunch of them . . . but they'll get you in the end. They'll bust you, even if they're busted, too, in doing it. They'll be riding against you quick now, mister."

X

"I know," said Hardy Young. He looked at the dead men and swore. "I didn't want this. I wouldn't have had that trouble with your drive at the Stinking Lakes. Clem Springer said it was forced on him." He shook his head. He looked older, deeply troubled, and something had happened to the bold drive of the man. "Maybe I asked for some of this," he said, partly to himself. "I've had to take my rights as I thought I found them. I've had to fight to hold my spread on the border. Trouble all the time down there. That's why I hired Springer, who'd been using his guns for years down in Mexico. He could handle trouble. But . . . I don't understand this."

"So Springer was down across the border, too?"

"Yes," said Hardy Young, staring.

Breck turned to his horse and swung in the saddle. And then paused alertly, holding the reins: "Here comes some of your men. Are you backing the law . . . or are you too big for the law, mister?"

Young looked at the dead men. "If the law can help now, I'll back it all the way. Any kind of play."

Breck's hard look searched the older man's face. "You didn't start any of this jerk roping, rustling, an' general hell raising?"

"All I want, and ever wanted, are my rights . . . and I never had to go after them that way."

"Then back me up. I want Clem Springer."

"He'll kill you, Coleman, if you try to shoot him."

"Who said shooting? Just back me up."

But Hardy Young was thinking of the dead at Stinking Lakes, and didn't believe it. The first four of his men to return were in high spirits until they met his cold anger.

"Who planned this?" he demanded bluntly.

"Springer got word they was comin' through here an' said orders was to bust 'em wide open if they started anything," said one of the men uncertainly.

"Where's Springer?" asked Breck mildly.

Two of the men grinned as they eyed him. You could see

what they thought the law was worth in this. One of them spat, still grinning.

"Clem run some of them jack rabbits on a piece. He'll be comin' back with the other boys."

"Keep your men inside Circle S fence," Breck told Hardy Young. "These dead men'll have to be cared for, too. The man who came with me is up over the top there."

Behind him, as he walked his horse down the trail, he heard Hardy Young giving orders. He met more Circle S men returning, laughing, joking. They said Clem Springer would be coming and were grinning, too, as they watched him ride on. Then Hardy Young caught up with Breck and was gruffly brief.

"I'll look around."

"Keep out of this."

Young shrugged, and then gathered the reins carefully and sharpened his attention as another bunch of his men were audible, riding into sight down a winding, grassy draw. Clem Springer led them, hat back on his head, one arm gesturing as he lounged sideways in the saddle, talking. He straightened up and pulled his hat forward, his face going expressionless as he saw Breck and Hardy Young, waiting.

"Springer, you've played the devil with . . . ," Young started ominously.

"Keep out of this," Breck cut him off, riding ahead so that he crowded abreast of the Circle S ramrod. "You're under arrest, Springer. Head toward town with me."

Springer's blurting was startled: "Git back, blast you! I'll run you to town after the others!"

He grabbed for his gun—but Breck's horse was already lunging against his and continuing on. Breck's arm hooked hard around Springer's neck and yanked him backward out of the saddle. Then a quick swerve of Breck's horse and a hard heave sent the ramrod flying helplessly through the air.

Springer's gun came out and fired once, wildly, as he was launched into space. Then he landed hard on his back and rolled, with the breath knocked out of him. When he pushed himself up, Breck's rope dropped over his shoulders and arms, tightened, and yanked him down, dragging him helplessly.

Hardy Young's voice crackled through Springer's bawling fury: "Hands off, men!"

"That's one trick Springer didn't catch on to across the border," Breck told them dryly as his alert horse kept the rope taut and Clem Springer helpless on the ground. "I've got him now. You men move back behind your fences."

Young lingered. "Coleman, you'll need help."

"You won't be help," said Breck. "There'll be gun play if you or your men are sighted down the valley. I'm trying to stop it."

Clem Springer was cursing as the rope slacked enough for him to sit up.

"You . . . you ain't gonna leave me here with him! He'll gut-shoot me soon as you're out of sight! He's been layin' for this!"

"I wouldn't blame him," said Young harshly. "I'd like to do it myself, after hearing what you've done!" And he rode after his men.

Breck rolled a cigarette and lighted it while the last rider passed out of sight and quiet closed about them. Breck's voice, when he spoke, was almost gentle, talking to no one in particular. "You take Pablo Moya now, he had tricks to make a man talk. Sometimes he'd have him roped like this an' start the horse walking. Just walking. We found a man once who'd been walked near twenty miles. Wasn't any use in it, either. He'd have talked inside of five miles. The general just didn't like him. He was a big fellow, too. Bet he weighed over two hundred when he started draggin'. He scraped off fifty or sixty pounds, anyway, along that twenty miles. I'll bet you ran across Pablo Moya while you were down in that country, Springer. He had some Anglos with him that were as bad as he was. After Moya was killed, they lit out of Mexico. Folks remembered them down there. They would've been killed on sight. You couldn't have been one of them, could you, Springer? Or Ory Shotwell?"

Clem Springer had gone taut, and then looked fearfully over his shoulder. He was sweating. He tried convulsively to loosen the rope that pinned his arms. The horse jerked it tight and dragged him down again. He shouted wildly for Young and the riders.

"They're gone," said Breck mildly. "The law's got you now."

Springer strangled on his words as the rope jerked him slowly over the hard rough ground.

"It ain't the law! It's what happened near the Stinkin' Lakes!"

"Wrong guess, Springer. We wouldn't be talking now if that was it. It's the law . . . only we're short-cutting things a little. There ain't much time. Not near the time the law gave you to get in your dirty work."

"I don't know what you're talkin' about!"

"I didn't think you would, Springer. You're as tough as they come. Bet you won't be so tough after a while. Bet you'll be begging for a chance to stop and tell me what's been going on around here. About those rustled cattle up on the mountain behind the T Slash. And who helped Monty rob the bank, and just who was aiming to pick up the chips after all the fighting was over here in the valley. I've read most of the sign anyway . . . but I'd like to hear you say it. You'll get a chance to say it, too, which is more chance than we got out there beyond the lakes, or those poor devils who were prodded into walking into the trap you laid for them. This is the law . . . the way I'm running it on the Tampiano today, Springer. There'll be killing again if it's not stopped . . . an' the law's out to stop it. Think it over."

Breck walked his horse over to Springer's, caught the reins, and twisted around in the saddle so he could watch as the long, slow trip to Tampiano started.

Clem Springer was tough. But his wild ravings went dry and husky in his thickening throat. The grass helped him for a time. Then there was sandy gravel for a space—and a low rough arroyo bank, rocks in the dry arroyo, the bank on the other side, and the rough hard trail that began to fray out and tear away the last protecting cloth on which Springer was dragging.

When the slow endless walk turned off the trail through broken country that stretched for miles toward the Bear Claw Crossing, Clem Springer stood it for a few minutes longer, and then broke, raving in his fear of the miles yet to come. Breck exhaled a long breath and stepped down to ask his questions.

XI

The sunlight was white and hot, and shadows were slanting past noon when they rode into Tampiano. They had come a slower way, keeping to the back country, out of sight. Clem Springer had wanted it that way, too. For word would have traveled ahead of them of the Circle S trap at Cedro Cañon and the man who had sprung it. They rode in from the east, where there was no road or trail. Springer's hatless head was bent down to hide his face from the first eyes they passed—but there was no hiding the tattered strips of shirt that failed to cover his raw, blood-smeared back. No hiding Andy Bradshaw's new deputy.

Questions were called; the first men on foot joined several boys who tagged after Breck and his prisoner, and then a man on horseback rode out of the first cross street, stared hard, and called: "That's one of the Circle S men, ain't it?"

"He's under arrest," said Breck.

The man whirled his horse and raced ahead of them toward the main street.

Clem Springer had kept a length ahead all the way. Now Breck whipped an order: "Get to the jail fast! Maybe I can't hold 'em if they catch you on the street!"

They hit the main street at a gallop and swung left toward the jail. With one quick look up and down the street, Breck read the sign. The word had long been in from Cedro Cañon, and spread out over the valley as it came. That first hard squall of trouble was swiftly gathering into a storm.

The valley men were gathering here in town; the small owners and the men who rode for them. Hitch racks already were filling along the street. Knots of men were standing in the open. Word flashed among them that the new deputy had brought in a man. Riders and men on foot were heading toward the jail when Breck dismounted behind the prisoner. Clem Springer looked fearfully toward them.

"They'll hang me," he muttered.

"Maybe," said Breck. "Get inside."

A foam-flecked horse was already hitched before the jail, but Breck was inside, slamming the door, before he saw Jean, on her feet beside the old desk.

"Talk to you in a minute," said Breck, hustling his prisoner on back to the cells.

Link Tucker's eyes popped.

"Clem! What happened? How'd you land in here?"

Clem Springer cursed the little T Slash man.

"He landed like you did," said Breck. "Bet his cards against the law and found his aces were deuces. Talk it over, you two curly wolves."

The heavy cell-room door closed them off from the office. Jean's voice was tight.

"Father said you were bringing Springer here. He said you were trying to stop all this . . . alone. I had to help if I could. I know Andy's friends. He still has some friends. You'll need them."

Breck put his rifle across one of the worn chairs. His smile banished for a moment the hard grim lines that had settled on his face. A young face, matching Jean's drawn youthfulness, but older, too, since that dry blistering day the Coleman men had crossed the border.

"I'll need something," Breck said, nodding toward the street.

They could hear the first riders dismounting, calling to one another. Breck stepped to a gun rack on the wall, selected a sawed-off shotgun, nodded with satisfaction when he found it loaded.

"When I open the door, walk out ahead of me and ride to your grandfather's house."

Jean shook her head. "I'm going to stay here. There might be something I can do."

Breck opened the door and stepped out. Men were already on the steps, the walk, and more were coming. Men heavily armed, grim and purposeful. The nearest one fired the general question while Breck was still coming out.

213

"Who's that you brought in?"

"The Circle S man who started the shooting this morning."

The man who turned on the steps and shouted to the gathering crowd was Cam Wilson, who had helped drive the cattle to Cedro Cañon.

"I knowed it looked like him! Bring a rope here! Let's fix this 'n' before we go get Hardy Young!"

"Wait a minute!" Breck called, and, when they quieted, staring at him, he said: "The law's got him. That's good enough right now."

"Good enough, nothing!" Wilson cried. "It ain't good enough for me, after what he did! Trot him out here an' we'll start on him first!"

The casual shifting of the sawed-off shotgun might not have had any meaning, for Breck was grinning thinly at them. "Wrong guess, Wilson. You'll be starting on the law. It tried to hold things down this morning . . . an' now it's got the man who started the guns popping. No use bucking the law right now, is there? I thought you men were kicking because the law didn't suit you. Now you're wanting to tangle with a load of buckshot because the law's on your side. Where's the sense in that? Hell of a note if I have to swear in a posse that's crippled up with buckshot."

It might have been the ready shotgun, or the ugly moment of tension. A man called: "You aimin' to help us?"

"The law'll settle everything," said Breck, still smiling.

They read it their own way. The threat was past. A loud voice called: "The young feller's all right, like Ory Shotwell said! That skunk in there'll keep!"

"Where's Shotwell?" Breck asked quickly.

"He's out spreadin' the word while his men get here from the ranch."

"I'll see him when he comes back to town."

And they read that their own way, too, and began to disperse, moving back toward the saloons. Breck stepped back inside and shut the door again.

Jean looked pale and tired. "So you're going to settle it by leading them against Father and his men."

"I didn't say that."

"Then you can't stop them."

"Maybe not."

"Father tried to explain things to me. He said you believed him. . . ." Behind that was her hunger for her own beliefs that had faltered at Cedro Cañon.

Breck nodded. "Hard-headed . . . maybe a fool about the way he's handled some of this . . . but not a killer." He shrugged as he turned back from the gun rack. "Although a hard-headed fool can be almost as bad as a killer sometimes. Your dad could have headed a lot of this off if he'd worked more with the law."

"I know," agreed Jean. "He knows it now . . . when it's too late." But she had reached across a gulf to Hardy Young again. She had back belief in her father that helped her fear of what was to come.

Now she had no scorn for Breck. He had known it since the brush at Cedro Cañon. The shabby little jail office shut them in together, and Breck was calm, almost content, as he closely examined revolver and rifle. One of the cluttered desk drawers held boxes of cartridges. He filled the loops of his belt and dropped an extra handful in his pocket.

"I don't understand you," Jean said, watching him. "This morning. . . ."

Breck looked up and smiled. "That was this morning."

"But you can see how they are. And you're alone. What can you do?"

215

"Maybe I'm not alone. I'm the law." Breck grinned at her. "That's something."

Jean brushed the words away with a quick, helpless gesture. "You said none of this means anything to you. And you'll be hurt, or killed, if you get in their way. What do they care about the law now?"

"That's the trouble," said Breck, smiling. "It's time they cared a little about the law." Watching her, he stopped smiling. "I promised my brother Steve, before he died, that I'd keep out of trouble until I found something worth fighting for. Steve was pretty smart. I reckon he'd think this was worth it."

"The law here in the valley?"

"That's one way of looking at it," said Breck. "Folks can't settle down until all this is straightened out. I've been thinking I'd like to settle around here." He chuckled. "Like to have me for a neighbor?"

"Why . . . yes," Jean said, and color crept into her face as she met his smiling look and read there the things he meant her to.

"I'll have money enough to buy a place," Breck said. "My mother called this God's country, an' always wanted to come back across the border. Her name was Jean. She'd like this, too."

Jean's eyes were bright—but dread once more was gripping her. "You can't settle anywhere, if you're killed, Breck Coleman. And you're alone. They won't listen to you unless you help them smash the Circle S."

"Hanged if I do . . . an' hanged if I don't." Breck chuckled. "You said Andy Bradshaw had friends. Tell me their names."

Jean turned to the desk and wrote a list of names. The act made her feel better, as Breck thought it would. But when he shoved the paper in his pocket, she confessed: "I'm still afraid. All this can't be stopped by talk."

"Maybe a thing's worth more if you have to fight a little for it," said Breck, smiling again. He picked up his rifle. "I'll go out an' look around. You'd better go to your grandfather."

"Andy's in good hands. I . . . I'll stay here."

"Then bar the door and don't let anyone in but me. Promise?"

"Yes."

Breck was smiling as he watched the jail door close behind him and heard the heavy wooden bar come down in the iron sockets. But when he went down the steps and turned toward the saloons, his eyes were bleak and cold, and he touched the holstered belt gun once or twice to make sure the hang was right for quick action.

XII

The word was spreading. More men were riding into town. Already the saloons were busy. Bitter tempers were not being helped by the whiskey and talk. Word had spread that the sheriff's office was with them. Now, as Breck walked among them, he was no longer a stranger, marked for trouble. Men greeted him, slapped him on the back, offered drinks. Breck grinned back at them, and moved on, watching the faces, stopping for a few words here and there, now and then lingering to talk briefly with some man.

A red-bearded, swaggering rancher, loaded with whiskey already, caught Breck by the arm as he came out of the

Gold Dust Bar. "When you gonna make us a posse, bub? We're r'arin' to go!"

"Plenty of time." Breck grinned, and moved on, leaving the man boasting loudly to bystanders about what he'd do when the fighting started.

Plans had been decided on and suited everybody. When enough men had gathered, they'd head for the Circle S and take the place to pieces. They'd burn the Circle S out, string up Hardy Young if they caught him. They'd come shooting and keep shooting until there wasn't any doubt about who was running the valley. Nobody was talking back to them that Hardy Young's hardcase riders might have something to say about it, that Hardy Young's outfit had battled trouble for years along the border—and wiping them out meant more than drinking whiskey here in town and riding out to find them. They didn't want to hear that now. They were friendly with the law because they thought the law was with them—and, when they found differently, they'd turn against all of the law that they could see. One man, a stranger to most of them, they'd brush him aside, with guns if they had to, and have their range war.

Breck walked slowly down one side of the street and up the other. Now and then he glanced at the list in his pocket, asked questions, or lingered longer to talk with some man he'd never seen before.

He stopped in the bank and talked with the banker, a short, heavy-set, nervous man named Dunbar. He was on the street when Doc Taylor's dusty two-horse buggy returned from the south end of the valley. Breck waved the little doctor down and climbed in the buggy with him.

"Ken Waters dead, Doc?"

"Not yet. He's got a chance to pull through. He'll have to stay at Young's place for a time, though. Can't move him."

"He tell you about that money belt I found?"

"Yes." The wiry little doctor drove on toward the livery stable. He was somber behind his short, iron-gray mustache. "There'll be work for me tonight. I told Hardy Young things were out of hand, and I see they are. He said you were doing what you could, young man. Not much luck, eh?"

"Depends on what you call luck, Doc. Maybe you can help me."

They were at the livery stable before the talk was finished. Huck Haines, the fat liveryman, had a mixture of emotions on his smooth pink face when he saw Breck step out of the buggy. "You lasted longer'n I thought, young feller. I hear you aim to lead 'em against Hardy Young."

"There's all kinds of talk," Breck said. "Mostly I'm whittling on my stick an' keeping close to the law. You might tell folks that, in case you've forgot."

Then, a little later, Ory Shotwell and his riders roared into town. All the men Breck had seen on the T Slash, and more. They tied horses before the Elkhorn Saloon, which had the biggest bar in town. From down the street Breck could hear Shotwell's bull bellow calling everyone in to free drinks. The rush filled the Elkhorn before Breck got there.

But men near the door saw him enter and a cry was passed along. "Here's the law! Let him get through to talk with Ory!"

The hard riding that Shotwell had done through the day had left him fresh and swaggering as he waited with a whiskey glass in his hand and his back to the bar for Breck to get through the crowd. And he was jovial, too.

"They tell me you're bringin' the law along with us, Coleman."

"I'm bringing the law."

Shotwell swept a bottle and a glass to the outer edge for

Breck. His loud voice went through the big room. "That's what we need. Coleman was there. He saw it. He knows what it takes to clean up this valley. And if I'd been him, I'd've killed that snake Springer that started the shootin' today. What good's he doing in jail?" Shotwell turned to Breck. "How'd you happen to get him?"

"Caught him riding back and brought him along."

"What'd he have to say?"

"He didn't like it."

Shotwell's cold stare relaxed. He grinned. "Don't blame him. Sooner he's took care of, the better. Me 'n' my men'll take him off your hands when we get back from the Circle S. Drink up, men. It's about time to ride."

Breck turned and lifted his voice, too. "It's time to get right with the law. I'll be waiting outside in the street. Everybody who's aiming to ride come out there where I am."

Somebody laughed. "Here's where we turn into a posse, boys! Andy Bradshaw'll have a foamin' fit when he hears about it!"

Breck was smiling, too, only faintly, as he pushed back through the crowd and went outside, and walked across the street to Doc Taylor's office. Taylor and the banker, Dunbar, were in the medico's little front office. Breck put his rifle in the corner, grinned at them, and said: "It's about time to do your talking. I'm having a little meeting out in the street. You ready?"

Dunbar was nervous. "I'll do as you asked me, Coleman. But I don't like the way you're going about it. No, I don't like it."

Breck chuckled. "I don't like it, either. Maybe a drink'll help him, Doc."

"I doubt it," said Doc Taylor dryly. "Come on, Dunbar, and speak your piece."

Men were already streaming out of the Elkhorn when they reached the middle of the street. The noisy crowd began to gather around them. "The doc an' Dunbar are ridin' with us, too!"

Dunbar licked his lips as that went through the crowd, but Doc Taylor's short mustache bristled at them. "Have your fun now," snapped the little doctor. "You won't be laughing when I get to work on you."

That sobered some of the men, brought their faces bitter and grim again. Ory Shotwell and his men came through to the center. Voices went silent as Shotwell said: "Here we are, Coleman. Let's get on with it. We got a long ways to ride an' plenty to do."

"This won't take long," said Breck. His face was expressionless now as his eyes ran around the crowd and noted certain quiet, unobtrusive movements behind Ory Shotwell and his men.

Then Breck's voice lifted, so that men back in the crowd could hear. "Listen to the man who runs the bank. I'm showing Dunbar a money belt full of money. He's already had a good look at it. Dunbar, what about this money?"

They could hear Dunbar's nervous voice well enough. "It's some of the money that was stolen from the bank."

"Sure of it?"

"Positive."

Dunbar had spoken his piece; he started pushing away through the crowd as exclamations and talk burst out. Ory Shotwell's rough voice lifted.

"Hang it, we ain't interested in that now! That's the bank's business! We got the Circle S to get!"

But most of these men had had money in the bank. They wanted to hear more. They were ready to listen when

Breck's hard voice ignored Shotwell. "Listen to Doc Taylor tell where I got the money!"

Doc Taylor knew them all, in their sickness and troubles. He wasted no words. "I went out to fix up Ken Waters, who was shot at Cedro Cañon this morning. Waters told me about the belt. He saw Coleman here take it off the man who pulled a gun first, against Coleman's orders. Monty was his name. He rode for Ory Shotwell." And Doc Taylor added more than he was supposed to say. Mustache bristling, he glared at Shotwell: "Maybe you can tell us about that bank robbery, Shotwell."

Taylor shouldn't have done it. Breck wasn't quite ready for the instant of stunned electric silence that was broken by Shotwell's bull bellow of anger. "You dirty little liar. I'll make you eat that an' cough it right up."

But something like this would have come anyway. Breck was bleak and easy as he stepped in front of the little doctor. "Hold back, Shotwell. You're under arrest, and you can do your talking in court."

He had known Shotwell and the T Slash men would go for their guns—as they did now when Shotwell's bawl of anger reached them. Every man there in the crowd recognized the fateful instant before guns roared, and did what Breck had counted on them doing. They were too stunned, confused, uncertain from what they had heard from Dunbar and Doc Taylor to take sides and want to start shooting about anything right now. There was a mad shoving and pushing and rush to get out of the way.

Shotwell's furious yell cut through the commotion. "Let's get this tinhorn deputy, boys!"

Shotwell's hand streaked for his gun as he said it—and he was fast and dangerous and furious to kill. He would have killed Breck but for those years south of the border,

222

when the Coleman men lived on trouble. Breck's gun was a streak out of the holster, too, as he met the showdown he'd known was coming. He met Shotwell on the same terms, to the death, so that other men might not die if the thin thread of the law was broken now by hesitation or weakness.

The hammer blast of the two guns blotted out all other sounds. Shotwell fired again, into the ground, as Breck's second shot hit him and drove him on down to the hot street dust. Another shot from a T Slash rider knocked Breck half around as it smashed into his left shoulder. His flame-spurting gun found that man over to the side and knocked him staggering. And still another bullet hit Breck's leg, so that it buckled under him. The lurch he gave was all that saved him from the following shot—and the man was thumbing for the third shot when Breck swiveled around on the good leg and shot the man squarely in the middle, so that he rocked, his arms going out with the shock, and then began to fall.

Eyes cold, face a mask, and half of him numb and useless, Breck looked for the next man. But three men were down, and the crowd had scattered away from them, to the sides of the street, and the other T Slash riders were standing in frozen positions with their hands up. Behind each T Slash gun hand was a grim man well along in years, who had taken a position behind one of Shotwell's men and put a gun in his back when the trouble started. Only there hadn't been enough of Andy Bradshaw's old friends to go around.

Three men down and the rest helpless for the moment.

"Hold 'em like that!" Breck called and, limping to Ory Shotwell, he pulled open his shirt and found the thick, heavy money belt Clem Springer had said would be there.

Breck straightened up, opening the belt, and satisfying

himself of the contents. Then he waved it at the scattered, confused crowd and called to them:

"Here's some of your bank money that Shotwell was carrying! He couldn't put it back in the bank an' it was safer on him than trying to hide it. Take a look. An' start thinking what a bunch of fools Shotwell played you for!"

They surged back toward the center of the street, and Breck limped up and down in the dust, showing them the flat, filled money belt and rasping the truth at them so they couldn't misunderstand him. "I knew there was something wrong when I rode into the T Slash yesterday, an' Shotwell tried to hire me for gun work an' then tried to dry-gulch your sheriff. But the sign was all mixed. I didn't get it straightened out until this morning. Shotwell and Hardy Young's foreman, who started the shooting at Cedro Cañon this morning, were old partners down in Mexico. When the Circle S had to move up here for grass, Springer and Shotwell got their heads together and figured how to take over the valley for themselves. They'd bust the bank first, and have that much more money to work with. They'd start rustling and cattle killing, and get you men fighting the Circle S. They'd get a first-class range war started . . . and, when everybody was losing at it, they'd start picking up the chips. There's rustled Circle S cattle up behind the T Slash now. Ben Jordan was right when he saw one of Shotwell's men at the burning of his house. Shotwell and Springer did that, to lay more dirt on Hardy Young. And Young didn't help it by being stiff-necked and willing to fight for grass he had to have. Andy Bradshaw tried to hold it off, and got talked about because he was kin to Hardy Young. And when Young played the fool and drew that deadline yesterday, Shotwell and Springer had their bets down just like they wanted them. All they needed was a few killings and the war was on. Hardy Young didn't know Springer had men posted at the cañon. He didn't want a trap laid like that.

"When I went out there with the law and tried to prevent trouble, one of Shotwell's men pulled his gun anyway. And when I shot it out of his hand, Clem Springer saw it was up to him if there was going to be any killings like he and Shotwell had to have, and he gave the order and ducked out of the way. I've got Springer in the jail now. He's told everything. But I couldn't try to lock up Shotwell, the way he had everybody aroused. Ain't a one of you wouldn't have thought that I had sold out to Hardy Young. I had to get him out here in the open where you all could see it. Now you've seen it. Now you've got a taste of what fools he's made out o' you. The law's got Shotwell now and the gun hands that were doing his dirty work. The law's going to settle things in this valley so a cow can walk from one end to the other an' a man won't look twice at it. The law's going to make your fences and your cattle an' bank safe. Hardy Young is already set back on his heels and anxious to have peace and stay inside his own fences. Are you going to stand behind the law, or will the law have to get on you to keep you from getting yourselves shot up more over something that's already settled? I'm asking you now. I'm giving you law an' order like you want, and Andy Bradshaw will carry it on soon as he's up and around. Who wants to start fighting with the law now? I'll lock him up with these gunnies of Shotwell's."

Limping, gun in hand, Breck hobbled between the packed rows of armed men, glaring at them because of the pain and the weakness that were cutting him down before it was all settled.

One bearded old rancher in the front row broke the

tension with a sheepish chuckle. "Looks like you've done all our fightin' for us, young feller. It sounds good to me an' I'm with you."

"Then let's get these men locked up," Breck said, and was grinning with relief as he took another hobbling step and fell down in the dust.

He heard Doc Taylor's voice, far away, saying: "Get him into my office!"

Then things went blank for a time, and, when Breck's eyes opened again, Doc Taylor had him on a table, shoulder already bandaged, and leg almost bound up. Later, men carried him, protesting, to Andy Bradshaw's house, where Jean was waiting.

They pulled off his boots, put him in bed between white clean sheets, and tramped out, grinning at his irritation. And Jean took charge, flushed and bright-eyed, and dead set on having her own way no matter what was said.

"Stay quiet, Breck Coleman. I just had to settle Grandfather in the other room, after he heard what had happened. He wanted to get up. Now I won't have any nonsense out of you."

"I'm going to collect that five thousand reward from your father. Do him good to pay it."

"I think so, too," said Jean promptly, and walked out of the room with Breck's clothes and no arguments left.

Breck stretched out between the clean cool sheets, and then grinned and decided to make the best of it, as he'd known he'd have to, ever since they brought him in the house.

"Jean?" he called.

"Yes."

"Come here," Breck said meekly. "I want to tell you what happened to Pancho."

About the Author

T. T. Flynn was born Thomas Theodore Flynn, Jr., in Indianapolis, Indiana. He was the author of over 100 Western stories for such leading pulp magazines as Street & Smith's *Western Story Magazine*, Popular Publications' *Dime Western*, and Dell's *Zane Grey's Western Magazine*. He lived much of his life in New Mexico and spent much of his time on the road, exploring the vast terrain of the American West. His descriptions of the land are always detailed, but he used them not only for local color but also to reflect the heightening of emotional distress among the characters within a story. Following the Second World War, Flynn turned his attention to the book-length Western novel and in this form also produced work that has proven imperishable. Five of these novels first appeared as original paperbacks, most notably *The Man from Laramie* (1954) which was also featured as a serial in *The Saturday Evening Post* and subsequently made into a memorable motion picture directed by Anthony Mann and starring James Stewart, and *Two Faces West* (1954) which deals with the problems of identity and reality and served as the basis for a television series. He was highly innovative and inventive and in later novels, such as *Night of the Comanche Moon* (Five Star Westerns, 1995), concentrated on deeper psychological issues as the source for conflict, rather than more elemental motives like greed. Flynn is at his best in stories that combine mystery—not surprisingly, he also wrote detective fiction—with suspense and action in an artful balance. The psychological dimensions of Flynn's Western fiction came increasingly to encompass a confrontation with ethical principles about how one must live, the values that one must hold dear above all else, and his belief that there must be a balance in all things. The cosmic meaning of the mortality of all living creatures had become for him a unifying metaphor for the fragility and dignity of life itself. *Dead Man's Gold* will be his next Five Star Western.